Calculated Risk

A Cross Security Investigation

G.K. Parks

Copyright © 2021 G.K. Parks

A Modus Operandi imprint

ISBN: 1942710283
ISBN-13: 978-1-942710-28-8

For my mom, who reads all my books.

BOOKS IN THE LIV DEMARCO SERIES:

Dangerous Stakes
Operation Stakeout
Unforeseen Danger
Deadly Dealings
High Risk
Fatal Mistake

BOOKS IN THE ALEXIS PARKER SERIES:

Likely Suspects
The Warhol Incident
Mimicry of Banshees
Suspicion of Murder
Racing Through Darkness
Camels and Corpses
Lack of Jurisdiction
Dying for a Fix
Intended Target
Muffled Echoes
Crisis of Conscience
Misplaced Trust
Whitewashed Lies
On Tilt
Purview of Flashbulbs
The Long Game
Burning Embers
Thick Fog
Warning Signs
Past Crimes

BOOKS IN THE JULIAN MERCER SERIES:

Condemned
Betrayal
Subversion
Reparation
Retaliation
Hunting Grounds

BOOKS IN THE CROSS SECURITY INVESTIGATIONS SERIES:

Fallen Angel
Calculated Risk

ONE

"You're in a good mood." Justin glanced at me as I entered the office, confused by my humming. "Did you get laid?"

"No, but on the bright side, I didn't get screwed." I picked up the stack of mail and flipped through the envelopes. Bill. Bill. Check. Junk. I put the junk in the shred pile, left the bills for Justin to pay, and tore open the check from our latest corporate security overhaul of Rathbone Enterprises. I turned to the desk behind me, but our receptionist was nowhere to be found. "Where's Gloria?"

"Breakfast run."

"But she's the receptionist. Why is she getting breakfast?"

"Lucien," Justin leaned back in his chair, "aside from the hired muscle and the one forensic expert you couldn't live without, it's just the three of us."

I thought for a moment. Cross Security and Investigations needed more assistants, more techs, and more office space. However, the first two would have to wait until after the move. And to do that, we needed more money. The settlement I'd gotten would put us on the map. But I wanted to make sure we had an ideal office location.

The bigger and bolder we looked on the outside, the better.

So far, the vast majority of clients I'd signed had known me from my days on Wall Street and trusted that my business savvy and head for wise tech investments that had made them millions would also safeguard those millions from hackers, thieves, and questionable employees. I'd only taken on a couple of unknowns since. They'd been mostly minor cases with one glaringly obvious exception. Jade McNamara. Again, I found myself humming. Shit. The smile tugged at the corners of my lips. This had to stop.

Rubbing a hand over my mouth, I tried to focus on the negatives. The scars on my back, the weeks spent in the hospital, and the weeks spent recovering were all checks in the con column. No amount of money could fix that or what I'd done to the man who tried to kill Jade and me.

Yet, I found myself focusing on the positives. The payout from the police department padded my bank account. It'd pay for our move. It'd even pay for the equipment Amir Karam forced me to agree to before he'd sign a contract to work for Cross Security. Plus, it meant something far more meaningful. Jade was safe, and in a few hours, she'd be coming home.

Justin quirked an eyebrow. "Seriously, Lucien, what's going on?"

"Nothing. I was just thinking Rathbone's check might be enough to hire someone to run errands."

"Isn't that my job? Or are you finally promoting me?"

"You already own a stake in the company. Isn't that enough?"

"I'd like my own office."

"We'll see. King Realty is scouting locations for us. As soon as they find something that lives up to Amir's lab specifications, we'll discuss your office situation."

"I hope this guy's as good as his reputation." Justin reached into the drawer for the checkbook. "Are you sure you don't want to set up automatic bill pay? What happens if I take a vacation and no one's here to keep the lights on?"

"I guess we'll work in the dark."

"At least you have a plan, boss."

"Don't I always?" I went into what had once been a closet and was now our break room and made a cup of coffee using the espresso maker. Then I made one for Justin and returned to the outer office. "What's on the agenda today?"

"You have a meeting with your new client at nine, lunch with Miranda to discuss extending her contract at eleven, and conference calls with prospective businessmen to discuss corporate security at two and four." He slipped the check into the envelope and sealed it. "Are you sure you don't want to try online trading instead? We're money guys. We served our time on Wall Street. We could take another stab at it. Don't you think we're better equipped to do that than this?"

"Hey." I narrowed my eyes, knowing my former intern turned executive assistant wanted to yank my chain. It served me right for coming into the office humming a pop song. Frankly, I should have been relieved he didn't shoot me on sight. Thankfully, he was still one gun safety class away from a carry permit. "I didn't get my P.I. license for nothing."

"Yeah, well, I just thought maybe after everything you might have reconsidered. We're blackballed from most of the investment banks and major trading companies, but you could start your own or invest for yourself. You have that kind of cash now."

"I had enough before."

"I never thought I'd hear you say that." Just as I opened my office door, he asked, "Are you sending a car to pick up Jade from the airport, or are you going to do it yourself?"

I turned. "How'd you know?"

"I might not have a fancy P.I. license, but I picked up a trick or two." He also organized my calendar and scheduled most of my meetings.

"I'm picking her up."

"Is she moving back?"

"I don't know."

Justin nodded and returned to paying the bills.

Settling in behind my desk, I reached for the intel I'd compiled on my newest client, Trey Knox. He'd seen the ad

I'd taken out on the back of a business magazine and decided to give me a call. I'd done the consultation over the phone.

Knox's home had been burglarized. His collection of valuable sports memorabilia had been stolen, along with whatever cash, jewelry, and other high-ticket items the thieves had been able to haul off. The police had yet to catch the culprits, and I doubted they would. Even Knox doubted them, which is why he came to me.

Specialty items like signed jerseys and MVP rings would be difficult to fence without catching someone's attention. That must have been what the police were counting on, assuming they even gave a damn about helping Mr. Knox recover his property, but I was biased.

I went to the police academy and almost graduated. Almost. But my father, Mr. Police Commissioner, made sure that didn't happen. Just like he let an asshole like Scott Renwin carry a badge.

Again, I found myself falling into the bottomless pit of anger and bitterness. So I shook it off. Mr. Knox had a problem. The cops hadn't helped him yet, so in the meantime, I might as well try. That's why I started Cross Security. It was time I put my money where my mouth was.

Shaking off the unexpected anger, I reread the copy of the police report Knox had sent me. The security system had been dismantled, not disarmed. Whoever broke into Knox's house had to be a professional crew.

Knox lived in a gated community. Getting in and out wouldn't be easy. The security guards and cameras didn't catch anything. The interior cameras had been shorted out, and according to the guards' statements, no one suspicious entered or left the area on the night in question. Knox didn't see anything, and neither did his neighbors. The police believed the thieves breached the residence by entering through a first floor window. But I had my doubts.

According to what I'd found, several break-ins had occurred in the area over the last few weeks. The police had no leads, but they assumed it was the same crew. However, none of those other burglarized locations had high-end security systems. So either the crooks had moved on to bigger and better things, or someone else broke into Knox's house, knew exactly how to get in and out without tripping an alarm, and knew what to take. That meant it might be personal.

"Tell me your secrets, Trey Knox." My fingers flew over the keyboard. *Knox, Trey.* No criminal record. I checked his employment history. He'd worked his way up to acquisitions manager at the same company where he first started interning seventeen years ago. That probably meant he was loyal and hard-working or unimaginative, complacent, and a kiss-ass. One or the other. It also meant his colleagues must know him well. They'd probably been to his house for barbecues or to watch the big game. That could make them suspects.

I wrote a note to ask about recent problems at work. Then I moved on to his social media presence, but I didn't find much. He remained professional online. Everything was buttoned up.

After a few quick searches, I found some fantasy sports leagues Knox belonged to, but that didn't tell me much about his real-life friends or acquaintances. I bookmarked the pages, figuring if nothing else turned up I could do a deep dive on these sports maniacs to see if one of them had the skills and balls necessary to conduct the break-in. As far as I could tell, Knox's main concern had been his stolen sports memorabilia. He had signed all-star jerseys, a championship ring, pennants, and game balls. And they had all been taken.

According to Knox, these items were irreplaceable. He didn't seem to give a damn about his watches, cash, or stolen electronics. Those he could replace. His precious collection was another story, and the longer it was gone, the less likely the police were to recover it. Even if they did, they'd hold the items as evidence until after the trial. When I mentioned that tidbit to Knox, he'd grown even more desperate.

I had e-mailed him my boilerplate contract to review and my daily rate. He told me he'd think about it, only to call back an hour later and say he wanted my help. That was two days ago.

I pressed the button on the intercom. "Justin, did you run a credit check on Trey Knox?"

"His credit's not stellar, but he has enough in the bank to pay us."

"What about his car and house?"

"Lease and mortgage."

"Credit card debt?"

"He makes payments every month. His cards have twenty thousand dollar limits, and they're each about three-quarters full."

"How many cards does he have?"

"Three."

"Student loans?"

"None."

That's a plus. "Did anything send up a red flag?"

"Not that I've seen." The intercom clicked, and Justin stepped into my doorway, giving me the look that told me he thought it was ridiculous we had an intercom when he was sitting fifteen feet away. "Do you think this is a scam? Insurance fraud?" He handed me a few printed pages. Most of the unpaid charges on Knox's cards were season tickets and box seats to football and baseball games and auction charges. A few were for online gambling and fantasy leagues. This guy really loved sports.

"He likes expensive toys, but if he just gave up his hobby, he could pay off his cards. So it's probably not a scam, but I'll ask him if he had his collection appraised or insured."

"You might want to take a look at his homeowner's insurance policy too."

I pointed a finger pistol at Justin. "Brilliant suggestion. Call Knox and ask him to bring it with him today."

My assistant glanced at the time. "He might already be on his way, but I'll see if I can catch him."

"Thanks."

TWO

"Do you have somewhere else to be?" I asked.

Knox shook his head, tearing his eyes away from the clock. "Sorry, I was just thinking about traffic."

I rocked back in my chair. "Is this everyone who's been to your house?"

"Yeah, I think so." Knox rubbed his forehead and leaned closer to check the list he'd made for the third time. "The police said the cleaning lady has an alibi, but I never thought she'd do something like this. None of my friends would."

"What about your colleagues?"

"Nah, they're cool guys. The only times they've stopped by were to watch games or help me crunch numbers for work."

"What about repairmen or delivery guys?"

"The house is still new enough that I haven't had to get anything repaired, touch wood." Knox knocked twice on the top of my desk. "The cable guy's the only person I can think of who's been inside that I didn't know, and that was when I first moved in. Everything was still in boxes."

"When did you move in?" I asked, too lazy to look at the paperwork.

"Four-ish years ago."

"Any problems with your neighbors? Any complaints or issues?"

"Look, Lucien, I've already been over these questions with the police. No one I know would do something like this. Whoever came into my house and stole my stuff is a complete stranger. I wouldn't affiliate with criminals or shady types." He'd even said it more than once for emphasis during our previous conversation.

"I wasn't suggesting that, but it seems the thieves might have had prior knowledge of your security system and the layout of your house. One might even entertain the notion that the thieves knew what was inside your house, which is why you were targeted."

"Perhaps." Knox reached for the list of stolen items. "Nowadays, everyone has a tablet. They probably just got lucky with my VR set."

"Did they just get lucky with two designer watches, a few pairs of gold cufflinks, and five grand in cash?"

"Yeah, I guess." Knox put the list down. "I'd like to get everything back, but I'm hiring you to find my memorabilia. That's your top priority. The rest is just icing."

I reached for the list. "Four signed jerseys, a World Series pennant–"

"Signed by every single player."

"Uh-huh." It was worth less than two thousand dollars, but just like everything else in Knox's collection, he thought it was priceless. "A few bobbleheads, two signed basketballs, a hockey puck from the Stanley Cup finals." I looked up from the paper. "No soccer?"

"What?"

"Soccer, the most popular sport in the world."

He stared at me in horror. "I like American sports."

"America has a soccer team."

"They suck." He jerked his chin at the list. "Football, American football, that's where it's at."

"Do they call them baseball cards?" I pointed to the page. "They're football cards, right? Since it's football." I might have been taking a little too much joy out of asking these pointless questions, but it made me feel like a real gumshoe. Perhaps, I needed the practice.

"You can call them trading cards. They have the player stats on the back. Mine were mint, all signed, and encased in protective sleeves."

"Good idea to keep your assets in protective sleeves." My thoughts drifted to Jade's impending arrival. I should make a stop at the pharmacy before I picked her up, just in case she missed me as much as I'd missed her these last few months.

Knox continued to talk about his collection, flashing photos of various pieces toward me as he scrolled through the content on his phone. I tried to pay attention, but this reminded me of second grade show and tell when that one geeky kid who had no friends insisted on showing us his action figures he kept inside their boxes. As a seven year old, I found the idea of having a toy and not playing with it asinine. And Knox's fondness and devotion to a collection of things that he kept framed and on display but served little to no use seemed just as asinine. "If nothing else, I want that MVP ring back. It took me years to find one for sale, and once I did, I spared no expense. That's what you have to find."

"Why didn't you keep your valuables in locked cases or a safe?" I asked.

Knox stared at me as if I'd said something in Klingon. "I bought them to enjoy them. I have them on display so I can see them. Now, when I go home, there's nothing but bare walls and shelves." He looked utterly distraught. "I'd do anything to get my stuff back. I can't believe someone would stoop so low to do something like this. Cash is one thing, but a man's prized possessions are something else entirely."

"So you think the thieves took your collection as a personal attack? To add insult to injury?"

"I don't know. I never thought this would happen." He scratched his neck. "You keep saying thieves. Why do you think it's more than one guy?"

"The police said a crew's been hitting houses in the area. They're under the impression they are responsible for the break-in at your place, which means once they try to fence or pawn your collection, they'll get nabbed."

"I don't want to wait for that to happen. By then, it'll be too late. It could all be gone." His breath became frantic, and his cheeks pinkened. "I didn't hire you to fall into line with what the cops think. During my consultation, you said you didn't buy into that. Have you changed your mind? Maybe this isn't the right fit for me after all."

He moved to stand, and I watched, waiting to see if he'd storm out. Instead, he stopped mid-squat, his hands firmly grasping the arms of the chair while he waited for my answer.

"You seem certain this isn't the same crew. What aren't you telling me?" I asked.

"Nothing, but you said recovering my stolen collection wasn't a police priority."

"It isn't, but I'll make it mine."

"That's not how it sounded a second ago."

I cleared my throat, forgetting how much hand-holding went into dealing with non-corporate clients. "In that case, I apologize for the miscommunication. However, you said taking your collection felt personal, which indicates whoever did this knows about your hobby and how big of a score taking these items really is."

"Like I was targeted by a professional thief?"

"Given the way the security system was dismantled, more than one individual was involved in the actual crime." I reached for the copy of the police report. "I've done my homework on your security system. In order to dismantle it so as not to trip the alarm, three people had to remove the connectors from these three boxes simultaneously. So it is a crew, whether or not it's the same crew who's been targeting other houses has yet to be seen. Since you are such a sports enthusiast, I'm guessing you must frequent auction sites and message boards. Have you bragged to anyone online about your scores?"

"Sure, I guess."

"Okay." I made a note to take a look at his browser history to see if another sports fan had gotten pissed and decided to take what he wanted instead.

"I have paperwork on everything that was taken. Certificates of sale and authenticity." He grabbed the attaché case off the seat beside him and pulled out a folder. "The information on the auction sites and houses where I made the purchases is included."

"Great." Too bad all my clients weren't this prepared. I took the folder and skimmed the information. This would require several phone calls, employee background checks, and possibly a peek into their records for details on the other bidders interested in these stolen items. If nothing else, the losing bidders might have their ears to the ground on ways to obtain these treasured pieces of sports history through less than legal means. I'd have to do some digging. "What about insurance?"

"My house insurance covers theft up to a certain amount. I didn't upgrade when I made these last few purchases."

I clicked the messenger icon on my computer and typed a message to Justin, asking him to see if Knox had made any inquiries into selling his collection or any of the more expensive pieces from the collection. Unless he had already sold off the stolen items, I didn't think this was an insurance scam.

"Do you think you can find them?" Knox asked. "They're all special, but that ring is one of a kind. It's my most prized possession. My dad had scrimped and saved to take me to that game. That's the game where my favorite player got named MVP and received the ring. My dad passed recently, so I never got to show him what I bought as a memento, but it has special meaning to me."

"I'll do what I can. You said your friends and colleagues wouldn't do anything like this. What about a vengeful ex?"

He shook his head.

"What about recent paramours? A crew broke into your house. Perhaps, they have a fourth working with them who picks out the marks, assesses the layout and security, and reports back."

"You make this sound like a heist."

"Wasn't it?"

"Yeah, I guess it was."

"So girlfriends? Hookups? Any new people come into your house or life in the last few weeks?"

"No one. I wouldn't put it past my college ex, but we haven't seen each other in half a decade. She's never been to my house or seen the MVP ring or my recent additions."

Thoughts of Jade drifted to mind, my blood boiling at the thought of her vengeful ex and the damage he inflicted. My back still pinched every time I turned too quickly, and my legs would go numb on occasion. The doctors said that was normal, and the symptoms should continue to improve as long as I continued doing the exercises and following their advice. Nonetheless, it pissed me off every time it happened.

"Yoo-hoo." He waved his hand in front of my face. "You still with me?"

"I'll look into her anyway." Picking up the pen, I remained poised to write until he finally gave me her name. While he expounded on what went wrong between them, I ran a quick background check and did several searches. She wasn't responsible. She didn't even live in the tri-state area. Sighing, I tossed my pen back on the desk. "Do you have any enemies or some sort of fucked up family drama or sibling rivalry going on?"

"Not that I can think of."

"Is it possible this could be a prank?"

"Hell no."

"Okay, so we're back to looking at a professional crew, most likely comprised of strangers." Still, the surgical precision of the break-in made me question that assessment. "Can you think of any other collectors who might want to take your collection from you?"

While Knox blathered on, I took notes, but strangers on the other end of the bidding wars wouldn't necessarily know where Knox lived or what kind of security he had in place. The break-in wouldn't have been this clean. Something didn't fit.

"When can you start searching?" he asked.

"I've already started."

"Okay. How long do you think it'll take?"

"For a recovery?"

"Yes."

"I'll reach out to fences, do some research, and see what's what. I told you before that I can't guarantee results. But your chances are better with me than the police department."

"What kind of odds are we talking?"

I'd never worked a recovery before, but finding stolen property and returning it shouldn't be that difficult, especially when dealing with one of a kind items like these. I could probably put the word out, offer a huge payday, and wait for the thieves to surface. The bringing them to justice part would be more difficult, especially since I was to recover the evidence, not turn it in, but that would be up to my client to decide. He just wanted his stuff back. "Fifty-fifty."

"All right, let's see what you can do." He shook my hand.

THREE

"You've got it bad." Miranda held the tiny coffee mug beneath her chin, letting the steam rise. "How long were you two together?"

"Come on, Miranda, we're here to talk about your business, not my personal life."

She made a pfft sound and stared at me with those big doe eyes. No wonder millions of people bought her albums, posters, and t-shirts. Sure, she might have been one of the biggest names in the music industry, but it wasn't entirely about her music. It was about her look. The sex appeal. The husky voice. The way she moved. We'd had our share of fun on a few occasions. That had been when I was in charge of investing her money and raking in the millions. "Don't give me that bullshit, Lucien. I asked for you to be put on my accounts because I could tell you were a real go-getter. I've just never seen you want to get someone before. This is new for you, isn't it? I bet women fall at your feet. You've probably never had to pursue one before. Flowers are good. Jewelry's better. Do you know her ring size?"

I ignored her prying questions. "You asked for me to be put on your accounts because I was the best looking guy in the office and you had an ulterior motive."

"That too. But I wasn't wrong about the go-getter part. You made me enough smart investments that I was able to tell the label to shove it and branch out on my own. And let's not forget the celebratory sex."

My hand went through my hair, a nervous tic I had yet to shake.

She laughed. "I love making you squirm." She checked her phone. "Want to check-in to a hotel for lunch?"

"We have business to discuss."

She narrowed her eyes at me, placed the cup on the desk, and picked up a pen. "Fine. I want a full detail to accompany me for the rest of my tour. Twenty-four hour protection, not just at the venues but in the hotels, at home, restaurants, clubs, whatever."

"You'll need more than six guards for twenty-four hour protection, if you continue to have a four-person entourage."

"My entourage is a lot bigger than four, but I know what you mean. At shows, I'll need six."

"I thought your band had a security team."

"It does. The business does, but this is personal security just for me. Band security does what it can, but they work more crowd control than anything. In private or when I am out without the party, I only need two."

"Eight then, at least to start." Twelve would be ideal, but I couldn't give her every trained security member I had on the payroll. Opening a note tab, I added another candidate search to the list of things to do and reserved two days to conduct interviews next week. Until we got the new offices, the security teams remained on call until I needed them. "We might want to revisit this in a few months and consider an upgrade."

She snickered. "Only if you sneak away for lunch."

"I can do lunch. I just can't do you."

"Pity." She signed the contract and slid it across the desk. "You were always good in the sack. What if I upgrade to two years instead of one? Do I get you as a perk?"

"You realize by signing with my firm, in essence, you're employing me."

She rolled her eyes. "I'm not harassing you, sexually or otherwise. If I were, you wouldn't be enjoying it this much."

That was true, and I didn't want to quibble. "Where would you like to go to lunch?"

She waved a dismissive hand at me. "You're really not going to tell me about the girl?"

"There is no girl."

"Justin said you're picking someone up from the airport."

"Justin's fired." I leaned toward my open office door and raised my voice a little. "Did you hear that?"

"What, sir? You'll have to use the intercom," Justin called from the main room.

Miranda giggled. "I don't see how you get any work done around here."

"We don't." I'd been useless most of the day as my thoughts kept drifting to Jade and what I needed to do before I picked her up and what would happen once I did.

Miranda climbed out of the chair. "Fine, don't tell me about the girl. But she must be something special to have you so smitten that you'd give up on lunch."

"I said we could go to lunch."

"That's not the lunch I was talking about." She leaned over and pressed her lips against my cheek. "I'll give you a raincheck for the next time I'm in town, but you might not need it. I hope things work out with you and the mystery woman. You're a good guy, Lucien. You should have everything you want. Just don't be a chickenshit, and make sure she knows what you want. Girls don't like games."

"Isn't that from one of your songs?"

She laughed softly. "Oh, if you think you're going to trick me into giving you a private concert, you're mistaken."

"I'll see you again in three months," I said. She quirked an eyebrow at me. "I'm in charge of your personal security. I know your schedule by heart. I probably know it better than you. You'll be playing a gig in the city in three months. I'll be there."

"You better be." She went to the door. "Remind me to have someone leave an extra ticket at the door for your lady friend, if that's still going on."

I walked her to the door and leaned against the jamb

while she said a few parting words to Justin and signed a t-shirt for Gloria's niece. Two Cross Security specialists escorted her out of the office and to the elevator.

"We need to hire more security specialists," I said. "Pull the resumes we have on file. If no one looks good enough, we'll have to reach out again and start another search."

"Yes, sir." Justin slid backward toward the filing cabinets and opened the middle drawer.

"And one more thing, don't mention Jade to anyone else."

"Miranda's different. You've known her for years. She's your friend."

"Still, this is business. Let's keep church and state separate."

"Can't do that if you slept with her," Gloria murmured, earning a surprised look from me. "Sorry, I just can't believe you slept with her. She's a literal rock star."

"Who said I slept with her?" I glared at Justin's back.

"She did," Gloria said.

I squeezed the bridge of my nose, feeling a headache coming on. "Don't believe everything our clients say."

"Or everything our boss says," Justin warned her. He placed the stack of files on the edge of his desk. "Do you want me to start on this now or continue looking into Mr. Knox's case?"

"Stick with Knox and see what you find. I'll skim through these and let you know what I want to do before I leave today." I also needed to review my notes for my next appointment. "Gloria, I hate to ask, but would you mind ordering lunch for the office?"

"First breakfast and now lunch. Shew, I'm gonna need a raise." She grinned at me and winked at Justin.

"Did someone put a sign on my back or something?" I bent my elbow and reached behind me, feeling the twinge near my left shoulder blade. But I refused to let that put a damper on my mood. "Did Mr. Knox ask you to take one of his signed baseball bats to my balls?"

"Sorry, sir," Gloria said. "What would you like for lunch?"

"Have the sandwich place down the street bring a

platter of half sandwiches, salads, and soups." My fridge at home was nearly empty, and I didn't want Jade to starve. The leftovers would suffice until I found out how long she was staying.

Gloria started dialing while I hefted the files off Justin's desk and went back into my office, coaxing the door to close by hooking my ankle around the bottom corner and giving it a yank as I went inside. It remained cracked open, but that was good enough. I didn't need complete privacy. After all, someone had to keep an eye on Justin and Gloria, or the inmates would be running the asylum in no time.

Settling behind my desk, I reviewed my notes in order to prep and practice for my afternoon meetings, but my mind was elsewhere. I tapped my pen on the legal pad, finding myself doodling in the corner instead of listing the bullet points of my presentation. Maybe I needed more coffee.

"Do you need something?" Justin asked when I stepped out of my office.

"A lobotomy."

"I'll give it a whirl."

"You would, wouldn't you?"

He laughed. "Do you want me to have a car deliver you to Miranda's hotel?"

Turning, I stared at my assistant, unsure if that was a joke. But he had the best poker face I'd ever seen. It rivaled mine on days when I wasn't losing it. "Actually, while you're pulling info on security specialists, see what you can find in terms of executive assistants."

"Are we in the market?"

I matched his look. "It's possible."

I made another espresso, grabbed three half-sandwiches to keep the acid from eating away whatever was left of my stomach lining, and went back into my office.

"Focus," I mumbled to myself. In a whisper, I ran through my presentation for my first meeting, hitting the high points. I jotted down a few more notes, checked the time, and revised my presentation again.

After lunch, I wiped away whatever crumbs there might be, tidied my appearance, and waited for my next potential client. The afternoon went by slowly, like a snail stuck in a wad of discarded chewing gum. But the meetings were advantageous. By the time six o'clock rolled around, Cross Security had two new corporate clients and an extensive list of things to do. That alone would keep us busy for the next month.

"We might have to hire a few freelancers to help us out on the IT side of things. I'll have to see if we can stagger our assessments. With any luck, I won't have to do two overhauls at the same time." Palming my keys, I checked the time again. Rush hour traffic could be a bear. In another ninety minutes, things would calm down, and I wouldn't have to spend the same amount of time stuck in traffic, trying to get to the airport. Perhaps I'd stop by the liquor store after dropping the leftovers off at home. Jade didn't like gin, which was my drink of choice, or scotch, which is what a lot of my clients enjoyed. She liked tequila, rum, and wine.

"Do you want me to see who might be available?" Justin asked.

I glanced at the empty desk. Gloria had gone home at 4:15, like she usually did. "No, that's okay. I'll handle that myself."

"All right. I have a list of four more security specialists that look promising on paper, but you never interviewed them. There were a few you wanted who initially had scheduling conflicts. I'll see if they're still looking for a permanent position."

"Okay." I nodded a few times. "Do another job posting online. Let's see who else might be interested."

"Roger."

I went to the door, turning as I opened it. "I'm calling it quits. That means you get to go home."

"In a sec. I just want to finish this up. I sent everything on Knox's case to your dropbox, so you can check it out later if you want."

"Tomorrow."

"Night, Lucien."

"Good night."

FOUR

The racks of souvenirs stared back at me from the airport kiosk. Magnets, pens, water bottles, t-shirts, and jackets. The last time I'd visited this particular kiosk was when I'd been observing Jade's abusive ex. The bad memories sent a shiver down my spine, but I shook it off and waited in line to make my purchases.

With the bag in hand, I made my way to baggage claim to wait for Jade. We agreed to meet here. Well, I agreed. She insisted I could pick her up outside, but that didn't sit well with me. So I told her I'd meet her at baggage claim. What kind of knight in shining armor didn't offer to carry a lady's bag for her?

The screens told me her flight should be arriving on time. Seven minutes. Then I'd have to suffer through the slow process of deplaning. That probably meant at least a half hour. I found an empty seat at the end of a row, placed the bag securely on my lap, and took out my phone to check my dropbox.

Justin had sent me details on the new potential hires and most of the information I'd asked him to dig up on Trey Knox. Since I wasn't in the right headspace to think about what security qualifications the new hires should have, I opened the Knox files. Knox's browser history and phone records were exactly what I expected to find. No surprises there.

I scanned the names of his contacts, but no one appeared suspicious. He didn't receive any threatening messages, and his call durations were standard. Threats usually happened in a matter of seconds with the caller hanging up. Still, I decided to err on the side of caution and sent a text to Knox, asking again if anyone had threatened him or shown an inordinate amount of interest in his collection. He said no.

No blocked numbers or burner phones called his cell. Everything appeared legitimate. I checked again, but I didn't see any two a.m. texts for booty calls or any personal or intimate messages. Knox had said as much, but I'd been warned not to take clients at face value.

He didn't have a spouse or girlfriend. Still, I shouldn't rule anything out, so I made a note to find out if he used any dating or private messaging apps. That would explain the lack of text messages and phone activity. It could also be how the crew determined Knox would be a great mark and when to strike.

It was no secret men liked to brag. For Knox, it wasn't how big his bat was, it might have been how special his collection was. Perhaps, he hadn't said those things to a potential love interest on a dating site, but I'm sure he'd said them to plenty of people on the internet—other collectors, sports fans, or anyone willing to listen.

His browser history didn't lead me to many message boards or social media pages. He didn't have photos of his prized possessions anywhere on his social media pages. For once, I'd stumbled upon someone who actually kept things private. But Knox didn't appear to have much time or interest in sharing his life with friends or strangers. He didn't have time with all the games and fantasy leagues.

I shifted my focus to those boards, but everything looked like rankings, stats, and smack talk. Knox never mentioned the MVP ring, at least not that I noticed. Justin didn't find any postings or intel which indicated Knox had tried to sell his collection, so that was out.

"Trade shows," I mumbled. Knox had spent plenty of time on online auction sites and memorabilia sites, along with generic shopping searches, but he often went to trade shows. He might have spoken to vendors there. One of them could have decided to target him and shared that intel with the crew. I'd need to go over each certificate of sale, track the seller, and see where that led.

I should have passed on the case. It was too tedious a venture, and Knox wasn't big enough to be worth this much time and effort. But he was the acquisitions manager at a big company. I wouldn't mind working on their security, so that had been part of the reason. The other part was because I wanted to have a client that I could point to and say I was helping him with a personal problem, something that would make Jade proud.

My thoughts drifted back to her, and I tried to imagine her life in Colorado. Was she seeing someone? We'd called things off when she left, not that we'd ever classified our relationship, but we had spent a lot of time together, mostly in the hospital and physical therapy. After what she'd been through, she had trust issues, particularly when it came to men. Despite everything, she barely trusted me, so I doubted she was with anyone else. It'd only been a few months, but a lot could happen in a few months.

"Pussy," I muttered.

The grey-haired woman two seats away looked up. "Shithead."

I winked at her, which caused her to emit an exasperated huff. That was a sign I should get back to business and keep my internal musings to myself, so I went back to work.

Knox's deleted browser history showed plenty of research for work, a dabbling into the realm of naked women, and lots and lots of sports searches. He'd even been on several sportsbook sites. Going back into my dropbox, I checked to see if Justin uploaded Knox's financial statements. With the frequency Knox visited these sites and other gambling pages, he must have spent some money.

A gentle hand touched my shoulder, and I turned,

knowing what I would find. "Hey, stranger." Jade trailed her fingers down my bicep as she circled around the chair.

Before she even had the chance to get in front of me, I was on my feet with my phone shoved into my pocket. In my haste, I knocked the bag to the floor, and we both bent down to pick it up, nearly colliding in the process.

Scooping it up, I straightened. "How was your flight? You look good. Beautiful." Her hair was the same fiery red. It cascaded around her face in smooth waves, contrasting nicely with her alabaster skin. The few freckles on her nose were more pronounced, as if she'd been spending time outdoors, and her green eyes were a clear aquamarine. My gaze drifted to her lips. Should I kiss her? Hug her? I'd always let her take the lead on these things, so I held the bag tightly in front of me to keep from doing something we'd both regret.

"The flight was fine." She studied the bag, searching for something else to focus on besides me. "Were you waiting long?"

"Not really."

"So you shop here often?"

"On occasion."

Her lips quirked up in the corners. She was teasing me. "I just traveled three thousand miles and this is how you greet me?"

I grinned. "Fuck it." I took her in my arms and squeezed her tight. "I missed you," I breathed against her ear.

"Ditto."

Her hands ran along my shoulder blades, stopping near the base on the left side to avoid the bullet wound while the other continued all the way up to the top of my shoulder. She pulled me against her, and I felt her lips brush my neck. I pulled back just far enough so we could kiss, and it was like she never left.

After we were both breathless, she pulled away, turning her head down and to the side. Her cheeks were almost as red as her hair. "My god, we're the ending to every rom-com known to man. Kissing in an airport. Could we be any more cliché?"

"I don't mind. I missed you."

"You already said that."

"Yeah, well, it needed to be said twice."

She shrugged out of my grip, so I ran one hand through my hair and held the bag out to her. She took it from me and peered inside. "Really? You got me an *I Love New York* t-shirt, a big cookie, and a chocolate bar."

"It's Swiss."

"My favorite."

"Is it?"

She rolled her eyes. "You can't fool me, Lucien. I have your number."

"In that case, you should use it more often." Her gaze dropped to the floor. "I was only joking." I nodded toward the luggage carousel. "Are you ready to get your stuff and get out of here?"

"Yes, please." Before she could lead the way to the carousel, the grey-haired woman mumbled something to her that I didn't catch. Jade laughed. "That's not possible." The woman looked utterly offended and gave me the stink eye as I made my way past her. Once we were at the carousel, Jade asked, "What did you do to that poor, old woman?"

"Nothing. I was talking to myself, and she took offense and called me something very unladylike." I narrowed my eyes at her, but she kept hers glued to the conveyor belt. "What did she say to you?"

"She said I could do better."

I watched the luggage spin around in front of us as men and women grabbed rolling bags and duffels. "She isn't wrong."

"Yes, she is." Jade reached for her bag and hefted it off the carousel before it could spin past. She dropped it to the floor and extended the handle. "I'd know, don't you think?" A bitterness crept into her voice, along with that fierce defiance that had been the strength she needed to survive.

I reached for her bag. "May I?"

"If you insist."

"Where would you like to go for dinner?"

She hooked her arm through mine and rested her cheek against my shoulder. The scent of her shampoo, vanilla and citrus, overpowered the plane and airport smell. "Can we order in? I just want to go home and take a shower."

Home. My ears perked up at the word. Was she back for good? I didn't dare ask. "Sure, whatever you want. You know that."

We were quiet for most of the drive back to my place. She stared out the window, taking in the city as if she'd never seen it before. She'd been here for years, since college, but it must look different now after being away. I considering asking her about Colorado and her mom but decided against it. Hope was a four letter word. I didn't dare risk bursting that bubble, not after the kiss in the airport, except I wasn't a patient man. No matter how hard I tried.

"Penny for your thoughts?" I used the fob to gain access to the parking garage beneath my building.

"I miss it. The city. Being here. Being with you." She turned in the seat to face me. "I probably shouldn't say things like that."

"Afraid you're going to inflate my ego?" I turned to look at her. "Because that ship's already sailed. But if it makes you feel any better, I miss being with you too."

"Stop that." Her features hardened, but her eyes looked sad. "We are not reenacting any more rom-com moments. Life isn't always a happy ending, Lucien."

Pulling into my assigned spot, I killed the engine. "What's wrong? What happened?"

"Nothing." She sighed and stared out the windshield. "I just don't think women like me get to have the fairytale ending. My prince doesn't get to slay the dragon and take me off to his palace to live happily ever after."

"It's not a palace. It's just an apartment with a good view. I understand why you might be confused." What I didn't understand was why she was talking like this or why she felt it necessary to stomp all over my heart. But I reminded myself we weren't together. Seeing me must be hard for her too, like not seeing me. As usual, I figured it was best to give her space. "You still get to have a happily ever after. You make that on your own. That has nothing to do with me unless you want it to."

She bit her lip. "Are you sure it's okay I'm staying here? Mary Beth said I could crash with her and her new roommate."

"I'd like you to stay with me, but whatever you want. I can make a few calls and get you a hotel room if that's easier." I opened the car door, grabbed the grocery bags from the back seat, and went to the trunk to take out her luggage. "It's up to you. Whatever makes you comfortable."

"You make me comfortable." She grabbed the grocery bags from my hand. "Just stop treating me like a princess or someone who's too fragile to do anything. That's not me. Not anymore."

"You're not fragile, Jade. You never were. You're the strongest, fiercest person I know."

"Do you really think so?"

"Absolutely." I pressed the button for the elevator, and we stepped inside. Again, my hand went through my hair, and she laughed. "What?"

"You still have that nervous habit. I guess that's my fault. This is really awkward, right? We talk on the phone every few weeks, so I don't get why this feels so weird."

"I have no idea." But I knew why. When we spoke on the phone, it was basic small talk. We discussed work and the weather. We kept things light. When she said she was coming back to the city, she didn't go into any details. We never discussed us or what her visit would mean.

"Maybe it's true what they say," she mused. "Maybe you can't go home again."

"To Colorado?"

She shook her head. "I want to talk to you about some stuff. I might need your help, but let's have dinner first. I'm starving."

"Sure." But her words worried me. "What are you in the mood for?"

"Everything."

FIVE

"Lucien, how long do you think I'm staying?" She stared at the liquor and treats I'd stockpiled for her return.

Forever. I cringed at the voice inside my head. No, forever was not a good answer or a good thought. That was a one-way ticket to crazytown, and Jade had already had more than her fair share of psychos.

I picked up the box of tea bags. "They were out of the twenty count. A hundred was the smallest box they had. I'll take whatever you don't use to the office. It's not a big deal. Gloria would probably prefer if you don't touch any of the cookies or chocolates. She has quite the sweet tooth."

"Gloria?" Jade cocked an eyebrow at me.

"My receptionist."

"Oh," her green eyes held an uncertain look, "I thought she might be your girlfriend."

"I wouldn't have kissed you like that if I had a girlfriend."

"Right." She appeared deep in thought. "What about casually? Are you seeing anyone?"

"Does it matter?"

She shook her head, her expression exaggerated in the same way my mother used to look at me when she wanted me to volunteer information without having to ask. "Nope."

"Good." I reached for the bottle of wine. "For the record, the answer is no. I'm not seeing anyone."

"Not since I left?"

"No."

Her lip twitched, as if trying to squelch a smile. My answer pleased her, even if she'd never admit it. "You should date. Go out. Meet people. Have fun."

"What about you?"

"What about me?"

"C'mon, Jade, don't be a buster. Answer the question. It's only fair."

"Since when do you play fair?" Her eyes twinkled. She found this amusing but turned away before I could ask anything else and walked across the kitchen and into the living room. "Your apartment looks the same."

"Did you think I was going to redecorate?"

She shrugged, and I realized this was to buy time to avoid talking about whatever topic was actually on her mind.

"What's going on?" I asked. "Why did you make this trip?"

She picked up the glass orb from my coffee table and studied the colored patterns inside. "How's work? Have you been helping the helpless and fighting the good fight?"

"It's been mostly corporate security gigs."

"I thought you had grander plans."

"I do. It just takes time. I can't exactly privatize policing and save the downtrodden without clients, capital, and a positive reputation. Cross Security and Investigations needs to be on the map to have a reputation for professionalism and excellence. Right now, the only people who know me were around for my previous career."

"And the shooting."

"That was barely a blip on anyone's radar. That was the point of the settlement. The police wanted it kept quiet. They didn't parade me around or accuse me of murdering a cop, so I was just a random victim of a violent crime. No one knows about it. My name didn't even make the papers."

Anger made her cheeks flush. "It wasn't random. Scott abducted me. He was going to kill me. If you hadn't..."

"I know, but I can't talk about it publicly. You know that." Was that the reason she came back to town? Did she plan to go to the press to tell them what happened? A part of me hoped she would, but I knew Mr. Almeada, my attorney, would see things differently. If she went public, my involvement would get out, which could hurt my reputation and my company. But I didn't care. It was Jade's story. I'd back her decision no matter what, even if I couldn't afford to be sued for violating a gag order. "Are you planning on making this public knowledge?"

"No. It's done. I told you that before I left. Maybe one day I'll come forward, but not today. Victims get crucified in the press. I don't want that. I don't want to become fodder for the talking heads or a joke on late night TV. What I want to do is help others like me, and I can't do that with reporters and crazies hounding me at every step."

"Did something happen in Colorado?"

"No, it's great. It's not the city, but it's okay. My mom and I are getting reacquainted, which is good. I missed her."

"But you needed a break?"

Her green eyes stared at me with that helpless look of desperation that I'd seen when we first met. That look could make me crumble. "I need a plan."

"Anything. Tell me how I can help."

"You can't. I just had to come back and get some stuff together. I'm going back to school."

"Really?" She'd be back in the city. We could pick up where we left off. I fought to keep from smiling. This thought obviously had her upset, so I had to be sensitive to that.

"Yeah, and I need Mary Beth to write me a letter of recommendation and help me fill out the application."

"Your roommate?"

"She was more than that. In some ways, she saved me almost as much as you did. She helped me put my life back together, to find myself, to move forward. She does a lot for the battered women's shelter here. I want her input on what I should include in my essay and what to avoid." She pulled her gaze from the spot on the floor she'd been staring at since the conversation started.

"You'll need money for tuition, books, and housing." I reached for my phone and opened my banking app. "I told you I set aside the money from the settlement for you. That's your account. Graduate school or post-grad," since she already had a master's degree, "can be expensive. Let me transfer more from the investment account into your bank account. How much do you think you'll need?"

"I don't want your money, Lucien. You've already done enough."

"Nonsense. I've done nothing. The only reason I received the settlement was because of the hell you endured. It should be yours. All of it."

"No. It's blood money. Yours. Mine. His." She shook her head vehemently. "I don't want it."

"It can be used for good. It should be used for good."

"Aren't you using it for good?"

"I'm trying." But I doubted my corporate clients counted in her eyes. Hopefully, Trey Knox's case counted.

"Keep the money. I just need a place to crash while I get all of this together."

"You can stay as long as you need."

"I fly back in two days."

"That's not long."

"No, it's not." She sucked in some air.

I picked up on the physical cues almost instantly. "Are you okay?"

She nodded, swallowing. "My therapist said it'd be hard returning to the city. Lots of bad memories. Lots of trauma and baggage that I still need to unpack, so to speak."

"You didn't seem this apprehensive before you left."

"It's worse coming back. It's like muscle memory, but it's not just that. Seeing you is hard too. I really do miss you, Lucien. You're the one regret I have."

"I'm sorry. I should have done more. I wish I'd figured out a way to stop him."

"No, not that. Leaving you. I thought by now you'd have moved on, but you haven't. I wish you would. This is burying me. It shouldn't bury you too."

"Jade?"

"I hate this." She turned to stare at me. "I hate that I'm still so afraid. I thought when I moved away the nightmares would stop. That I wouldn't find myself staring out the window, half-expecting to see him lurking in the shadows across the street or waiting for me when I get home from work. Isn't that crazy? He's dead. I know it, but I still can't shake it. I just want to feel safe again."

"Is that why you decided to take this trip?" I didn't need her to answer. It was obvious.

She didn't turn, but her head bobbed. "Leaving was stupid. It didn't solve anything."

"What can I do?"

"Nothing. This is something I have to work on. My therapist thinks coming back to the city and confronting the memories and my demons might help. Mary Beth agreed."

"You're going to be okay. It just takes time."

"And help. But you're right. I will be okay."

"Would you like some tea? We have plenty."

She laughed. "That would be nice."

I filled the kettle, turning to find her standing beside me at the counter. We didn't speak, but she stood close enough that her side brushed against mine. I should have done more to help her.

The kettle let out a shrill whistle. Exhaling, she turned off the burner. After filling her mug, she put the kettle back on the stove.

I placed the honey beside her and took a spoon out of the drawer. She took it from my hand, and our fingertips brushed. "So you're going back to school. What are you thinking? Doctor? Lawyer?"

"I want to face my fears head on. I'm thinking social work."

"Really?" That surprised me, even though it shouldn't have. That job could be dangerous, and she'd have to work closely with police officers in some instances. Domestic abuse was a common issue social workers faced. This seemed wrong on every level imaginable. "There are plenty of ways to give back. You could do something else."

"No. This is what I'm meant to do." She squeezed a large dollop of honey into her cup and stirred it with the spoon. "Scott took my joy, my independence. And now that I'm finally free, I'm afraid I'll run into another Scott, but these women are already dealing with men just as bad or worse. Someone has to help them. I understand what they're going through, so it should be me."

"Are you sure?"

"Yes." But she didn't sound sure.

"You have time."

"I know. That's what school and therapy are for." She spun, nearly shoulder-checking me in the process. "How do you cope? How can you go to work and take cases, knowing any one of them could be your last?"

"Gin. Lots of gin."

"Lucien, be serious."

"Fine. If you must know, the first thing I did was take a page out of your book. After that, I stopped thinking about it. If necessary, I force myself not to think about it. It won't serve me to dwell. It's over."

"It's that simple?"

"Most of the time. If not, there's always booze." I held up my glass. "Cheers."

She picked up her teacup and clinked glasses with me. After savoring a few sips of the chamomile tea, she eyed me curiously. "What do you mean you took a page out of my book?"

SIX

She traced her fingertip along the outline of the angel's left wing. "This must have taken forever."

"Thirty-five hours." It was a lot of line work, no shading, and very few things filled in. I'd been considering going back to add more details, but the pain held little appeal.

"Are you insane?"

"Are you?" I asked. "The leopard on your leg took almost as long, and you did that before you even fully healed. I'm surprised the tattoo artist let you get away with that."

"I couldn't deal with the scars. I wanted something fierce. Something protective."

"So did I."

She pressed her lips against my spine above the ink. She knew, despite the tattoo, the scars were still tender. "You got the angel of death tattooed on your back, Lucien. How is that protective?"

"I'm not sure it's my spirit animal or whatever, but it was only fitting." I watched her over my shoulder as she gently traced the lines that concealed the scars hidden beneath. "Since the angels had such a firm grasp on me that day, I figured I might as well embrace it. What do you think?"

She ran her fingers down the angel's body and off to the side. Tracing the one extended wing, she circled around to my front where the tattoo ended at the end of the bullet graze. "You should have mentioned it during one of our conversations."

"Surprise."

She gave my shoulder a shove. "What's the point of keeping in touch when you don't tell me what's going on with you?"

I could say the same thing, but I didn't want to start a fight. "Didn't I offer to send you some shirtless photos?"

"Yes, but I thought..." She blushed. "Did Kai do yours too?"

"Uh-huh." Until Jade had gotten a tattoo to cover her scars, I'd never considered getting anything this extensive. I had a small one on my chest, the result of a drunken dare, but this was different. It had taken three and a half months and nine sessions to get it done.

"Did it hurt?"

"I didn't feel it in most places."

"And some places were excruciating," she said knowingly. Her hands ran up my chest. "I did say you were my guardian angel. I guess this proves it."

"I thought you told me I was a fallen angel."

"Is that why you got the tattoo?"

I shrugged. "I missed you."

"You keep saying that." She looked up at me from beneath her lashes. "What would have happened if I stayed? Would you still have gone through with this?"

"Probably." I cleared my throat, uncomfortable with the question and unwilling to move when she was standing so close, touching me. Even the slightest twitch would cause her to retreat, and I didn't want that. "You could have come with me and kept me company. If you don't like angels, you could have talked me into getting something else."

"A giant panda bear."

"A panda bear?"

"They're cute and cuddly."

"I thought we were going for fierce and powerful."

"You shielded me with your body. You're already fierce and powerful. You didn't need a tattoo to prove you're a badass."

"You think I'm a badass?"

"Shut up." She took a step back, and I fought to keep from reaching for her. "You didn't answer my question. What would have happened if I never left? Would we be dating? Would you be my boyfriend? Would we live together?"

"Don't you think we might be rushing into things?"

"We slept together for months, but what, we would just hook up from time to time?"

"Jade, our first night together might have been a hookup, but it meant more to me than that. Despite everything, the next few months we spent together, recovering, healing, that wasn't something casual. You mean too much to me to be a fling." I turned and reached for my shirt and pulled my arms through the sleeves.

"You never said anything."

"What was there to say? You needed to get away from here. I wasn't going to stop you. Long distance wouldn't have worked. It's not fair to either of us, not when I'm here and you're there."

She pressed her palms against my cheeks. "Say it." She grasped my hands as I tried to button my shirt. "I need you to say it."

"I wish you never left. Is that what you want to hear?"

With a sad smile, she stood on her tiptoes and kissed me. "That's all I needed to know." Then she took my hand and pulled me toward the bedroom.

*　　*　　*

Hugging the pillow beneath my arm, I faced Jade. Her fingers had found their way to the ink on my back. "What would you like for breakfast?" I asked.

"I'm still on Colorado time. My body thinks it's four a.m."

"Okay." I leaned over and gently kissed her. "I'll try to be quiet. Go back to sleep."

She grabbed my arm before I could get out of bed. "Are you going to work today?"

"I'm sorry, honey. I have a few meetings I can't miss and some research I need to do for a client, but I'll have Justin cancel my afternoon. By the time you wake up, I should be back."

"Don't do that. I'm meeting Mary Beth for lunch, and I have to swing by the university to get copies of my transcripts. I probably won't be here most of the day. I don't want my visit to disrupt your life. You should do whatever you have to."

"How about we have dinner?" I climbed out of bed and opened one of my drawers, searching for my spare apartment key. "We could go to the Mexican place you like."

"I was thinking Chinese."

"That works too." I pulled out the key and placed it on the bedside table. "I can leave my car if you need transportation."

"Lucien, what did I say yesterday?"

"Right, sorry." I put the key down. "Here's the apartment key. Feel free to come and go as you please. If you have any problems, you have my cell number."

"And the office. And Justin's cell." She shut her eyes and let out a little moan.

"Jade," but I chickened out of saying what was on my mind, "I'll see you tonight."

While my internal voice berated and belittled my cowardly ways, I showered. The water stung my back, and when I dried off, I found a few smears of red. Turning in the mirror, I ignored the pinch and laughed at the scratches Jade had left on my back. She'd been careful not to put her hands anywhere tender, which was good since she hadn't taken it easy on me.

When would we find our even keel? Last night, she said we should hook up whenever we were in the same time zone, but from the way she said it, I wondered when that would be. If she were going back to school, wouldn't she be moving back to the city? Or was she applying elsewhere? Maybe she didn't want to go to her alma mater, the place that had led her to Scott.

I had to stop. This was ridiculous. I wasn't some love-struck teen. I was Lucien fucking Cross. And I loved her. The thought shocked me, mostly because I'd never realized it until now. I didn't want her to leave again. She should stay. But that wasn't my decision. It had to be hers. Colorado had been the right choice, but maybe she would come back. But the voice in the back of my head knew the truth.

Once I was dressed, I left the apartment, making sure it was locked and my security system was armed. She knew the codes, so I wasn't worried. On my way to the office, I grabbed breakfast for everyone. As usual, I was the first to arrive at work.

I left the bag of bagels in the break room, made coffee, snagged a cinnamon raisin, and went into my office. I didn't have much scheduled for today since I planned to spend it with Jade. But now that I had extra time on my hands and Trey Knox needed help, I might as well pick up where I left off.

"Morning," Justin called. A moment later, he came into my office holding half of an everything bagel while he squeezed cream cheese onto it. "You brought a bag of comfort food for breakfast. That's never good. How was your night?"

I gave him a look.

"Not good?" he asked around a mouthful.

"Let's just get to work."

"Whatever you say, boss."

SEVEN

Trey Knox liked sports, and he liked to bet on sports. That had led to a chunk of his credit card debt, but he'd stopped using the online sportsbook sites several months ago. His credit cards weren't maxed out, and his more recent expenses involved buying more items for his collection. Did they have a support group for obsessed sports fans? I didn't know, nor did I care. That was Knox's problem. I had enough of my own.

The sportsbook sites he visited were automated transactions. No forums. No message boards. No interactions. I didn't have to worry that someone targeted him from there, which left all the auction and store sites. "This is going to take forever."

I resisted the urge to get another cup of coffee. I already had a headache, which the last cup of espresso exacerbated. Instead, I popped a few aspirin and grabbed a bottle of water. Maybe I needed to hydrate.

Pressing the intercom button, I said, "Justin, what did you find on the auction houses?"

"The physical ones?"

"Yes."

"No other reported problems. I'm still working on background checks, but so far, everything's been inconclusive. They don't hire ex-cons."

"Okay. What about the delivery drivers?"

"Knox picked everything up personally. Nothing was ever delivered."

I crossed that off my list. "I'll look into the security firm that installed his home security system while you finish up the auction houses. I already reached out to area pawn shops and posted a few listings on the dark web for anyone who could fence these items."

"Do you think you'll get a bite?"

"We'll see."

Opening a new tab, I went to the security firm's website, read every bit of information they had listed on their home security systems, performed several other searches, and found an online video tutorial on how to bypass the system. That meant any idiot could have broken into Knox's house. At least I knew it had to be a three-man team, at the very least.

Returning to the security firm's website, I searched for a list of employees, but they didn't broadcast that information. So I did some more digging until I got a roster of names. Three of their tech consultants had records for B&E and one for armed robbery.

I checked their criminal records, but those hadn't been home invasions. They'd been high-end heists. Obviously, these reformed cons had gotten positions in the company by assessing the security system's weaknesses.

I'd keep them on my radar, but they'd been on the straight and narrow far too long. And given what they were making at the company, stealing Knox's collection wouldn't be worth it. They stood to lose far more than what they could gain. But I had to perform my due diligence, so I checked their business records for other security systems that had been installed and cross-referenced them to reported break-ins. Nothing lined up. Knox was the only person with that particular security system who had suffered a break-in within the last two years.

Scribbling down their names, I did a quick social media

search, checked their known associates, and texted Knox their names and photos to see if he recognized any of them. A moment later, my phone rang.

"Cross Security and Investigations," I answered, my focus on the computer screen in front of me.

"Do you think these men are responsible?" Knox asked.

"Mr. Knox," I never expected him to call back so soon, "I'm just checking into every possibility. Do you recognize any of them?"

"No. Should I?"

"That's not how this works. The only answer I expect is an honest one." According to the records I'd seen, the security system had already been installed before Knox moved in. He had no reason to interact with these men unless one of them had targeted him.

"No. I've never seen any of them before."

"Thanks."

"Does this mean you're making progress?"

"Leaps and bounds," I deadpanned, already on to a more thorough analysis of the forums Knox frequented. "While I have you, what can you tell me about trade shows?"

"They're great."

Swallowing an exasperated sigh, I asked, "Do you go to them often?"

"Every chance I get."

"You must have interacted with tons of other sports fans. Did you ever tell them about your collection or recent acquisitions?"

"Of course."

"Did you ever exchange names or contact information?"

"With a few guys."

"I'll need that. Did you invite any of them back to your house?"

"No. It was more like 'I'll let you know if I stumble upon that signed rookie card if you keep an eye out for the championship game ball'."

"Did any of them keep in touch?"

"A few. We usually meet for drinks to exchange merchandise or to catch a game."

"All right. Send me their contact information. Do you always go to the same bar?"

"Yep. McGinty's."

A sports bar. I wasn't surprised. Adding that to my list of places to visit, I asked Knox the few questions I'd come up with while at the airport last night, but he didn't have any private messaging apps on his phone. "You don't date?"

"How is that any of your business?"

"It isn't, but I'm curious."

"I meet plenty of women. Plenty." He exaggerated the word the second time he said it. "I'm more of a one and done kind of guy."

"You don't take them back to your place?"

"Nope."

"May I ask why not?"

"They want to stay the night. They use my toothbrush. They want to get breakfast and plan a second date. One chick even wanted to plan our wedding. It's awkward when I have to kick them out to go to work in the morning. There's always a scene. It's just better to love 'em and leave 'em. Am I right?"

Though I shared several of Knox's views, at least when it came to picking up random women, hearing him say it bothered me. "Uh-huh."

"So I go to them."

"Were you with someone when your house was broken into? According to the police report, it happened around ten p.m."

"No, I was at work. Acquisitions involves a lot of overseas calls and dealing with different time zones. I work late a lot."

"Okay." That marked another possibility off my list.

"I have to go," Knox said. "Good luck. I hope you find my stuff soon. I'm dying to get that ring back."

He hung up before I had a chance to respond. All right, so he didn't subscribe to a dating app. He didn't invite random women to his house. From what I gathered, Knox didn't do anything that would make him an easy target. He didn't broadcast his location or habits. The only thing he did was talk a lot about his cool toys in online forums and to other die-hard fans. That could be troublesome, but his name was common enough. No one should have been able to find his house and plan the perfect heist that way, but someone did. And that someone brought an entire crew with him.

After staring at the screen for several more minutes without having brilliance strike, I got up and went into the outer office. "I'm going to the precinct to see if the responding officers can tell me anything that isn't in the file."

"All right. I'll let Mr. Almeada know he should be prepared to bail you out of jail." Justin reached for the phone.

"Why?" I shook my head. "Never mind. If you dig up something concrete, text me the details."

"Will do."

EIGHT

"Hey, Sara." I ran my hand over the edge of the counter.

"Lucien?" Sgt. Sara Rostokowski looked up from her spot behind the desk and automatically tucked a piece of grey hair behind her ear. "It's good to see you, kid." She studied me. "Are you good? You look good."

"I'm good."

"Really?" She glanced around to make sure the other cops working intake could handle the phones while she came around to the side. "It's nice to see you upright and walking again."

"Yeah." I stared at the posters on the walls. "Thanks for bringing food over and visiting me in the hospital."

"No, of course. It's the least I could do." She reached for me. "Is it okay if I hug you?"

I laughed. "You've known me my entire life. Since when do you have to ask?"

"I just... I didn't want to..." She gave me a gentle hug and pulled back. "Are you staying out of trouble?"

"Trying."

"But you're here. Do I want to know why?"

"A client hired me to recover his stolen property."

"Did he file a police report?"

"Yep."

She returned to her spot behind the desk. "Okay, give

me the details." I gave her the location and date. Before I could give her the case number, she pulled it up. "It's still under investigation."

"Obviously. I want to talk to the responding officer and whoever's primary and see if they have anything to add."

"And you think this is a good idea?"

I snorted. "Why? Are you afraid another cop is going to shoot me?"

"Lucien—"

"Yeah, I know." I slapped my hand over my mouth.

She shook her head. "Let me check and see who's around that you can talk to."

"Thanks, Sara."

I moved away from the desk and took a seat near the front door. A few officers glared at me from where they were working intake. I'd always had a reputation, first as the commissioner's washed-out son, then as a troublemaker who got out of assault and destruction of property charges because his daddy pulled strings, and now as a cop killer. No wonder Justin said he'd tell Almeada to expect a call. I'd be lucky to get out of the station in one piece.

"Lucien," Sara said, distracting me from giving the officers my most potent death stare, "Officer Gallo will be out in a sec to talk to you."

"Thanks."

A few moments later, a career patrolman turned a corner. "Lucien Cross?"

"That'd be me."

He cocked one eyebrow up and gave me a thorough once-over. "Joe Gallo." He held out his hand, but his eyes didn't hold malice. He seemed intrigued, possibly even pleased, to meet me. "I've crossed paths with your old man several times over the years. He's one of the good ones."

"Sure." Gallo didn't know dear old dad the way I did.

"He always brags about his boy. It's nice to meet'cha. What can I do for you?"

"I wanted to ask you a few things about a recent break-in." I gave him Knox's address.

Gallo nodded a few times. "Yeah, that was a week ago.

Week and a half. I remember it well. The security firm didn't alert us. The owner did. The system had been taken apart from the control boxes, and the owner's valuables had been cleaned out. But most of the house was pristine."

"What do you mean most?"

He led me into an empty room off to the side and closed the door. "Break-ins are usually messy. Wires hanging all over the place from where the TV and electronics got yanked, broken glass, tossed drawers, ripped furniture. But this place didn't have any of the usual telltale signs of a break-in. It was clean. Not a lot of damage to report."

I removed the copy of the police report Knox had given me from my breast pocket. "Just a busted bathroom mirror, right?"

"That was it." Gallo read over my shoulder. "The pieces had red paint on them, like someone spray painted them, but I don't know for sure."

"There's no mention of that."

"The owner said it was decorative."

"Spray paint's decorative?"

"No, he said the mirror had a red design etched on it and that's what we were seeing. It didn't look like it to me, but he was so distraught about his stolen stuff, I didn't want to press and make matters worse. You're working for the guy?"

"Trey Knox."

"Yeah. He was nearly in tears over losing his shit." Gallo chuckled. "I'm not used to seeing grown men acting like that. He acted like the big kid snatched the juice box right out of his hand."

I glared at Gallo. "Isn't that what happened?"

The officer held up his palms. "Hey, I'm on your side here. I want to get this guy's stuff back and find the bastards who did this. That's my job. Any help you can provide is a plus in my book."

Narrowing my eyes, I wondered if he had known what recently transpired or if he wanted to be my pal because of his prior connection to my father, a.k.a. his boss. Perhaps the gag order had gone both ways, but I didn't have time to worry about it now. "Mr. Knox didn't hire me to help you do your job. He hired me to recover his property."

"I hope you can." Officer Gallo reached into his wallet and pulled out a card. "When you find his stuff, give me a call. I doubt this is the first time this crew has struck." He leaned in and lowered his voice. "Off the record, this isn't the first break-in in that area. It could be the same crew. We're working to stop them now."

"It's not the same crew."

"How can you be sure?"

"Different MO. Whoever broke into Knox's place disassembled the security system. They didn't cut some wires or trigger it. They took it apart."

"We already looked into the home security system people, but they're clean."

"I know."

"You looked too?" Gallo asked.

"Someone has to make sure the job's getting done." I resisted the urge to crumple up his business card and toss it on the floor. Officer Gallo might be a good cop or a wolf in sheep's clothing. I didn't know enough about him to make a judgment call either way, but as a rule, I didn't trust any of them. I hadn't in a long time, and given my history, that wasn't about to change anytime soon.

"Glad you're on it." Gallo winked at me and put a firm hand on my shoulder. "You're making your pops proud."

I tried not to let those words irritate me as I left the precinct and headed to the first of many pawn shops. Even though they had policies against dealing in stolen merchandise, I'd done enough checking to determine the least reputable. I'd start there and make my way down the list.

My best bet was to pose as a buyer. I had the car, watch, and suit to let them know I was serious and wasn't a cop. The police didn't dress this nicely. I'd been assured of that fact only a few minutes ago. When I entered the first store, with the bars over the windows, I wondered if I should have entered armed.

The guy behind the counter looked like a barrel. The black hairs sticking up on his shoulders from underneath his wifebeater were almost thick enough to carpet my hardwood floors. He turned with a permanent angry expression on his face.

"Buying or selling?" His eyes came to rest on my watch.

"Buying, I hope." I tugged on my sleeve and straightened my cufflink. "Do you have any sports memorabilia?"

"Yeah, sure." He led me over to a display counter of photographs, jerseys, and game balls. "Anything specific?"

I browsed the display, but none of it matched the items stolen from Knox's collection. "None of this is quite right. I'm looking for a gift for my boss. Maybe a championship ring or something."

"I got these." The guy opened a locked cabinet behind him and pulled out a row of rings that looked like they belonged to famous rappers.

"No." I sighed. "I was hoping for a specific item." I gave him the details on the ring, but he didn't have one.

"What about something else?"

I rattled off a few of the pricier items from Knox's collection, but he didn't have anything in stock. "I'd be willing to pay through the nose if you could get your hands on this ring. I'm looking to make partner, and with my boss's birthday coming up, this is the perfect opportunity. If you could get your hands on it, I'd pay you fifty percent over the asking price."

The guy just shrugged. "Sorry. This is all I got. I don't do a lot of sports shit in here." The store had mostly electronics, knives, and guns. "Check out Pauley's Pawn. They might have what you want."

"Thanks."

NINE

Pauley's Pawn looked like most discount stores, not a pawn shop. The place was huge. Rows of everything from knockoff Gucci bags to designer sunglasses to ancient weaponry filled the locked cases and shelves. Yet, the clientele inside the pawn shop made me uneasy.

Several rough-looking men were clustered around the back wall, which had racks of mounted weaponry and cases of bullets, blades, and what appeared to be grenades. The friendlier items were closer to the front.

I meandered the aisles, checking out the tablets and computers. Any one of them could have belonged to Trey Knox, but that'd be next to impossible to determine without checking serial numbers.

"Can I help you?" A woman popped her gum and studied me with mild indifference. The wrinkles around her mouth told me she smoked, probably a pack a day given the harshness to her voice.

Giving her a winning smile, I approached the counter where she stood. "I'm shopping for a specialty item for my boss. He's a big sports fan."

"What sport?"

"All of them." I told her about the MVP ring I was

hoping to acquire.

She whistled. "Have you tried ebay?"

"I couldn't find one."

"They're hard to come by. Anything else on this guy's wish list?"

"How about a World Series pennant signed by all the players?"

She scratched her head. "Let's see." She led me to a section of the store I hadn't browsed yet. "We might have a few more things in the back. Look around while I check."

"Sure, thanks." I crouched down to get a closer look inside the display case while watching her unlock a door and step into the back. Something about this didn't feel right. I straightened and leaned over the glass to get a better look at a few signed game balls, noticing the two men nodding in my direction.

I shifted, wondering if they'd noticed the bulge at the back of my jacket. After my visit to the previous pawn shop, I'd decided it was best to enter these establishments armed, as long as they didn't have metal detectors. The men went back to their conversation, but they kept one eye on me. Perhaps, one apex predator had simply sensed another apex predator, but I wasn't delusional enough to think of myself as an apex predator. They probably noticed my watch and cufflinks and figured they'd mug me on my way out.

"Yo," the woman called to me, "I found this in the back." She held it up, and I studied it carefully.

"Do you have a certificate of authenticity or anything like that?"

Her eyes went wide, and she popped her gum again. "Do you want it or not?"

I nodded down at the triangular piece of fabric. "How much?"

"Twenty-five."

"Dollars?"

"Hundred."

I gave it another look. "Let me think about it for a minute." I pointed at a hockey puck inside the display case. "Can I see that?"

She let out a huff, practically rolling her eyes at the inconvenience. "Which one?"

"On your left."

She pulled it out of the case and placed it on top of the glass. Picking it up, I checked to see if it had the same scuff mark on the side that Knox's had, but it did not. Stepping back, I examined the pennant again. "I'll give you $1800."

"Twenty-two."

I let out a sigh. "Fine. Do you take credit cards?"

She nodded, picking up the pennant and carrying it to the register. We passed the men, who looked away as I approached, but once I was past them, their eyes were back on me. Ignoring them, I examined the other items on the wall and in the display case near the register.

"Do you think you might get a championship ring in? That would really cinch things for me."

"This won't do it?"

"Nope."

"Rings are hard to find, and they get expensive. Tens of thousands."

"I know." I watched her carefully. "I'm prepared to drop seventy-five grand on it."

She nearly choked. "Are you serious?"

"As a heart attack."

"Where do you work?"

"An investment bank. The partner buy-in is almost two-fifty. Another seventy-five to make sure I don't get skipped over again is worth it."

She put the pennant into a large flat box and slid it across the counter. "Check back next week. We're supposed to be getting some new stock in on Thursday."

"Great, thanks."

Lifting the flat box off the counter, I kept it horizontal as I made my way to the front door. The two men remained in the store as I unlocked the trunk and put the box inside. I couldn't be sure this was part of Knox's stolen collection, but it'd be easier to verify at the office than in the middle of the pawn shop.

Before pulling away, I made a few calls. While I was on the phone, one of the men left the shop. He walked past my car and continued down the street. Beneath his jacket was a concealed handgun. Whether that had been a recent purchase, I didn't know. Perhaps he had planned to knock over the pawn shop until I showed up. But I didn't think that was the case either.

The first thing I had to do was determine if this place was hocking Knox's collection, and if they were, I had to find out who sold it to them. The lady said a new shipment was coming in on Thursday, but everything I knew about pawn shops didn't indicate they received shipments. Items came and went, as did the customers.

Some people just wanted cash, but if they were getting shipments, the thieves might be unloading their wares on a regular basis. Phoning Justin, I gave him the store name and address and told him to run the business and everyone associated with it. Then I made a quick detour back to the police station.

This time, I didn't go inside. I stayed in my car and called Sara to ask what she knew about Pauley's Pawn.

"We've busted them a couple of times for selling stolen property," she said. "But we've busted all the stores a time or two."

"Is there anything else you can tell me?"

"No, sorry. They aren't on the radar."

"All right, thanks."

"You just left a couple of hours ago. You can't seriously have a lead already."

"I never said I did."

"Just be careful, Lucien."

"What fun would that be?" Hanging up, I was glad I didn't waste a trip inside. The only reason I made the call from the parking lot was in case they had open files that I'd want to sneak a peek at. But they didn't.

Once I got back to the office, I laid the signed fabric out on my desk, scanned it in, and blew up the photograph Knox had provided. I placed one image on top of the other. The signatures lined up perfectly. Every swirl, dot, and line hit precisely.

"They're numbered," Justin said from the doorway.

"What?"

"In the bottom corner. They do that on some collector's items." Justin watched me compare the number to the info on Knox's certificate of authenticity. "Does that belong to our client?"

"Yes."

"That's a new record for you, solving a case in twenty-four hours."

"It's far from solved. This is just one part of his collection. I didn't see anything else." Another thought hit me. What if the thieves had spread Knox's collection out over several stores? It'd be harder to track them down that way. But the way the woman told me to come back for the ring made me think she knew where it was, which meant she might know where the rest of Knox's collection was being held. "What did you find on Pauley's Pawn?"

"Step into my office and I'll show you." Justin stepped back into the outer office. "Oh wait, not my office, the reception area."

I gave his shoulder a shove for good measure while he brought up the info he'd ascertained. "What do we know about Lenmere LLC?"

"Filings look good. They have a few holdings, Pauley's, a self-storage center, and another pawn shop. Both pawn shops have received citations and fines. The owner's clean. No criminal record, just plenty of moving citations."

"Who owns it?"

"Dmitri Lenmere. He's sixty-two. This is his second act. He used to drive a taxi, retired, and bought a few shops. From what I gather, he's hands-off."

"All right." I stared at the screen. "No B&Es in his past. Did you find any known associates with a history of break-ins?"

"Nothing, but cabbies meet a lot of people."

"That's a stretch."

Justin pulled Dmitri's driver's license. He didn't live in the city anymore. If he was still driving a cab, I'd have wondered if he and Knox had crossed paths and if Knox had bragged to him about his collection, but that couldn't be the case.

"What do you want me to do?" Justin asked.

"Run Dmitri's name and photo by Knox. I'm guessing our client doesn't know this guy from a hole in the wall." I rubbed a hand over my mouth. "We were hired to find and retrieve Knox's property, not figure out who took it or why. That being said, if this was a random break-in," which I still didn't believe, "we just recovered one stolen item. I'm going to follow the breadcrumbs back to the source."

TEN

I'd seen a few cameras inside Pauley's Pawn but none outside. Still, cameras were everywhere. I just had to figure out which ones covered the pawn shop and hack into them. That shouldn't be too hard, except each one was on a closed circuit. That would make life more difficult.

Since I couldn't access the cameras remotely, I checked the time, went with plan B, and set out for a few more pawn shops. Even though they all had shelves dedicated to sports memorabilia, I didn't spot any of Knox's collection. I asked about several of the other pieces and the ring, but no one made any solid promises the way the woman at Pauley's had.

Most of the pawn shop owners weren't willing to send me away empty-handed. They could tell I was a potential big fish. They weren't going to toss me back into the ocean the way the first pawn shop I visited had.

"Come back in a few days. We have constant turnover. There's no way to know what we'll have, but I bet it'll be something great," one of them said.

"Give me your number, and if I get a line on one of those game balls or that ring you're so anxious to find, I'll let you know. And if anything else comes in that might strike your fancy, I'll set it aside so you can have first pick," another one said.

Reluctantly, I gave them my personal number because I didn't want to risk this tracking back to my P.I. firm. Pawn shop owners didn't like cops. And while I was the farthest thing from a cop, something told me they'd lump me into the same category as the boys and girls in blue.

After hitting those dead ends, I dropped by to see a fence I knew. He called himself a concierge because he could get anyone anything at any time. When I'd been trying to be a big shot on the money scene, I'd gone to him for different things, everything from dime bags of coke to Renaissance art.

"Lucien Cross, I'll be damned." Freddy Giles ushered me into the penthouse apartment. He wore a silk kimono and nothing else. He tugged on the belt. "What can I do you for?" He sniffed and wiped at his nose with the back of his hand. "You want to do a line?"

"No, I'm good." I glanced around his place, wondering how he'd made such a vast upgrade since the last time I'd seen him.

"I'm housesitting for one of my clients." He strode to the bar. "At least have a drink."

"Sure, that sounds great."

He poured a gin and tonic, light on the tonic, and brought it over to me. Movement from the bedroom caught my eye. A woman in nothing but a lace thong crossed in front of the doorway. Freddy handed me a glass and took a seat on the couch across from me.

I sat back in the chair and stared at the crown molding, hoping Freddy would take the hint and close his knees.

"So what exactly is it you're looking for? You said something about sports shit on the phone."

"I'm looking for this." I pulled a photo out of my breast pocket and held it out to him. He scooted forward on the couch, enabling me to stop staring at the ceiling. "That's the most expensive piece from the collection, but there's more. A lot more."

Freddy whistled. "That's a one of a kind piece. It'll be hard to come by."

"I know. The rest of the collection isn't as prestigious,

but the original owner wants it all back."

"Stolen?"

"Yeah."

"Recently?"

"Less than two weeks ago."

"So it's smokin' hot right now." Freddy picked up the two fingers of scotch he'd poured for himself and took a sip. "Unless the thief already has a buyer lined up, it'd be imbecilic to try to move this."

"Uh-huh." I sipped my drink. "Do you think you can find it for me?"

"Hey, I'm Freddy G. When have I not come through on something for you, huh?"

"Never."

"Damn straight." He pointed a finger at me before flopping back against the couch cushion and spreading his arms out wide. I resisted the urge to stare at the ceiling. "Have you already put out feelers?"

"I made a listing or two on the dark web, checked the usual online auction sites, and visited area pawn shops. I might be on to something. Pauley's Pawn, do you know it?"

"They do a decent business. They get some nice stuff from time to time, not that I do much business with them."

"Are they legit?"

"Is any pawn shop?"

"Maybe."

Freddy chuckled. "Well, they're the poor man's concierge. Did they promise they'd get you results?"

"I was told to check back next week."

"All right. I'll see if I can do you one better. Let me know if they come through in the meantime."

"Do you know where they get their merchandise?"

"The same place we all get our stuff. It fell off a truck."

"The Rembrandt you got me didn't fall off a truck."

"No, that deal was brokered by yours truly. All legit. Paperwork's golden. But I'm guessing since your pal lost his shit and you're looking to reappropriate it, you know this isn't going to have legit papers to go along with it."

"I'm just trying to recover his stolen property."

He cringed. "I don't like that word. Let's call it

redistributable merchandise."

I finished my gin and stood. "I don't care what you call it, Freddy. I just need to know who has it so I can get it back."

"No, Luci, that's not how this goes. Either I get it and act like a middleman and the two sides never meet, or you're on your own."

"Fine." I hated it when he called me Luci. "Find the ring, and we'll negotiate terms on how to go about recovering the rest of the redistributable merchandise."

He grinned. "See, I taught you something new."

The woman stepped out of the bedroom, practically naked, and moved over to the couch. She sat down beside Freddy, running her hand along his arm until she was leaning against him, and stared at me from beneath fake lashes. Her eyes were almost as glassy as his. Licking her lips, she whispered something in his ear.

"She wants to know if you'd like to join us," Freddy said.

"I can't. I have a dinner date."

He snorted. "When did you become so reputable?"

"You should try it sometime." I put the empty glass on the bar. "I'll see myself out."

"Hey, Lucien," Freddy called, sounding more serious and a tad more sober, "I can be a reputable businessman when the situation calls for it, but that's not why you came to see me tonight."

"I guess you're right."

"I'll see what I can do. Just remember, my name never comes up with your pops or with your client. I'm not getting involved in a police investigation because I do have a reputation."

"Thanks." I eyed the woman. "Have fun."

Shaking off the nagging at the back of my mind that always came following a trip to Freddy's, I called Jade to let her know I was on my way to pick her up. As I walked out of the apartment building, I felt eyes on me. But when I looked around, no one was there. Visiting Freddy had made me paranoid, as it so often did. No matter how old I got or what I did, being that close to someone with that much contraband always made me nervous. I probably had my father to blame for it.

As I drove away from the building, I made sure to maintain my speed and not violate any traffic laws. I kept one eye on my rearview mirror, but I didn't see any police cruisers or tails. That helped squelch the uneasy feeling that had wormed its way into the pit of my stomach. By the time I opened my front door and found Jade waiting for me, it was no longer even an afterthought.

"Hey, honey, how was your day?" I took off my jacket and grabbed a hanger from the coat closet.

"It was okay, I guess." She picked at a hangnail, her gaze darting from me to the floor.

"Did something happen?"

"Nope, everything's great. I saw Mary Beth." Her chin quivered a little. "We talked about some hard stuff."

"Are you sure you're okay?" I crossed the room and knelt in front of her, reminding myself she didn't like to be touched.

"I'm fine. Stop asking me that."

I held up my palms. "Okay. Give me five minutes to change into something else and then we'll go." I'd just pulled a black button-up with silver pinstripes from the closet when I noticed Jade lingering in the doorway. "Enjoying the view?"

"Yes." She chewed on her bottom lip for a few moments, a mischievous grin on her face.

After changing into something stylish but casual, I closed the closet, went into the bathroom to wash my hands, ran a hand through my hair so it'd do that sexy, messy thing Jade liked, and grabbed my keys. "Still in the mood for Chinese?"

"Absolutely. I'm starving." From the way she'd been looking at me, I wasn't convinced it was food she wanted, but the rest could wait until after we ate.

While I set the alarm, she stepped into the hallway. I followed her out and pushed the button for the elevator. When we made it to my car, I opened her door and waited for her to get in.

"You're such a gentleman." She kissed my cheek and slid into the passenger seat. After I put the car into drive, she took my hand in hers. "You really haven't dated anyone since I left?"

"No."

"Why not?"

"Jade, come on, why are we having this conversation?" I already knew it would lead to no good.

"Humor me."

"I've been busy. When would I have had time?"

"What about before?"

"Before what?" I glanced at her before returning my eyes to the road.

"Before I showed up at your office that day. Before we met. Before Scott…"

Since she had taken my free hand prisoner, I didn't have to worry about demonstrating my usual nervous tic. Instead, I found my throat had gone dry. After clearing it, I shrugged. "I haven't seen anyone steady in a long time."

"Except me."

"I guess, if you call what we had steady."

"We weren't casual."

"No."

"You let me stay over whenever I wanted."

"I'd let you do anything you want. You know that."

She fell silent. Unsure what minefield I would wander into by pursuing this line of questioning, I let the quiet linger for a while. When I couldn't take it anymore, I turned on the radio, flipping through the presets on the steering wheel controls until I found something fun and poppy. Jade squeezed my hand and sang along until we parked at the restaurant.

The hostess greeted us and asked for our names. After marking something on the chart, she led us to a table near a window. I pulled out Jade's chair and pushed it in after she sat. Since she thought I was a gentleman, I figured I better act the part.

A moment later, someone arrived to take our drink orders. We started with cocktails and a variety of appetizers. After he disappeared, Jade carefully studied the menu.

"I haven't had good Chinese food in a long time." She

frowned at the selections.

"Is something wrong? If you'd rather go somewhere else, we can leave."

"No, it's not that. I just can't decide what to get. It all looks so good. General Tso's chicken, beef and broccoli, shrimp lo mein, moo shu pork." She looked up at me. "What are you getting? We can split our entrees, right?"

"Jade, you don't have to pick. This is your last night in the city. You can have whatever you want. It's my treat."

"No, I can't eat that much. Maybe we should have gone to one of those buffet places."

I cringed. "Didn't you say you wanted good Chinese food?"

She laughed. "You got me there."

The appetizers came, and while Jade was distracted by the shrimp toast and spare ribs, I ordered a selection of soups, white and fried rice, and told the server we'd need a few minutes to figure out entrees. Jade appeared to be in heaven as she crunched on the fried shell surrounding an egg roll.

After limiting our ordering to one item from each protein category, I settled into my chair, watching Jade nibble little pieces of everything. When the soups came, she picked out two to sample. Halfway through her cup of hot and sour, she abruptly put her spoon down and wiped her mouth.

"Stop staring at me. Aren't you going to eat anything?"

"Sorry. I just forgot how cute you are." I grabbed the bowl of wonton soup and scooted it closer. "Is it good?"

"It's fantastic." She nudged the tray of appetizers closer, and I snared one of the egg rolls since she had no interest in them besides a single bite. I'd forgotten she didn't like them. "That's better. You were making me feel like a glutinous pig."

"You're not a pig. You've barely made a dent in anything."

"It all adds up."

"Don't tell me you're watching your figure. You're perfect no matter what."

"You mean that, don't you?"

"I wouldn't have said it if I didn't."

She stopped eating and wiped her mouth on the napkin before placing it back on her lap. "It's quite possible you're the most amazing guy in the world." The way she said it made it seem like that was a problem, but no matter how I twisted it around in my head, I couldn't figure out what was wrong with that.

ELEVEN

"Should we splurge and get the green tea ice cream?" I asked.

Jade stared at me with wide eyes. The server had already taken back our five entrees to box up, along with the leftover appetizers and soups. "You're joking."

"It's green tea ice cream. Didn't you drag me out of the house at one a.m. that time to get green tea ice cream because they wouldn't deliver and you had to have it?"

"I didn't drag you. Plus, you skipped PT that day. You were supposed to walk around. I just wanted to make sure you got your exercise."

"Uh-huh."

"I needed exercise too."

I snorted. "Fine. If you don't want to split a scoop of ice cream, I'll have to eat it all by myself."

"I don't want it."

"Okay." When it came, I picked up one of the two spoons, took a bite, and waited. Just like our first encounter, Jade stared at the food on the plate in front of me, except this wasn't a giant cookie, it was ice cream. After another spoonful, I pushed the bowl to the middle of the table. "All right. I'm done."

While I was pulling my wallet out, Jade snared the second spoon and sliced off the other side of the ice cream globe. She closed her eyes to savor it, triggering a pain in my chest. This should be just another day for us, not a second goodbye.

"Where are you applying to school?" I asked.

"What?"

"You said you had to get your transcripts. Don't schools usually send those upon request?"

"Sometimes, but I needed an unofficial copy." She finished the rest of the ice cream. "I think I'm going to pop."

She didn't answer my question. My inquisitive nature demanded a response, but I didn't push. Instead, I paid the check and picked up the bag of leftovers. Knowing Jade, she'd want a snack later tonight, and whatever was left I could take to the office for lunch. Justin would bitch about eating my leftovers, but this was one of the hottest new restaurants and he wouldn't pass up the opportunity to sample the cuisine.

"Lucien," she nudged me as we made our way to the car, "you just disappeared. Where did you go?"

"I'm right here."

"No, you're not." She took the bag from my hand and slipped into the car. When I got in on my side, she had one knee up on the seat so she could face me directly. "We can't keep doing this. We can't pretend what we have is nothing."

"I never said it was nothing. It's not nothing, but you don't want to be here. And I won't ask you to stay."

"Why not?"

"Jade, it's not fair."

"No, it's not. None of this is fucking fair." She pressed her fingertips to her eyes to wipe the tears, breaking my heart. "He did this to me. To us. The worst part is I wouldn't even know you if it hadn't been for him."

My throat felt tight. "I know, but he can't hurt you. You're safe. You're safe here. You're safe in Colorado. Wherever you go, you'll be safe. I promise."

"A part of me wants to come back. I just... I don't know."

She turned to face the windshield and put on her seatbelt. "Let's go home."

I pulled into traffic. A light rain had started to fall in sync with Jade's tears, which she fought against. I paid attention to the rearview, noticing a silver SUV turn when I did. He pulled past me on the next street, and my eye caught a dark blue sedan a few cars back. I wondered if it was an unmarked police car. From here, I couldn't tell, but I thought I spotted the bars and spotlight.

"Today was hell, Lucien. After I left your apartment, I went to Mary Beth's. Her roommate's going through a similar situation, but her ex isn't nearly as psychotic or dangerous. He calls a lot. The phone kept ringing. Maybe it was her nervous energy that I picked up on, but after that, I was anxious all day. It felt like people were watching me, following me. I can't tell you how many times I turned around and thought I saw someone tailing me."

Her words worried me. "What did he look like?"

"Scott." She laughed. "I know. It's crazy. And then when I took the train, I saw the cops down in the station, and god, those uniforms, you'd think I was a wanted criminal or something with the way they freaked me out."

"It's okay."

"No, it's not. I want to take control of my life. I don't want to be freaked out for no good reason."

"Are you still freaked out?"

"No. After I got back to the apartment, I didn't feel like I was being watched anymore. I felt safe. You always make me feel safe. Your apartment feels safe. You let me stay with you a lot after it happened. Your place is like my second home. Maybe my only home in this city. You're my home, Lucien. This place isn't."

"You can stay with me as long as you like." Recalling our conversation from yesterday, I asked, "Do you want to live together? I didn't think that was something you ever wanted to do again."

"I...I don't know."

"Okay."

"Is that something you want?"

My hand went through my hair. "This can't be my

decision."

"Why not?"

The dark sedan turned, but the silver SUV which had passed me and parked at a hydrant while I'd been stopped at the red light pulled back in behind me after I passed. It sent an uneasy feeling through me. Then again, this conversation had already spiked my blood pressure and adrenaline, so I couldn't tell if my reaction had anything to do with the SUV or if it had everything to do with Jade and our relationship status.

"Why not?" she repeated.

My gaze flicked from the rearview to the side mirrors. I took the next turn, wondering if the SUV would follow. It did. I took the turn after that.

"Lucien, where are we going? What's wrong?"

"I'm not sure."

She paled, turning to glance behind us. The SUV had dropped back two car lengths, but its high profile made it easy to spot over the Mazda coupe behind me. I took the next turn. The Mazda went straight, and the SUV turned too. One more turn, and we'd have gone in a complete circle. So I made the last turn, but the SUV didn't follow. It turned in the opposite direction.

Letting out a sigh, I checked a few more times to see if anyone else was following me, but we were in the clear. Jade's paranoia must have been contagious. "We're okay," I said, hoping to soothe her. "False alarm."

"Who do you think would be following you?"

"I don't know."

"You don't know?"

"No, but it's not beyond the realm of possibility. The cops have it out for me, more now than before. And with my clients, you never know who I might piss off."

She swallowed, fidgeting with the seatbelt and drumming her fingers against her thighs. At that moment, I knew she couldn't stay. It wouldn't be fair to her. She needed to feel safe, and my life wasn't safe. I wasn't safe, just ask the angel of death.

We returned to my apartment without incident and had passionate, life-affirming sex. When I opened my eyes after a brief nap, I found Jade curled up on the window seat with her legs tucked beneath her. She wore my shirt with the sleeves rolled up to her elbows.

"It's still raining." She scooted forward, so I could slide in between her and the wall. I rested my back against it and placed one foot flat on the window seat beside her. She settled into the space I made with her head resting just beneath my chin. I brushed the soft waves of her red hair with my fingers. She put her hand on my knee. "Maybe I should delay my departure date."

"You can. We have tons of Chinese left to eat."

She laughed, but her focus remained out the window. We were so high up, it was hard to see much beneath us, especially in the dark. Still, I spotted a large silver sports utility vehicle parked at a hydrant. The bike rack on top reminded me of the one from earlier. A lot of people in this building owned similar vehicles, so I resisted the urge to investigate further. I didn't want to freak Jade out, and right now, I wanted to spend every remaining moment close to her.

"Any interest in moving to Colorado?" she asked. "I'm sure they could use privatized policing, security consultants, or private eyes." She tilted her head to the side to look at me. "What do you even call yourself?"

"Most days, Lucien. Sometimes, Cross. It just depends on my mood."

"That's not what I meant."

"It depends on the client. The guy I'm working for now needed a private eye. So that's what he got. Miranda needed a security consultant, so that's what she got."

"You're like a chameleon. They blend in to whatever environment they inhabit. See, you could live in Colorado."

"I could." But I didn't want to. "Perhaps, one day I'll be able to expand to the West Coast. Maybe open an L.A. office. What do you think of Los Angeles?"

"That'd be nice."

"One day, but not today or tomorrow." I cleared my throat. "Jade, I lied to you earlier. I said you were safe here, but I don't know if that's true. Being around me is unpredictable. I don't exactly get paid to find lost dogs."

"You're in the business of making enemies." She shivered. "I know. I've seen firsthand what happens when you piss people off."

"I'm not asking you to leave now or tomorrow or ever, but I want you to be aware of what could happen."

"I am." She turned to check the time. "My flight leaves at 1:20. I should be at the airport by 11:30."

"You don't have to go," I said, but we both knew that wasn't true.

"I don't want you to wait."

"At the airport? You want me to just drop you off?"

"That's not what I'm talking about. I'm talking about you. Your future."

"Honey, I'm still getting this office off the ground. I can't expand yet."

"No, Lucien, I meant I don't want you to wait for me. You should go out, have fun, date. What we've been doing since I left hasn't been healthy for either of us."

"What have we been doing? We talk once or twice a week. We're friends, right?"

"Friends who have sex."

"They call those benefits," I said.

She let out a sigh and pulled away from me. "We have to move on. I have to move on. You have to move on."

"I didn't realize I was stopping you." I fought to keep the anger out of my voice, but I wasn't sure I succeeded.

"You haven't, but you're stopping yourself. I don't want to feel guilty or responsible for that. I'm not ready to date yet, but one day, I will be. If you're still burning a candle for me when that time comes, I don't know what will happen. But I can't come back here. I just can't."

Nodding, I got up and went into the kitchen. This conversation required a drink. Several drinks. While I poured a shot of whiskey, Jade went to the fridge, heated some leftovers, took her plate to the table, and sat down.

"Don't be mad." She slid the food around on the plate for something to do.

"I'm not." I swallowed the shot and resisted the urge to pour a second one. The last thing she needed was to see me drunk and angry. That would just bring back bad memories from relationships past. "Do I remind you of him?"

"No."

"But when you see me, you think about what happened that night, right?"

She stared at the table, barely nodding.

"Well, fuck." I dropped into the chair across from her, picked up the extra fork she'd grabbed, and skewered a piece of chicken. I didn't scare her, but I reminded her of all the things she hoped to forget. The city might not be the problem, but I was.

We sat in silence, picking our way through the chicken and vegetables. Neither of us had an appetite, but it was something to do. The food tasted like wet cement, but it eliminated the need for conversation, apologies, or arguments. When we were done eating our late night snack, I cleaned the kitchen while Jade brushed her teeth and went back to bed.

After I joined her, she curled up against my chest and fell asleep. I watched her for the longest time, glancing occasionally out the window at the suspicious-looking SUV. Around dawn, my eyelids drooped.

"I love you," I whispered before falling asleep.

TWELVE

By the time we left for the airport, the SUV was gone. I kept an eye out for possible tails, but in the light of day, none of that seemed real. Our conversation from last night had numbed me.

I pulled to a stop at the end of the drop-off line. Jade leaned over, running a hand over the stubble on my jaw. "Lucien—"

"I know." I took her hand and pressed it to my lips. "You have to go. The reason you left was to put this behind you."

"Maybe one day I will."

"Maybe."

She leaned in and kissed me on the mouth. "Don't wait. Promise me."

"I won't."

She swallowed, her lashes wet from the impending tears. "Good, because I'm going to want progress reports."

"Some things are best left unsaid."

"You're going to date, whether you like it or not."

"Jade, I'm not much of a dater."

"Fine, go get laid. I don't care. Just be safe. And I mean that every which way imaginable."

"Yes, ma'am." I watched her reach for the strap on her duffel. "Are you sure you don't want me to park and walk you inside?"

"No, it's time we said goodbye."

"Call me when you get home?"

"I will." She kissed me again, a desperate, passionate yearning that had me leaning so far over the seatbelt nearly choked me. Then she grabbed her bag and slammed the door.

I waited until she was safely inside before parking the car and hoping she'd change her mind, even though I knew it was best that she didn't. After her flight took off, I paid the two hour parking fee and headed back to the office. My mind on nothing but the smell of her shampoo and the taste of her lips.

"Hey, boss." Justin looked up when I didn't mumble back a greeting. "Is everything okay?"

"Uh-huh."

Justin exchanged a look with Gloria before following me into my office. He had a stack of files in his arms which he dropped beside my computer. "No hits on your listings on the dark web. I made those calls you asked me to, but none of the other pawn shops had the items I requested."

"Did you ask if they could get them?"

"They were dead ends."

Pouring a hefty amount of scotch into my empty coffee cup, I took a sip. "Call Pauley's and ask about Knox's basketball collection, but use one of the burner phones we have in the cabinet. I don't want them to connect that to me."

"I can be vague. Anything else?"

"Did Freddy call?"

"No."

It had been less than twenty-four hours. I had to give the man time to work, but my patience had grown thin. I wanted this case to be over. "Have you set up interviews yet for the new security staff?"

"They start tomorrow at noon and run through the following day."

"What about new applicants?"

"The posting went out yesterday. I mentioned we'd interview on Friday of next week."

"Fine." I swallowed more scotch, burning the back of my throat. "I'll get started on the work I promised our two new corporate clients. Once I get the employee background checks out of the way, I'll move on to their internet security assessment. If I do it myself, we won't have to hire freelance IT guys." I waved a dismissive hand in Justin's direction, not wanting to look up and see the question or concern on his face. But he didn't move.

"The last time I saw you like this was two days before you threw our boss's chair through the window."

"It's a good thing I'm the boss. Now get back to work."

The hours went by without me noticing. Background checks were time consuming, but they didn't require much brain power. Type, skim, print. I could probably do it in my sleep if only I knew how to sleep with my eyes open and fingers moving.

Justin brought a plate into my office and put it on the edge of my desk. He didn't say anything, but I thanked him for the pizza. The smell made my stomach growl, even though I hadn't noticed I was hungry.

Folding the slice in half, I chewed on the end while I stared out the window. Why was it suddenly so dark out? A glance at the clock told me it was almost ten. No wonder my legs were numb. After I finished the slice, I used the desk to push myself into a standing position and locked my knees, waiting for the blood flow and feeling to return before I tried to walk. Before going home, I'd have to put in some time at the gym or I'd regret it tomorrow.

A worrisome thought came to mind, and I went into the outer office. "Did I receive any calls?"

"Nothing."

I returned to the office and called a contact I had with Jade's cell phone carrier. Her phone was turned off. I pulled up her flight information and found that due to bad weather her return flight had been rerouted to Atlanta and delayed a few hours. Now I felt like a stalker, no better than her previous ex. "This has to stop," I muttered.

"What, boss?"

"Working so late. You should have left hours ago."

"Then who would be here to assist you?"

"Don't be a smart ass."

"I finished writing the reports you wanted and left them in your dropbox to review before you send them to our clients. I also invoiced Mr. Rathbone for next quarter to include the advanced services he requested, and I have three interviews scheduled for new applicants next Friday. As far as Mr. Knox's case, Pauley's didn't bite when I asked about the basketballs. I did some more checking but found nothing. No one has. Whoever stole Knox's stuff is keeping a low profile. Do you think it's another collector with no interest in the monetary value?"

"Could be, but why did he hire a crew to commit the theft and pawn the signed pennant?"

"Maybe the thieves don't like baseball."

"It's possible, but it doesn't seem right." I leaned my hips against his desk, stretching one leg and then the other. My back pinched, and I bit back the wince. "I checked the intel you sent me on the company, but it was rather vague. Did you dig anything else up on the LLC or Dmitri Lenmere?"

"Nope."

"Me neither. It looks like a reputable business, at least as far as pawn shops go. I even checked the employees, but that didn't get me far either."

"You need to identify their sellers. Perhaps you should try the direct approach."

"Too risky. It could tip 'em off." I went back to my office, shut down my computer, removed my gun from the drawer, tucked it behind my back, and put on my jacket. "What do we have tomorrow morning?"

"Not much. A few interviews with prospective clients."

"Good. If I'm late, you're in charge. You know what to do. I trust you can take care of it."

"What are you going to do?"

"Identify the seller and drink myself into a stupor."

"I take it she left."

I nodded, not wanting to say the words but needing to tell someone. "She's not coming back."

"You could visit her. Go away for romantic weekends every so often. You have the money."

"Originally, I thought maybe that'd be something she'd want." Come to think of it, I didn't know. She said we could be together if and when we were in the same time zone, but then she insisted we had to move on. Perhaps, I'd ask for clarification. "But I'm pretty sure we're done."

"In that case, invite someone to drink with you. Miranda might still be in town."

"No, she's a client. I'm not crossing that line."

"Since when?"

"Right now."

*   *   *

I stared at the neon sign for Pauley's Pawn. It was no longer lit. The woman who'd helped me yesterday had left forty-five minutes ago after pulling down the metal gate covering the front door and windows. A few dull lights remained within, probably from the display cases.

The place wouldn't be easy to breach. They had an alarm system and not a cheap one. The front would be too obvious and draw a lot of attention. Even though the pawn shop closed for the night, several adult shops and a few bars on the street did a good business. Someone would notice the idiot in the suit breaking in. And even if they didn't, one of the nearby security cameras would. Deciding it was best to rethink my plan of attack, I assessed the neighboring exterior cameras, figuring I might be able to pull footage of the thieves entering Pauley's Pawn with Knox's memorabilia instead.

The Stop-n-Shop on the corner had the best angle of the pawn shop's side door. So I spent the better part of the next two hours attempting to hack into local networks and access the nearby security feeds, but I had no luck. Either I didn't have nearly as many computer skills as I liked to pretend I did, or the security feeds were hardwired or non-networked. From the looks of the security cameras I'd seen, I was betting on the latter.

That left me with two options, go into the nearby shops and politely ask for access to their exterior security footage for the last few days or wait a few more hours and do it the hard way. The first option would bulk up the incidentals I'd charge Mr. Knox. Also, I didn't know if the surrounding shop owners would comply with my request. Something told me the nature of their businesses would make them less likely to want to help a private investigator. If they didn't want to help, I'd have to resort to plan B anyway. So maybe I should just start there.

Circling the block, I entered the Stop-n-Shop. The guy behind the counter was watching a video on his phone but looked up when the bell above my head chimed. He nodded at me and went back to his video. Another employee was mopping around a caution sign where blue slushie covered the floor and continued to drip from the machine.

"Bathroom?" I asked.

The guy with the mop jerked his chin toward the narrow hallway between the coolers and the hot dog machine. "It's unlocked."

"Thanks."

I went down the hall, hoping to find an office or back room where the security system might be. Unfortunately, the only door in the hallway led to a unisex bathroom. Shaking my head at the disgusting smell that assaulted me the moment I pushed open the door, I retreated, having no desire to even pretend to use the john.

Neither man noticed when I returned to the main area, so I went around a few of the shelves until I happened upon another door. This one was open and led to a storage room with janitorial supplies, excess stock, a couple of lawn chairs, and a rusted aluminum TV tray covered in cigarette ashes and squished out butts. Again, no security system.

"Hey, what are you doing?" The guy with the mop wheeled it into the room, not bothering to empty the muddy blue water from the bucket before shoving it into a corner. "The bathroom's down the other hall."

"I don't need the bathroom."

He sized me up. "So what do you want?"

"I'm looking for your security system."

"Why?"

I reached into my pocket and pulled out my wallet. Flipping it open to my P.I. license, I flashed it at him like a TV cop and tucked it back into my pocket before he got a good look at it. "The camera outside covers the street and a few of the other shops. I wanted to check something out. I need your footage from the last two weeks. I can make it worth your while."

The guy cocked an eyebrow at my jacket. "All our camera shit is behind the counter. You got a warrant or something?"

"I have a few Benjamins to award to anyone who wants to help out."

"How many?"

Laughing at the shakedown, I pulled out two, crisp one hundred dollar bills. "One for you and one for your pal." I handed them both to him. "I just need a copy of the footage."

"You got something I can save it on?"

This wasn't the first time someone wanted the footage from this shop. I handed him a blank USB drive. He pocketed it.

"All right. Buy some chips or gum or something. I'll meet you out front," he said.

Following him out of the storage room, I picked up a bag of pre-popped popcorn and a cola before making my way to the counter. By then, the guy who'd been watching TV had gone to service the coffee machine. I placed the items on the counter for the other guy to ring up. After I paid, he slid the USB back to me with my change.

"Have a nice day."

I gave him my hard stare, wondering if he'd bilked me out of two hundred dollars. I guess I'd find out soon enough. "Thanks."

Once I got back to my car, I circled around to another spot farther down the block, grabbed my laptop, and plugged in the drive. The store clerk had copied all the footage from the last fourteen days. I scanned back to the night of the break-in at Trey Knox's apartment, cracked open the bottle of cola, and wrote down every license plate that parked outside of Pauley's Pawn.

A white van appeared four different times, every three days since the break-in. The driver, a man wearing a trench coat and bowler hat who kept his face turned away from the cameras, always went to the side door with a large cardboard box. I had no idea what was inside, but since I never spotted anyone else entering the store with anything large enough to hold Knox's collection or even just the pennant, this had to be one of the thieves. Now I just had to figure out who he was.

THIRTEEN

The last place I wanted to go was back to the office. Instead, I went to Charlene's, an upscale speakeasy I used to frequent a lifetime ago. The smell of cigar smoke and expensive liquors permeated the air. I recognized a few faces, but it'd been years since I'd talked to most of those people.

"What'll it be?" the attractive bartender asked.

"Scotch and soda."

"Cigar?"

I shook my head.

"Do you want to start a tab?"

"I'll pay as I go."

"Great."

She poured while I fished some cash out of my wallet. I probably should have started a tab since I was running low on green and had no idea how long I'd be here. I gave her a twenty dollar tip, took my drink, and found a comfy chair next to a mahogany side table.

This gave me the perfect spot to drink and work. While I sipped my scotch, I ran the plate number on the van. It was registered to a storage facility. So I did some checking on the storage facility. It was just like every other climate-controlled, self-storage facility around, except it was owned by Lenmere LLC.

Anything could be inside those units. The white van was available for rent from the place. Not only could you pay to store your stuff but you could also rent the van to move your crap to and from the unit. That was genius. The place was full service. Idly, I wondered how to make Cross Security more full service. So far, I offered security consultations, investigations, and protection. What else would clients want or need?

"Mind if I join you?" a woman asked.

I looked up. She wore ridiculously high heels, which made her already too thin legs look even thinner. She had a cocktail in her hand and practically crawled over my lap to get to the chair on the other side.

"I never said yes."

She pouted at me. "Don't you want company? You look lonely." Her hand ran up my thigh.

I laughed, picking up on just a hint of an accent. "How much?"

"Depends."

"No, it doesn't." I shook my head, feeling like I was being punked. Charlene's was upscale. Then again, so was the woman in the high heels. I'd crossed plenty of lines in my day, but hiring a sex worker was something I'd never even consider. "What are you drinking?"

"A gimlet."

"That's funny. I'm normally a gin guy."

She smiled demurely. "What else do you like?"

"I'd like you to take your hand off my leg."

She leaned forward, her cleavage spilling out from the top of her dress. I'd say it was designer, probably last season or the season before. It tied in the front, but it didn't scream cheap. And until she bent over, it didn't scream sex either. "Why?"

Looking around the room, I clocked the crowd. The waitstaff appeared attentive. They knew the regulars, the troublemakers, and exactly what was going on. From the glances they kept giving a table near the back, I had my own suspicions. Adjusting in the seat, I closed my laptop and tucked it back in my bag.

A man and woman sat at the back table. He looked comfortable, but they only had water glasses in front of them. He kept stroking her arm, gesturing animatedly with his drink hand and doing his best to appear drunk. She appeared to be bored out of her mind.

Raising my glass in his direction, I smiled and nodded. For the life of me, I couldn't remember his name, but I remembered his beefy face and the scar tissue around his nose. He'd played high school football and a little in college until he got kicked off the team for a knee injury. I'd heard the story a dozen times in the academy. Ellis, Elvis, Elmer, it was something like that.

"Friend of yours?" she asked.

"Nope." I scanned the rest of the room, but I didn't spot her pimp. He might be outside, or she worked for a service or herself. It was hard to tell with the way the sex industry had broken down, but I hoped her actions were her choice, the johns treated her well, and management wasn't abusive. "I'd suggest you take the night off unless you want to spend it in a cell. I might be lonely, but I don't pay for company. Call it a pride thing. It's just how I am. No offense."

She shrugged it off. "Are you a cop?"

"No," my gaze remained on the two across the room, "I wasn't cut out for it."

"Okay," she said uncertainly.

Downing the rest of my drink, I grabbed my computer bag and headed for the exit. On my way, I detoured to the table in the back corner and gave Elvis a pat on the shoulder. "You following me?" I asked.

"Shit. Cross? Is that you?"

"In the flesh."

"Jeez, what's it been? Like five years?"

"Something like that."

He gave his head a shake and nudged the woman. "This is Lucien fucking Cross." He turned back to stare at me. "Are you shitting me right now?"

"Are you following me?"

"You? Fuck no. We're hoping to find some crumbs

that'll lead us to the big cheese."

I gave him a cockeyed look.

"This is Tanya, my partner." He alternated between staring at me and the prostitute who had now moved on to a broker seated at the bar.

"You're blowing our cover, Mr. Cross," the other vice cop whispered.

I held up my palms. "You need to dress better if you want to blend in at a bar like this. The place has standards."

"You always were a dick," Elvis mumbled.

"Glad I could be of assistance. Have a lovely night, officers." My voice carried, and half the bar turned to stare at the cops seated at the table.

As I left Charlene's, Jade's fears played through my head. She said someone had been following her. My gut said that SUV I spotted last night had been tailing us, even though it broke off pursuit. Could it have been a few police officers hoping to rattle Jade for revenge? They might also want to rattle me, except I didn't rattle. That might explain Elvis and the prostitute. The working girl could have been an undercover vice cop.

When I made it back to my car, I made a point not to put the keys in the ignition. If the cops were out to get me, I wouldn't give them a slam dunk on drunk driving charges, even if I doubted I was beyond the legal limit. Instead, I locked the doors and surveyed the area. A silver SUV with a bike rack sat parked a few blocks away. I couldn't make out much from here, but since I didn't see any exhaust, I had to assume the engine was off. It could belong to the cops inside. Elvis was enough of a creep to follow me as a form of harassment.

So I waited, wondering if I'd be stopped once I pulled out of the parking space. Maybe Jade's fears had fueled my paranoia. I couldn't be sure, so I remained in my car for another thirty minutes while I finished the work I started in the bar before the prostitute interrupted me. Perhaps, she was working with vice in exchange for a reduced sentence, and this was a sting to arrest a few johns. Boy, were they barking up the wrong tree.

My phone rang, and I laughed when I saw Jade's name on the display. "Hi."

"You're in a good mood," she said.

"I was just propositioned."

"Wow, you don't waste any time." She sounded hurt.

"I said no."

"Why? I told you to move on."

"And this morning you were in my bed. I'm not going to move on that quickly. How was your flight? Did you just land?"

"A little while ago. We were redirected. I'm home now." She sighed. "Tell me about the woman who propositioned you. Was she pretty?"

"She's a professional."

"Well, you like professionals."

"Not a business professional, a sex worker."

"Oh." Jade paused, unsure what to say. "Don't have sex with a prostitute."

"I wasn't planning on it."

"Good. Don't."

"Any other rules I should be aware of?"

"No."

"Jade, honey," I sucked in a breath, "I don't like how we left things. I want to ask you something. It's probably too soon, but in the event I find myself out west or traveling somewhere fun and exotic, I was thinking if the two of us are unattached at that time, maybe we could meet up for a few days and have some fun together, like you originally suggested. Is that something you might still consider?"

"Isn't that counterproductive?"

"I don't know. Is it? I'm not saying we wait. I'm just saying if I'm free and you're free and we're in the same place at the same time, why can't we make the most of it?"

She didn't say anything, but I could picture her biting her lip and fidgeting with whatever was nearby. "Let me talk to my therapist about it."

"Whatever you want. I just wanted some clarification." I counted to ten. "I'm glad you got home safely."

"Me too."

"Before you go, I just had one more question. The guy

you thought was following you yesterday, did you see him get into a vehicle?"

"No, why?"

"No reason." I stared out the windshield at the SUV. "I should let you go. Sweet dreams."

"Goodbye, Lucien."

Every time she said it, I hated it more and more. Irritated, I shook off my paranoid thoughts as nothing more than a consequence of my fucked up romantic situation and headed for the gym. If the police wanted to pull me over, I'd make their night a living hell. But I arrived at my destination without incident.

After changing in the locker room, I stretched, warmed up on the treadmill, and hit the free weights. After too many rows and dead lifts, my lower back ached, but at least my legs weren't numb. Too spent to do much else, I showered and headed home.

FOURTEEN

"You've got to be kidding me." I adjusted my rearview mirror so the morning sun wouldn't be quite so blinding. Could this be a paranoid hallucination? I turned in my seat and looked behind me. Nope, not a hallucination. The silver SUV was two car lengths away. I'd seen it pull out of the parking space across the street from my apartment as soon as I pulled out of the garage. This was no coincidence.

I turned. The SUV turned. This was getting ridiculous. As I approached the next traffic light, the car between us switched lanes, placing the SUV directly behind me. Due to the sun's glare and that reflective plastic sheet he had over his front plate, I couldn't get his license plate number.

I kept going straight, but he stayed with me. At the next intersection, I came upon a stale yellow. It'd turn red before I made it to the white lines. Oh well, I needed to get a new car, anyway. Slowing down, I came to a practical crawl as I approached the light. The moment it turned red, I gunned the engine and flew through the intersection.

Despite the angry beeps and shouted expletives, the SUV kept pace with me. Whoever this asshole was, he must not know who he was messing with. At this time of morning, I wasn't in the mood. I took a sharp turn and another. I thought I lost him, but I spotted the SUV making the first turn I'd already made.

"Nope, we're not doing this." I cut through an alley, ignoring the posted signs prohibiting such action, and pulled out directly in front of him. For a moment, I didn't think the SUV would stop before it T-boned me. But it screeched to a halt. The shriek of the brakes still echoed as I threw open my door and aimed my gun at the driver. "Let me see your hands."

The driver looked up from whatever it was he'd been staring at on his lap, fear marring his features. He raised both hands as I maneuvered around my car, the engine purring as it idled. He didn't open his door or make any move whatsoever.

When I got closer, I wondered why some college-aged guy was tailing me. He didn't look like he posed a threat, but that didn't mean anything. He could be fresh out of the police academy or a military reject working as a hitman. From the way he trembled, I doubted the likelihood of the second, but it was best to be prepared for anything.

"Open the door." I kept my gun trained on him.

"Okay. Okay. Whatever you want. Just don't hurt me." Slowly, he unlocked the door.

As soon as I heard the click, I grabbed the handle and yanked the door open. The guy wore khakis and a blue polo. "Why are you following me?" I asked.

"Following you? I'm not following you."

Grabbing his collar, I tried to yank him out of the seat, but the belt held him in place. Instead, I took his wallet from where he'd left it on the center console and glanced at his ID. *Will Esposito.* He was twenty-six, just a couple of years younger than me, but he looked like he'd be carded at bars.

"You can have my money. The car. Whatever. Just don't hurt me." He cowered as I leaned closer, my gun in his face. "My mom said I'd get carjacked in this neighborhood. Just let me out and you can take it." He hit the seatbelt release with his right hand before raising his palms again. "Take it, okay? You can have it. I won't fight you."

He tried to get out of the car, but I blocked his exit.

Allowing him to move about freely wasn't tactically sound. None of what I was doing was tactically sound, but that was beside the point.

I stared at him as if he were nuts. "Do you see what I'm driving? Why would I want this piece of shit?"

"I dunno."

I took a step back. "Why have you been following me?"

"I haven't. I'm not." He swallowed.

"You made every turn I did until I circled you. You followed me through the red. I saw you parked outside my apartment the last few nights and at the bar. Who the hell are you? What do you want?"

"What?" He shifted again, and I realized he'd wet himself. "I'm looking for 127 Claremont. I'm not following you." For the first time, he realized we weren't even on a main thoroughfare. Two or three cars had driven past us, but no one had stopped. No one wanted to intervene in a dangerous situation. He pointed to his phone mounted to the tray beneath his stereo. "I wasn't paying attention to the traffic lights. I was just keeping up with the flow while I figured out the maps on the GPS."

Nothing about his story rang true, but I had no way of disproving any of it. And with a few more cars approaching, it was only a matter of time before someone called the cops to check it out. "Don't let me see you again." I pointed down the street. "Turn left, then right. It'll put you on Claremont. 127 should be on the left, about halfway down."

"Uh...thanks."

I got back in my car, wrote down his plate number, and waited for him to drive away. The cars behind us honked, annoyed by the inconvenience, but I didn't care. I'd led him to a secluded area, but no city street was secluded during morning rush hour.

After hitting speed dial, I gripped the steering wheel to combat the jitters. "Justin, I need you to run a plate for me." I gave him the SUV's license plate number. "See what you can dig up. After that, run a name. Will Esposito. If everything checks out, call Mr. Almeada and see if he can squeeze me in. The sooner, the better."

"Are you all right, boss? You sound a little out of breath."

"I'm fine. I'll see you soon." Turning my car around, I headed in the opposite direction. No silver SUV tailed me, but I couldn't shake the feeling someone was following me. "You're losing it," I told myself as I zipped through traffic and pulled into the parking garage near the office.

Slowly, I checked each level, but nothing suspicious caught my eye. I replayed my morning, wondering if I'd overreacted. The kid would probably call the cops. Traffic cams in the area would identify me in no time. By lunchtime, the police would have me in cuffs. My attorney better return my call. The best defense would be to have one ready to go before we had to scramble to come up with something, and right now, I had nothing, no proof of being stalked or followed. I couldn't even be positive the silver SUV I kept seeing had been the same silver SUV. Today was the first time I'd gotten a plate number.

When I opened the door to Cross Security and Investigations, Gloria greeted me with a cup of coffee and a friendly smile. "Good morning, sir."

"Thank you." I took the coffee, wanting to hug her for the unexpected act of kindness, but I refrained.

"Mr. Almeada is in a meeting right now, but he'll call you back as soon as he's finished. He knows it's urgent," Gloria said. "Justin is conducting a consultation in your office, but he left the information you requested up on his computer screen."

"Fabulous."

"Is there anything I can do?"

"You're wonderful, you know that?" I took a seat behind his desk and read the report. The SUV was registered to Lilian Esposito, a fifty-two year old woman. Will was her son. He had no criminal record.

"I do, but it's nice to hear it," she said.

"I'll keep that in mind. I don't imagine we'll have any walk-ins today, but if we do, give them an appointment for later in the week and organize our calendar. Also, if you wouldn't mind making arrangements to have breakfast and lunch delivered the rest of the week, something to keep the break room stocked for the interviewees and new client consultations we'll be conducting, I'd appreciate it."

"Do you need the bar in your office restocked?"

"Always." I clicked a few keys and checked Will's social media, not sure what I hoped to find. According to recent posts, he was starting a new job today. "Shit."

"Is everything okay?"

"It could be worse." I could be Will. A part of me hated that I'd possibly ruined this guy's new job, and another part of me knew a silver SUV, just like the one he drove, had been following me for the last few days. I wasn't convinced Will hadn't been tailing me, but if I'd gotten the wrong SUV, that meant whoever was tailing me was still out there.

Going into the break room, I peered out the tiny window, but I didn't see any suspicious vehicles parked in front of the building. All right, I had to let this go. I didn't have time to chase ghosts or lunatics. I had a lead to follow on Trey Knox's case and plenty of work to do in the office.

The phone rang. "Let me see if he's in." Gloria stepped into the break room. "Mr. Cross, a Mr. Freddy is on the phone. He didn't give his last name."

"I'll take it at your desk." This was just another reason why I needed a bigger office with more actual offices. Perhaps the break room, which had been a closet, should be converted into an extra office, but where would we put the espresso maker?

Gloria stayed in the break room to take inventory and figure out what we should keep on hand while I answered her phone.

"Hey, Luci, how's it hanging?" Freddy G asked.

"What do you have for me?"

"So I called my guy who knows a guy. He's been hearing whispers about that ring you're looking for. He says he can't get a hold of it since it's already been promised to someone else, but he'll keep looking in case there's another one around. Then again, we could just have one made."

"No, I need that one. Who's it promised to?" With any luck, the answer was me.

"I don't know. I tried to press him on it, but he didn't

like that. This isn't exactly how I normally conduct business, and he knows it."

"What do you normally do, Freddy?"

"If I can't get it from one source, I go to another."

"What happens if they all run dry?"

"They never all run dry, baby."

I waited for Freddy to connect the dots.

"Yeah, okay, I'll do some more asking around. Just know, if this were anybody else, I'd have one custom-made and pass it off as the real thing, but I know that won't help you."

"No, it won't. Did your guy happen to mention anything about Pauley's Pawn?"

"No." But from Freddy's tone, I didn't entirely believe him. "You got a connection besides me, Luci?"

"Yeah, me." I took a breath. "If you find out who it's already been promised to or who the seller is, let me know."

"That'll cost you."

"I'd expect nothing less."

Freddy laughed. "Drop by the penthouse around midnight. I should have something for you by then. I expect the usual payment."

"You got it." Assuming the cops didn't arrest me for assault with a deadly weapon.

Just as I hung up the phone, it rang a second time. Gloria poked her head out of the break room, but I shook my head. I hadn't gotten to where I was without having to answer a phone a time or two.

"Cross Security and Investigations. Lucien Cross speaking."

"Since when do you answer your own phone?" Mr. Almeada asked. "Did the hired help finally mutiny?"

"Don't bust my balls. I'm having a hell of a morning."

"Do I want to know?"

I told him what happened, including what I thought and where it occurred. "I don't know if he'll press charges."

"He should. You got his name, right? Maybe I should give him a call and make a suggestion."

"You're not funny."

"Maniacs with guns shouldn't scare the piss out of people on their way to work," Almeada said.

"I'm aware."

"You need to act like it. I'm guessing you never filed a report or spoke to anyone in the police department about your stalker."

"There was no point."

"Did you tell this guy who you were?"

"No."

"All right. Let's hope he's too embarrassed to say anything or make a report. You gave him directions, after all. That was nice of you."

I rolled my eyes. "What would you suggest I do if the police come knocking?"

"Throw yourself on the mercy of the court, or do what you always do. Keep your damn mouth shut and wait for me to show up to save your ass."

"Thanks."

"Seriously, Lucien, I wouldn't worry about it. You didn't harm him or cause any property damage, so you might be able to write it off as road rage. You tried to make amends at the scene, and if pushed, we'll say you're willing to go to anger management. Now if you don't mind, I have clients with actual problems. I'd prefer if you don't turn into one of them, so stay out of trouble the rest of the day."

"We'll see."

"I don't like the sound of that."

Ignoring the comment, I said, "While I have you, I wanted to let you know I'll have half a dozen or so new employee contracts that need review by the end of the week."

"Send them over. I'll add it to your billables, along with this phone call. You know, if you keep this up, I won't have to take on any new clients. Maybe I'll just work for you."

"Cross Security could use in-house counsel. What do you say?"

"Talk to me when you have a nice benefits package and partner perks to discuss."

"I'll have Justin draft a proposal."

"Save yourself some time. I'm already at your disposal

twenty-four seven, and I have too much invested with Reeves to jump ship now. My name's on the fucking door. And I don't think you have any desire to rename your company Almeada and Cross."

As usual, my attorney was correct. Unfortunately, I had a terrible habit of not listening.

FIFTEEN

While my assistant conducted consultations and scheduled appointments, I dug deeper into Lenmere LLC. Since the company owned Pauley's Pawn and the self-storage facility which supplied the rental van, I wondered if the pawn shop used that to hold their surplus storage or if something much more sinister was going on. Whoever broke into Mr. Knox's home and stole his collection could have stored the stolen items in one of the many climate-controlled units. However, I couldn't get names or unit numbers from inside my office.

"I'm going out." I grabbed my keys and slipped on my jacket. "Forward any calls to my cell."

"You got it, Mr. Cross," Gloria said.

On my way across town, I kept an eye on my mirrors, but I didn't spot a tail. The self-storage facility was near the water and guarded by a tall fence. The top had razor wire and spotlights posted around the perimeter. It looked more like a high-security prison than a place for people to stow their belongings.

The office was nothing more than a cinderblock shack with a glass door. Pulling open the door, I was assaulted by the pungent aroma of stale paint. From the looks of things, the place had probably been painted a couple of weeks ago, but without any windows or obvious means of ventilation, the fumes remained.

A man looked up from behind the desk where he'd been reading a textbook. "You looking to rent a unit?"

"Maybe." I gazed at the price chart on the wall behind him. "What kinds of things do people keep in these units?"

"Furniture, boxes, y'know, just whatever."

"Do you have a key to the units?"

"Nope. You bring your own lock." He marked something in the margin of the book with his pencil, stuck a piece of paper inside, and closed the book. *Physical Science.* "What are you hoping to store?"

"Baseball cards."

"You're serious?" He gave me a cockeyed look. "How many baseball cards do you have?"

"Thousands." I watched his reaction, but he looked shocked. If the thief used one of the units to stow Knox's collection, he hadn't shared that info with the guy working behind the counter. "Is that weird?"

"Whatever floats your boat, man. I don't ask. We have a list of prohibited items." He pointed to another sign before running his pointer finger across a pile of pamphlets. Pulling one out, he spread it open and pushed it across the counter toward me. "That's what you can't keep here, and you can't live inside the unit. Nothing flammable or dangerous, either. Other than that, we don't care what you put in your unit."

I skimmed the brochure. "What about moving vans? I thought I saw a white panel van with your logo on it."

"Yeah, we have a few parked out back. If you need to move things, you can rent one. We charge a daily rate and a mileage fee on top of that." He grabbed a leaflet from a drawer and handed it to me. "Those are the rates, along with the sizes."

"And your unit sizes?"

"They vary, but our largest is twelve by thirty. They all have drive-up access. You saw the electronic gate. You have to have the code to get in and out. It's self-serve, so any time of day or night you can get your stuff or put stuff in. If you want us to accept deliveries for your unit, you can schedule those ahead of time. We can let the delivery driver in, but it has to be during business hours, and we won't go in your unit. If the package is small enough, we'll hold it here until you arrive. If it's too large, we put it in our waiting area, but you can only get it during business hours, and we ask that you schedule a pickup appointment."

"So I can't get inside without the code?"

"Correct."

"And to get the code, I have to rent a unit."

"Also correct."

I read the price sheet. "Give me the five by five."

"We rent on a monthly basis, but if you want to sign up for six months or a year, you can save ten to twenty percent."

"Let's go month by month."

"Sounds good. I just need you to fill this out." He handed me a clipboard with an attached pen.

The best way to figure out what kind of customer information he possessed and where it was kept was by going through the process myself. So I filled out the form and handed it back to him. He entered the information in the computer while I did my best to lean over the counter and read over his shoulder.

"Did you want to rent a van to move your items in?"

"Is it another form?"

"No, we just add the charge here." He looked up. "We already have a copy of your license for the unit rental, so it's nothing more than checking a box."

"Yeah, all right." I could check the inside of the van for clues, but I had to make sure he gave me the same one I spotted outside Pauley's Pawn.

He grabbed a set of keys off the board and handed them to me. "Give me one sec." He held up his pointer finger while he waited for the circle on the screen to stop spinning. "You're all set." He came around the desk. "Let me show you around."

On our way out the door, he flipped the open sign to say, "Back in five." Then he led me to the electronic gate. "The code is 2-2-1-7. We change it on the first of the month, every month, to encourage our customers to remember to pay."

We went through the open gate, and I watched it close behind me. He led me down a row of units to the fourth one on the right. A-6.

"Is this my unit?" I asked.

"Yep." He lifted the gate to show me the interior, which was nothing more than a five foot by five foot square with ten foot ceilings. "The thermostat is here. As you can tell, it keeps out the humidity and elements to keep your valuables safe. I'm sure you don't want your cards to get damaged, so just set it and go. Should any malfunction occur, we are insured. However, if you'd like to take out additional insurance, we can do that for a fee." He frowned, realizing he was supposed to have tried to upsell me while we were still in the office.

"No, this is fine. I'm sure nothing will go wrong."

He showed me how to seal the unit and secure my lock, once I returned with one. Then he led me down a few more rows until we reached the vans. The keys he tossed to me belonged to a different van than the one I'd seen on the surveillance footage. "Can't I take that one, instead?" I pointed to the van in question.

"What's wrong with this one?"

"The rear tire looks a little flat, doesn't it? I bet it has a slow leak. See how it leans."

"Yeah, fine. Let me grab the other set of keys. Wait right here."

"No problem."

While he was gone, I wandered down the row of units, but every occupied one was locked. I'd have no way of knowing which unit belonged to the thieves, if my assumption was correct. There had to be a way to figure it out. Returning to the van, I peered at the fence, hoping to spot some surveillance cameras, but there weren't any.

The guy returned with the new set of keys. "Here ya go."

"Do you have security cameras?"

"At the front gate."

"That's it?"

"That's it."

That wouldn't help either. I could always set up my own security cameras. However, this place was vast. I'd have to do it strategically, and that would require the thieves to return to the unit.

I thought about the facility's records and computer system, but just because Knox's collection was stolen two weeks ago, that didn't mean the thieves hadn't been doing this for a while and already had the unit set up. My best bet of figuring this out would be tracking down who rented the van on the dates in question. Since it was linked to the unit rentals, I'd figure out which unit, pop it open, and look around. This shouldn't be that hard. If it wasn't a registered unit but instead one Lenmere saved for its holdings, that would lead me back to questioning the people at Pauley's and possibly paying Mr. Lenmere a visit.

"What are your hours? I want to make sure I get the van back to you before you close."

"We close at nine and open at eight."

I took the keys from him and opened the van door. "Any idea who rented this last?"

"Why? Now what's wrong?" Obviously, his patience had waned.

"Nothing, I was just curious. A buddy of mine recommended this place. He rented a van last Saturday. I thought it'd be funny if it was the same one."

"I don't know who rented it. I just type up the paperwork. It all blends together."

"Could you check?"

He cocked an eyebrow at me. "That's private. Why does it even matter?"

"You're right. It doesn't." I'd just have to find out on my own.

* * *

The interior of the van proved useless. No GPS, no tracking system, and the front and rear had been cleaned. The only usable prints I found inside matched me. The rest weren't in the system or had been smudged beyond use.

"Are you sure there's nothing in the back?" I asked.

Amir Karam stepped out of the van and pulled off his gloves. "Trace amounts of cocaine and gunpowder residue. Neither means much on its own, and it's not enough to establish anything."

"I take it there isn't any forensic science mojo that could magically tell me if this transported valuable sports memorabilia in the last two weeks."

"You'd be correct."

"What about technological means to tell me where the van has been?"

Amir blew out a breath. "This is old school. The system is computerized, but it doesn't have any of the usual suspects. It doesn't even have roadside assistance or satellite radio."

"How would you treat this if it had been part of a federal investigation?"

"I'd sweep the van, like we just did, and possibly take tire treads to compare to crime scenes or run the dirt to see if there was something odd about it, but that's only if it connected to an out of the ordinary crime scene."

"That's not gonna help us any."

"No kidding." Amir looked around the top level of the public parking garage. "It's probably for the best. This isn't the ideal workspace either."

"I'm working on it."

He nodded and closed the doors. "I have one other suggestion."

"What's that?"

"Stick a tracker on the van. If your thief uses it to make another delivery to the pawn shop, you'll know about it."

"Already done." When I returned the van to the rental place, I'd make sure to stick trackers on the other vans too. Then all I'd have to do is keep my eye on them until the pawn shop received another delivery.

I opened the driver's side door and climbed in.

"Mr. Cross," Amir said, "are you sure you need someone with my skills? This isn't exactly the type of thing most private investigators need. I'm sure you're more than capable of pulling and running prints, and I don't see a private security firm needing much more than that."

"I will one of these days. For now, I could use some help when it comes to your other area of expertise. A team broke into Trey Knox's house. I've dug through his online activities and habits, but I didn't see any red flags. I'm guessing the thieves targeted him some other way. They knew precisely how to disarm the security system and when Knox would be out. I need to identify them."

"Do you think they're renting a unit from this storage facility to hold their ill-gotten gains in between pawning the merchandise?"

"Basically, or the pawn shop is using the storage facility to hold hot merchandise until it cools down enough to sell. Either way, I have to figure out the connection and who's responsible. Can you find the overlap?"

He considered the facts. "I'll need exact times and dates. I can't make any promises. It'll be slow going. Molasses slow."

"I appreciate anything you can do."

"I'll ping cell phone data and compare it to traffic cams and surveillance footage I find, but given hardware limitations and lack of staff, you're more likely to find these guys through other means."

"Get started on it anyway."

"Fine, but I'll tell you now, this is a waste of my time."

"Humor me."

SIXTEEN

After sticking a padlock on my empty storage unit and tagging the other rental vans, I drove around the city. Procrastinating, that's what my mother would call this. Lazy is what my father would say. There was always more work to do at the office, but Justin assured me he had it handled. I trusted him. Come to think of it, he was one of the few people on the planet who held that honor. Though, given the givens, it might have been a curse.

During one of my drive-bys, I noticed Pauley's Pawn was rather crowded, but I didn't spot any delivery vans. They hadn't called about the ring or any of the other stolen memorabilia, so I decided to wait. Appearing too eager might tip them off.

Instead, I went by Trey Knox's place of business. He was in a meeting, but his assistant didn't mind letting me wait. She had a pretty smile and toned legs. Every few minutes, she'd look up from her computer screen and grin at me. I found myself grinning back.

When Knox's door opened and a harried-looking man in an Armani suit stepped out, barking a few final words to Knox, I climbed to my feet. His assistant held up a finger that I should wait a moment. She knocked gently on his doorjamb and asked if he had a few moments to spare.

"Send him in," I heard Knox say.

She stepped back and nearly bumped into me in the process. "He can see you now, Mr. Cross."

"Thanks." I sidestepped, allowing her to pass, before entering Knox's office and pulling the door closed behind me. "Sorry to intrude."

Knox tidied his desk, shoving files into drawers and pens into a cup on his desk. "It's not a problem. Did you find my stuff?" He tapped a few folders harshly on the desktop until they were uniform in height.

"I'm meeting with a fence tonight. I also set up surveillance on the vehicle I believe the thieves might be using. As soon as the suspect is en route to sell your items, I will intercept."

"Excellent." Knox leaned back. "So what are we talking? A day? Two days? A week?"

"I don't know. Aspects of this case don't make much sense to me. The thieves are probably professionals and must have researched you. I'm still curious who would have that kind of access or intimate knowledge of your comings and goings." I glanced behind me. In between the waiting and grinning, I'd asked Knox's assistant about his schedule, but she'd only offered me available appointment times. She never told me where he'd be or when he'd be there.

"I told you, Lucien, the only thing I care about is getting my stuff back. I don't care who took it. I just want it. The ring is the most important thing. If that's the only item you can recover, I can accept that."

"I didn't realize you were such a defeatist. After getting back that World Series pennant, I figured you'd be more optimistic than this."

He stopped shuffling the papers around long enough to stare up at me. "I'm not. I'm just accepting reality."

"There are other rings." I studied him. "I could get you a replacement in a matter of days."

"I want mine."

"Okay. I'll do my best." Now wasn't the time to press him on the issue, but I had to know. "Did you ever notice a silver SUV following you around?"

"A silver SUV?"

"Uh-huh."

He made a face and shook his head. "Nah."

"You're sure?"

"Yep." He hit the intercom button. "Margaret, tell Stone I'm on my way." He grabbed the stack of files. "I'm sorry, but I have to prepare a pitch. Thank you for keeping me updated on the situation. If there's anything else I can do, call or text. I'll get back to you as soon as I can." He lowered his voice to a whisper once he was beside me and put his hand on my shoulder and mouth near my ear. "I don't want anyone around here to know I was the victim of a burglary. I'm sure you can understand that."

"No problem."

"Great." He shook my hand, and I resisted the urge to wipe the sweat from his palm onto my pants leg. "We'll talk again soon."

"You can count on it." I gave Margaret a goodbye grin with a wink, found the nearest men's room, and washed my hands. Trey Knox was nervous. I just had no idea why. So I decided it was time to check out the scene of the crime.

Since Knox lived in a gated community, it was difficult to get in without issue, but I found a way. A nice suit and luxury car could get a person into plenty of places, and when that failed, bribery often worked. The neighborhood was nice. Quiet. His house didn't look that different from any of the others. Small, multi-story, and expensive, with a postage stamp sized yard that was maintained by the HOA or whatever governing body ran the place.

The dismantled security system had been reinstalled. I knew the code from our earlier interviews, so I let myself in. Knox hadn't been smart enough to change the code, but since the thieves hadn't entered it, changing it wouldn't have made a difference.

The motion sensors outside must have picked up on my presence, but by disarming the system, I doubted Knox would be alerted. If he was, the doorbell camera would have shown it was me. He'd call to find out what I was doing. While I waited to see if he received an alert, I wandered around inside.

It was clean. Getting in and out without using one of the doors would be difficult but not impossible. However, it would be detectable. Perhaps, that's why the thieves dismantled the system and raised one of the windows. It was easier than breaking the glass and triggering the alarm.

Could this be an inside job? That theory had lingered around the back of my mind since the beginning. But Knox didn't have the ring insured, and that's the only item he had repeatedly insisted I recover. Did he point me to that just to distract me from something else?

I checked his home office and safe. He didn't have a computer here. His laptop was with him. The rest of his computer equipment had allegedly been stolen. Surely, if he used it for work, he'd have to tell someone what happened. So why the secrecy when I showed up at his place of business?

Entering in the code to his safe, yet another thing he'd disclosed to me, I pulled the lever to find it nearly empty. Inside were important documents, bills of sale, letters of authenticity, and policy information. No cash. No jewels. Nothing tangible that could be sold.

Most of the walls, shelves, and display cases remained bare. A few knickknacks remained, but they didn't have much value. They appeared to be the kinds of items one would find on the wall of a sports bar. Unsigned team photos, sports equipment, and a few ruddy balls.

The police had already checked everything inside. They dusted for prints and checked for trace evidence and found nothing. They may have missed something, but I knew I wouldn't find it, whatever it might be.

Moving on, I performed a quick search of the rest of the house, focusing mainly on his bedroom and bathroom. Aside from finding a fedora with a silk rose on top of his dresser, which struck me as odd, nothing else was of any interest. Knox hadn't lied. He didn't entertain guests, female or otherwise, and if he did, he made sure they didn't leave a single article of clothing or toothbrush behind.

Unsure why I wasted a good portion of the afternoon

snooping around my client's house, I reset his alarm system and returned to my car. Sitting inside, I surveyed the area, but I didn't spot any silver SUVs. A white Escalade idled on the corner. Had I seen it before? When I pulled out, I kept an eye on it, but it didn't pursue. I chalked it up to paranoia and decided the only way to combat it was by having a few stiff drinks and some dinner.

My favorite steakhouse required reservations, but since I knew the owner, I got a table in the back. I didn't dawdle. When I finished eating, I left a hefty tip, my thoughts on Jade. We'd come here several times on dates. She liked the silver and white table linens, the candlelight, and the understated flower arrangements on each table.

"Stop it, Cross." Shaking my head in the hopes of knocking the melancholia from my mind, I returned to my car. 8:23. I had three and a half hours to kill. Pushing the potential consequences aside, I drove to the only bar I knew where no one would flirt with me.

"What'll it be?" a barmaid I didn't recognize asked.

I stared at the bottles behind her. "Do you have any Hendricks?"

"Oh, hell no," a gruff voice from the other end of the bar snapped. The bar owner shooed her away with the wave of both of his hands. Crossing his arms, he leaned back against the counter and stared down at me. "What the hell are you doing here?"

"Hey, Jim. Nice to see you." Icicles clung to my words.

"What are you doing in my bar?" Jim Harrelson, retired cop, asked.

"I'm just trying to get a drink."

"And every other establishment and store in this city suddenly ran out of liquor?"

"It's possible."

"The hell it is." He grabbed a glass from beneath the bar and poured the clear liquor into it. Shoving it toward me, he said, "Drink up and get out of here."

"I can't."

"Why not?"

"This is a cop bar. I'll probably get arrested for drinking and driving if I just drink this and leave."

"You're not drunk. That won't make you drunk."

"I don't know." I stared down at the glass, carefully wrapping one hand around it and giving it a gentle swirl. "This stuff could probably double as lighter fluid."

Jim let out an exaggerated sigh. "Are you in trouble?"

"No."

"Your face says otherwise."

"My face doesn't say a damn thing."

"The last time you came around here, you were tailing a cop." Jim leaned over, resting his forearms on the bar in front of me. "And you nearly got yourself killed because of it. Your pops and I go way back. I don't want you getting into any more trouble, especially on my watch."

"You're not in charge of me."

"Are you sixteen?"

I glared at him and knocked back the cheap gin in one gulp. "Give me a beer. If I drink any more of that shit, my insides will corrode."

He grabbed a pint glass and filled it from the nearest tap. I didn't specify what I wanted, but I never had a problem with the beer at KC's, just the liquor and clientele. Jim continued to stare at me while I sipped the beer.

"Why are you here?" he asked.

"Honestly, I don't know."

He frowned and wiped the bar in front of me, as if I needed constant supervision. "What you don't realize, kid, is I know you. I watched you grow up. This is Uncle Jim you're talking to. Remember? You came here tonight itching for a fight."

"No, I didn't."

"But you're miserable."

"So are ninety-five percent of the people who drink alone at bars. What's your point?"

"When you're miserable, you get self-destructive. You do it all the time. Over and over."

"I do not."

"Uh-huh. Sure."

I snorted derisively. "How is drinking at a bar self-destructive? I already told you I have no intention of drinking and driving."

"Whatever you say."

Now he was pissing me off, but I shut up. He could think what he wanted. It didn't matter to me.

"Lucien, you can't fool me. You came to this bar because you want to punish yourself. Maybe your pops, too." He sighed. "Don't pick a fight. The last thing I need is to have to mop your blood and teeth off the floor. The cops in here will kill you."

"One of them already tried." Glaring at him, I wrapped both hands around the glass and stared at it until he went away. I came here to be alone, not to be bothered. This was a mistake.

"Hey," a man with a wrinkled, untucked shirt took a seat on the stool beside mine, "have you made any progress?"

It took me a moment before I realized the man speaking was Joe Gallo. "Have you?"

"Is that why you came here?" He sipped his mojito. "Did Rostokowski tell you I like to come here after shift?"

"No."

"Oh," Gallo nodded a few times to himself, "Jimmy and your pops were partners, right? You must come here all the time."

"Have you ever seen me here before?"

"Well, no."

"That's right."

Gallo turned to me and grinned. "See?" He pointed a finger in my face, his cheeks slightly flushed. "I knew you came here to talk to me. This is about as off-the-record as we can get, yeah?" He glanced behind us. "All right, let's get a booth so we can talk in private. I'll give you an update on our progress and you can ask me whatever it is you came here to ask me."

Before I could say a word to the contrary, he climbed off the stool and headed for a booth in the back. Picking up my beer, I followed him, wondering if I got knifed or poisoned if anyone would do a damn thing about it. Who was I kidding? They'd probably celebrate with a round of drinks for everyone.

SEVENTEEN

"We think it's a group of teenagers. Young, rich kids who enjoy the rush." Officer Gallo swallowed more of his mojito. "You know how people like that can be." He gestured at my appearance.

"No, how can they be?"

He chuckled uncomfortably. "Hey, I didn't mean anything by it, but you were one of those troublemakers."

"I didn't grow up rich. This," I indicated my shirt and jacket, "I made for myself. As far as being a troublemaker, I'd call it more of a whistleblower." I fought to keep my expression neutral.

"Sure, whatever. I didn't mean to offend you."

I tucked one hand in my pocket to keep Gallo from noticing my fingers were clenched into a fist. "So you think the break-in at Trey Knox's house was conducted by teenagers?"

"I can't say for certain, but we think the other recent home invasions were. A tip came in, and after some digging, we found some online videos of a group of kids inside two of the burglarized homes."

"Do you remember the link?"

Gallo glanced around as he removed his phone from his

pocket. "I have a copy here." He hit play and held it out.

I watched the footage for a moment. Three girls and one guy. I couldn't be certain of their ages, but from their clothing, builds, and word choices, they might have been kids or young adults somewhere in the fifteen to twenty-five age range. At least they were smart enough to wear masks. "Are you sure they're just kids?"

"Yeah, that one," Gallo paused the video and zoomed in, "is wearing a varsity jacket for a local high school. There's the mascot, and if you look closely, you can make out the HS right there."

I squinted briefly at the feed before tapping play. "How much damage resulted from these home invasions?"

"Not much. They stole some jewelry, cash, and a few smaller electronics and appliances, just like what happened to Mr. Knox."

"Do you know how they gained access to these other homes?"

"We're still working on it, but they might have been there before for parties or whatnot."

"Parties?"

"The victims all have children under the age of twenty-one."

"Knox doesn't."

"No, he doesn't, which is why I'm not sure the crimes are connected." Gallo stared down at his phone. "Like I told you at the precinct, we're on the same side. Help me out here. Have you found anything to contradict this? I want to help Knox, but I can't do that when the detective in charge is chasing a bunch of bored, rich kids."

"Why does he think they're committing these crimes?"

"For the adrenaline rush, probably. It could also be based on a dare or some form of revenge or hazing. We assume the perpetrators must know the kids who live in the homes they targeted, which is how they knew when the families would be out."

"Sounds plausible. Any idea what they are doing with the jewelry and electronics?"

"We're not sure. We've checked area pawn shops but found nothing. We have feelers out and asked several of the owners we trust to let us know if a kid comes into the store, but no one's seen or heard anything."

"Or they just aren't telling you."

Gallo pointed a finger at me. "Brilliant deduction."

I leaned back in the seat and rubbed my eyes. "Check online. Depending on what kind of jewelry they've taken, they might just mail it off to one of those cash for gold places."

The cop gave me a cockeyed look. "You're actually helping?"

"Call it what you want. It was just a suggestion."

"Huh." Despite Gallo's earlier proclamation that we were on the same side, followed by his veiled insults, he genuinely seemed surprised that I'd offer a suggestion, which meant my reputation preceded me. "I'll look into that. Is that what you're doing to track down Knox's belongings?"

"You said the police checked area pawn shops. What do you know about Pauley's Pawn?"

He chuckled. "Is that how you answer a question? With a question of your own?"

I remained silent and nursed my beer. He didn't have to answer since I was certain whatever he said wouldn't be the least bit helpful, but I had asked anyway. After all, I didn't know what I didn't know.

"You must get that hard ass thing from your father."

"I also get my piercing stare from him, but that's all the bastard gave me."

"Yeah, we checked Pauley's. They're one of the biggest pawn shops in the area. They got everything. Microwaves, vacuum cleaners, hunting rifles, knockoff handbags. But they didn't have any of the stolen merch."

"Have they been problematic in the past?"

"Not really." He narrowed his eyes. "Why? Are you on to something?"

"Nope."

"That's bullshit, and we both know it. C'mon, tell me what's going on."

I'd already said more than I should have, but I wasn't worried. I wanted to know what the cops knew. "Quid pro quo?"

"Yeah, sure."

"Pauley's was a bust, but a couple of the guys in there made me uncomfortable." I stared at him, searching his face for microexpressions. "And ever since I paid that pawn shop a visit, someone's been following me."

"Who?"

"I don't know." The genuine intrigue on Gallo's face convinced me he didn't know the answer to my question. That didn't rule out the possibility it was a cop. After all, Gallo was a career officer who had misplaced affection for my father. He might have been kept out of the loop intentionally. However, his ignorance reassured me that Will Esposito hadn't filed a police report against me, so that was a plus.

"What do these guys look like?" he asked.

"The ones from the shop?"

"Yep."

I shrugged. "Guys. Rough-looking. You know the type—beefy. You could sand a table down with their faces. Those kinds of guys."

"So, not a pretty boy like you?"

"I'm not pretty. Remember the piercing stare?"

Gallo shook his head. "Is it a requirement to be a smart ass in order to get a P.I. license?"

"It depends."

"No wonder we call you private dicks."

I continued to stare at him.

"What about the guy tailing you? What does he look like?"

"I don't know. I've never seen him. I saw two rough-looking gentlemen inside the pawn shop, but I can't be certain it's either of them."

"Then how do you know someone is following you?"

"Call it intuition."

"I call it paranoid." Gallo eyed me again, the lightbulb flickering on over his head. He'd heard stories. "Maybe you shouldn't worry so much about it. It's probably just a hazard of the job. You spend too much time watching dirtbags, you start imagining they're watching you back."

I didn't say anything. Almeada would want me to give the officer a few details, but something told me that offering up extraneous information would bite me in the ass. I just wasn't sure how, but it would. "So kids, huh?"

"That's the theory."

"They shouldn't be hard to ID. You know what high school they go to. Ask around. If you find one, you'll find them all."

"That's what the detective in charge said." Gallo finished his mojito and placed the empty glass beside mine. "Do you want another?"

"No. I'm on my way out."

Gallo looked at his watch. "Yeah, the missus will start wondering where I am if I don't get home soon." But he lingered.

"What?"

"You know something. I just don't know what, but we both know Knox had no reason to cross paths with a bunch of high schoolers."

"Maybe they bonded over sports. Your male suspect has a varsity jacket. That could be your connection."

"You're shitting me."

I shrugged. "No stone unturned, remember?" I tapped the table twice and headed for the door. I didn't believe for a second that teenagers were responsible for the break-in at Knox's house, but suggesting they were might be enough to distract Gallo away from my investigation. Sure, I offered up Pauley's Pawn, but that was so I could see if the cops had any interest in it, which they didn't. That only reinforced my opinion that they had no idea what they were doing. Unfortunately, neither did I.

The cool night air brought my senses to full alert. Instead of going straight to my car, I decided to take a stroll. The FOP stickers and decals on several of the cars told me they belonged to the cops and retired cops inside drinking. Ignoring them, I looked around, but I didn't spot any silver SUVs with bike racks. Instead, I spotted two black, one white, a red, and possibly a green SUV parked within a block of KC's.

This was pointless. I'd determined as much earlier. Yet,

here I was, standing on the sidewalk playing *I Spy*. "You need a life, Lucien. Jade's right. You probably need to date, or at least get laid." And now I was talking to myself. Shaking it off, I returned to my parked car and climbed inside.

When I pulled out of the space, no one followed me. On the drive to meet Freddy G, I made sure to maintain my speed, use my turn signals, and obey traffic signs. I wasn't drunk. I wasn't even close. But after listening to Jim's accusations, I had a nagging desire to prove I wasn't self-destructive. And since I hadn't come to blows with any cops inside the bar, that meant I needed to avoid coming to blows with any cops outside the bar too. At least for tonight.

When I arrived at the apartment building where Freddy was housesitting, I took the elevator to the top floor. The front door was cracked open. "Freddy?" I called.

This wouldn't be the first time he left the door open. Last time this happened, I'd found a trail of lingerie which led to a dozen women in the midst of a naked pillow fight. One of Freddy's other clients had requested a very specific porno, and Freddy was in the midst of filming when I'd come to pick up something unrelated.

"Freddy?" My hand traveled to the gun at my hip, just beneath my jacket. "It's Lucien. Are you here?"

The living room looked like it had been tossed. The couch cushions lay scattered around the floor. A chair had been overturned, and pieces of broken glass crunched beneath my feet.

I continued deeper into the apartment and checked the bedroom. The corner of the sheet hung from a lopsided lamp. Every drawer had been yanked from the dressers and dumped onto the floor. The sound of running water came from the attached bathroom.

"Freddy?"

Light filtered out from the crack in the door. I nudged it open with my gun hand, reminding myself that I should use my free hand to open doors. *That's why cops always keep their gun hand empty*, the voice of one of my academy instructors whispered in my ear.

Freddy turned sideways to look at me. "You're late."

"Yeah, sorry—"

Blood ran from his scalp down the side of his face. A large welt had formed near his temple, just above the corner of his left eyebrow. He turned back to the sink, squeezing his eyes shut as he grabbed the edge to steady himself.

I stepped closer, noticing the blood droplets on the tile floor and the cracks in the mirror. "What happened?" I asked.

Freddy rinsed the washcloth one more time before holding it against his face. "I need to sit down." His knees buckled, and he dropped to the floor like a brick.

EIGHTEEN

"Are you sure you don't want me to call an ambulance?" I rubbed a hand over my mouth and surveyed the damage.

"I'll be okay." Freddy sat on the edge of the bed, staring at the mess before him. "Fucking assholes."

"Who did this?"

"It doesn't matter."

I fought the urge to protest. "What did they want?"

"You need to leave this alone."

I raised my palms and took a step back. "Fine."

Freddy tried to stand, wobbled, and plopped back onto the edge of the bed. He leaned forward, supporting his head in his hands.

"You probably have a concussion. Maybe worse. You need a CT scan."

"Lucien, stop. I can't. The paramedics will see this mess and call the cops."

"Fine, I'll drive you to the hospital. It's no big deal."

"No."

"Urgent care?"

Glaring at me, he dragged himself off the bed and headed back into the living room, too stubborn to accept the help I offered. "I can't risk it. They might draw blood, and that'll land me in jail, at least for the night. I'm not getting arrested because of this."

I looked around the room. "When's the last time you used?"

"A few hours ago."

"Yeah, that's not going to work."

"No kidding." Freddy sat in one of the few chairs that remained upright, eyeing the drink cart across the room. "I can't get the ring."

"That doesn't matter right now."

"Yes, it does." The look on his face worried me. "You have to let this go. You want to get some guy's sports collection back, but it's not worth it. Tell him to start over. What's done is done. I can't help you find the ring or get it back. I'm sorry."

Picking up one of the fallen chairs, I placed it beneath the table and reached for another one. "Tell me who did this."

"I don't know. They busted in here, searching for something."

"What'd they take?"

"A half a brick of coke and about ten grand, give or take."

"Shit."

"It could have been worse." Freddy laughed. "It's not like I can report them to the police."

"I can handle it."

"Let it go, Luci. I mean it. You need to back the fuck off." He exhaled and peeled the towel away from his face, checking to see if the wound was still bleeding. "They came here tonight for a reason, and if you'd been on time, you would have been here when they barged inside."

"You're telling me they came here for me?"

"I don't know, but my customers don't typically shove a gun in my face or cold-cock me. Only warm cocks are allowed around here."

Freddy G dealt with plenty of shady types, from drug dealers to fences. Any one of them might have wanted revenge, but Freddy had been in the business for the better part of a decade, possibly longer. He cultivated relationships and exchanged favors. Pissing people off wasn't something he did.

"Did you welch on a debt?" I asked.

"Not me."

"What is that supposed to mean?"

"I don't know, but one of them said this would serve as payment for the additional trouble, whatever that means."

"What are you working on, besides tracking down the ring for me?"

"That's about it. Like I told you, I'm housesitting. I've hosted a few parties. Nothing out of the ordinary. Lately, it's just been a lot of little things. Box seats, sold out tickets, a few dime bags here and there, intel on a competing corporate entity. Let's just say, I haven't dealt with anyone who would act this uncivilized or violent. My clientele doesn't bust into my place of business brandishing weapons. They know better. I have a no tolerance policy."

"So this is about the ring."

"Whoever stole it doesn't want to give it back, and he sure as hell doesn't want to be found. You should drop the case. These shitheads mean business."

Crossing to the security panel on the wall, I removed the front and peered at the wiring. The penthouse didn't have any cameras inside, which worked in Freddy's favor but not mine. "The building has security cameras. I saw one in the elevator. They might have more. Once I get the footage, I'll figure out who's responsible and sit them down for a nice chat."

"Not too nice." Freddy got out of the chair, slightly more stable than he had been, and rinsed the washcloth in the sink before wringing it out and holding it against his temple. "Is this the kind of thing you do now?"

"Security? Yeah, it's my schtick. Didn't I give you a business card?"

"Not that." He swallowed. "When I started out a million years ago as a runner, I promised myself if I got out, I'd never deal with those types again. Occasionally, we cross paths, but it's always business. Congenial. Whatever happened here tonight is some back alley shit that I want no part of." The attack had freaked out Freddy G, the guy who could get you anything at any time.

I stepped out of the apartment, but I didn't spot any cameras in the hallway. The one in the elevator would have to do, so I rode down to the lobby. After some cajoling, I was granted access to the security office. The footage didn't show much, but the two guys who rode the elevator to the top floor around 11:30 had to be the men who assaulted Freddy. I printed a few stills and went back upstairs.

Freddy had fixed the couch cushions and leaned his head back with the washcloth pressed against the still bleeding gash. At the sound of the door, he opened his eyes and peered at me. A six-shooter sat on the seat beside him.

"I come in peace." I eyed the gun. "I've never seen you with hardware."

"I know a guy."

"You know lots of guys." I handed him the printed photos. "Do you know these guys?"

"Aside from our run-in an hour ago, I've never seen them before."

"What exactly did they say and do?"

"They forced their way in as soon as I answered the door. I didn't expect it. I thought it was you."

"I'm sorry."

Freddy waved a hand dismissively. "Serves me right for not checking the peephole." He turned the photo facedown and gave the bar another furtive look. "They asked if I was alone. One of them dragged me into the bathroom while the other searched the place. I elbowed the son of a bitch, and that's when he rammed me head first into the mirror. After that, everything's foggy. I remember the second one flashing the money and coke at me and saying that was payment for the added inconvenience or whatever. I asked what they were talking about, and they said I better mind my business if I knew what was good for me. I imagine the same holds true for you."

I thought about the silver SUV. Did the assholes follow me to Freddy's? Is that how they knew I'd be here? Or had Freddy's hunt to track down Knox's ring turned the thieves' attention toward him?

"Luci, why do you look constipated?"

I pulled out my phone and brought up Will Esposito's driver's license. "Do you know this guy?" I handed him my phone.

"No."

"What about anyone who drives a silver SUV?"

"How much time do you have?" He slid off the couch and headed for the bar. A few glasses and bottles had been smashed. That's what caused the glass to crunch beneath my feet, but the tequila and bourbon remained unharmed. Freddy opened the tequila and took a swig before I could stop him. "Everyone and their brother drives an SUV."

"You shouldn't drink with a concussion."

He looked at me with his one good eye and took another swig from the bottle, just to be spiteful. Still holding it, he returned to the couch and slumped down. Taking the tequila out of his hand, I swallowed a mouthful and placed it on the coffee table, out of his reach.

"C'mon, man, don't be like that. I got my brains scrambled tonight because of whatever shit you got me involved in."

"Which is why I'm doing what I can to keep you alive." I watched as the washcloth slowly soaked through with his blood. "You need stitches."

"I already told you—"

"You're Freddy G. You must know some doctors who work off the books."

"I'm not in the mood to deal with anyone else remotely sketchy."

Tapping my fingers against my phone, I thought about the people I'd crossed paths with. Surely, someone must know a concierge doctor in the city who wouldn't report this. Out of the list of celebs and corporate types, very few would answer my calls, and I couldn't risk going to a valuable and reputable client with this kind of request. Still, there was a very good chance the reason Freddy had been attacked was because of me. I couldn't let that stand. I was supposed to protect people, but I'd repeatedly done a lousy job.

Scrolling through my contacts, I stopped on Miranda's personal line. She was clean and sober and had a good head on her shoulders, but she was in the music business. That hadn't always been the case. I dialed her number and waited. After a brief exchange, she said she'd get someone to text me a doctor's info. A few minutes later, my phone chimed. I read the details and made the call.

"Help's on the way," I said to Freddy. "For once, I'm the guy who knows someone who knows a guy."

He laughed. "I'm surprised you don't have medics on your payroll."

I snorted, though that might not be a bad idea, especially when dealing with clients who might find themselves in similarly problematic situations. I filed that thought away for later consideration, wondering about the insurance and legal ramifications of such actions.

While we waited, I called Justin and asked if he could get back to the office to run the photo I e-mailed him through facial rec. Since Freddy shouldn't be left alone, I couldn't do it. I didn't think the men would return, but I didn't trust the fence not to drink himself into a coma or die of a brain bleed because he was too afraid to seek help. So I waited.

"Stop pacing. You're making me dizzy."

"I'm not pacing. I'm cleaning up this mess." Actually, I was looking for clues. But according to Freddy, the men wore gloves. Regardless, I hoped to find something damning, but the place looked clean. Even though Freddy had elbowed his attacker, I didn't find any drops of blood anywhere except around the bathroom sink, which I assumed came from him.

By the time I finished my search of the apartment, the concierge doctor had arrived. He examined Freddy while I tidied up. The prescription pill bottle full of pre-rolled joints and the pills I found in the cabinet hadn't been touched. Either the men who broke in had no interest in them, or they missed them. The expensive stereo system and AV equipment remained undisturbed, as did several pricey antiques. I was surprised the thieves hadn't taken them or smashed them.

This wasn't a robbery. It was a warning. And it wasn't meant for Freddy. It was meant for me.

NINETEEN

"You have no idea who would do this?" Justin asked.

"No, but it links back to Knox. It has to." I just didn't know why the men who assaulted Freddy didn't empty out the penthouse. Perhaps they'd been in a rush since they knew I would be arriving, but how did they know? And if the point was to threaten me, why didn't they wait for me? I should be the one with a dozen stitches and a concussion, not Freddy.

"Freddy G's not exactly Mr. Upstanding Citizen."

"No, he's not, but he conducts his business according to a specific set of rules. It's very civilized."

"How can it be? He doesn't know what a client will want or what he'll have to do to get it. He could come up against all different types. People far less reputable than some pawn shop owners and those responsible for home invasions."

I looked at the clock. "Trust me. This is about Knox." It was too late or too early to call, depending on perspective. But as soon as seven a.m. rolled around, Knox's phone would be ringing.

"Facial rec will take a while. The footage you got from outside the building didn't get a look at the vehicle, so we can't cross-reference that." Justin yawned.

"Go home. It's late. Take tomorrow morning off. You deserve it."

He gave me a look. "You only call when it's an emergency."

"It wasn't, but I wanted to get this started. And I couldn't get back to the office until I knew Freddy was squared away."

"What did the doctor say?"

"He'll be okay as long as he stays away from the drugs and liquor for a while." I didn't know how likely that was, but I couldn't control Freddy. He'd do what he wanted. The doctor agreed to stay and monitor him during the night, something that had cost me a cool grand. But time was money, and since I had work to do and couldn't stay, this was the next best thing.

"Do you think they'll return?"

"No. They made their point." They wanted me to back off, but now I was more intrigued as to why they targeted Knox in the first place and why they'd taken so much offense to me helping him. "They won't be back, but it doesn't hurt to make sure. Who's next up on the roster?"

Justin handed me the info on the unassigned members of our security detail, and I called the first two names on the list and had them stake out the penthouse apartment.

"I'll send you a photo of the attackers. If you see them anywhere near the building, hold them, and notify me immediately," I said.

"Yes, sir," one of them said.

"Should we call the cops?" the other asked.

"Yes, let them know you detained a prowler. I'll handle the rest." Disconnecting the three-way call, I gave Justin another look. "You're still here."

"I'm going." He grabbed his jacket. "I'll see you at lunchtime. If you need me sooner—"

"I won't."

He laughed. "Whatever you have to tell yourself, Lucien, but we both know that's not true."

Alone with my thoughts, I couldn't figure out where to start. Too many things needed to be done. I had to pick one and run with it. So I did.

Facial rec ran in the background while I homed in on tracking down the SUV. I thought about the times and places I'd been, but most of it was a jumble. The only time I had been certain I'd been followed was on the way back from the Chinese restaurant, so I phoned in some favors and got access to DOT footage.

After an hour of scanning the feed in the hopes of finding the exact moment I passed through the intersection, I backtracked until I spotted the SUV I was sure had been tailing me. With the plate number in hand, I pulled up the vehicle registration information.

Danny Foster. According to this, he didn't live anywhere near me or the Chinese restaurant. He could have been lost or running an errand, but I swore I saw the same SUV parked outside my place later that night. Luckily, I'd also requested DOT footage from outside my apartment building on the same night, so I switched to that feed and fast-forwarded. The silver SUV parked less than ten minutes after I entered the parking garage. Unfortunately, the angle was shit. City footage from stationary cameras left a lot to be desired.

I tried zooming in on the driver, but no one ever got out of the vehicle. Whoever it was either remained inside the SUV the entire night or timed their exit perfectly to match with that of a passing truck. I couldn't tell either way.

Dialing the number for the building manager, I left a message and asked if he could call me back. My apartment building didn't have the best security system, but it wasn't bad. Getting in and out was difficult for anyone without a fob, but I wasn't sure how many exterior security cameras the building had. The garage had plenty. Cameras covered each door and emergency exit. But I didn't know if any of them pointed that far down the street. I hoped so.

Now what? I turned back to the computer program, but it'd be hours, possibly days, before we got a match. So I let myself into the backdoor of the police department's database and did some digging into Danny Foster. He served in the military and currently owned a gun, so his prints were in the system. He was thirty-eight years old. I checked his driver's license photo again and compared it to the photo of the men who attacked Freddy, but Danny wasn't one of the two men in the elevator.

Could Danny Foster have crossed paths with Trey Knox? Grabbing the Knox files, I skimmed the list of names, but Foster's didn't pop. As far as I could tell, he didn't work at any of the auction houses or websites where Knox purchased a part of his collection. Foster could be involved with the trade shows. I hadn't had much luck getting the vendor list and names of everyone who had a booth at every show that Knox had ever gone to. All I knew for certain was Danny Foster wasn't one of the guys he exchanged merch with or contacted.

I dug into Foster's social media presence. He had a single profile image. When I did a reverse lookup, I found one photo, and that was it. The only things he posted were articles, pictures, and stories that he'd taken from somewhere else. He didn't put anything personal up. He had hundreds of friends. As far as I could tell, he rarely sent or received messages from any of them, unless they were all done in private.

Unsure what Foster had to do with anything, I locked the office and headed to his home address. When I arrived, I scanned the surrounding streets for the silver SUV, but I didn't see it anywhere. So I parked my car in clear view of his front door and waited. Since he'd been so desperate to follow me, I'd make it easy for him.

At 4:30 a.m. the front door to the apartment opened and a man matching Foster's description stepped out in running shorts, compression leggings, and an olive green hoodie. He lifted one leg and tugged his knee to his chest a few times before repeating the stretch on the other side. Since I was in no mood to chase him through the streets, I got out of the car and approached the stoop where he was now doing hamstring stretches.

"Danny Foster?"

He didn't look up.

"Mr. Foster," I said a little louder. It was pitch out. The only light came from the streetlamps half a block away and the two porch lights on either side of the door.

He stopped stretching and reached into the pouch of his hoodie. When he finally looked up, he noticed me. Sliding the earbuds out of his ears, he tugged off the hood. Anxiety etched his face.

"Mr. Foster?"

"Yeah," his eyes darted from one side to the other, "what can I do for you?"

"I have a few questions."

"Who are you?"

"I'd think by now you'd know."

"Look, pal, I don't know what this is or what game you're playing, but you don't want to mess with me."

"Ooh, scary." I wondered if I could take him in a fair fight. It didn't matter. I was armed. He wasn't. "You probably should have thought of that before you started following me."

"Hey, you came up on me." He took a step closer to the door. "I'm not looking for trouble."

"Again, you should have thought of that before."

"I'm going inside and calling the cops. You don't want to be here when they arrive."

"Fine by me. I'll show them the video footage I have of your SUV following me home the other night."

He took a deep breath and held up his palms. "Look, I don't want any trouble. Are you sure it was my SUV?"

I rattled off the license plate number, even though I had no doubts.

Danny rubbed a hand over his close-cropped hair. "That's not mine."

"It's registered to you."

"So call the cops. I didn't do anything illegal."

"Stalking is illegal."

"I'm not stalking you." He tried to push past me, and I shoved him back toward the door. Anger burned in his eyes. His chest puffed out, and he shoved me. I moved with the momentum, putting some distance between us and pulling my piece before he got too close. He raised both palms. "Whoa. Take it easy."

"Tell me the truth."

"I wasn't following you. I was following her."

Jade. "Why?"

He glanced to the side, his face contorting. "She used to date a buddy of mine. Some serious shit went down. He's dead now." He gave me a look. "You should steer clear of that bitch."

My blood boiled. "Stay the hell away from her."

"Fine, whatever. She's toxic anyway."

I bit my lip, turning back toward my car, my breath coming in angry huffs. For a moment, the only sound I could hear was my own heart beating. Everything moved at half-speed as if in slow motion. Then time caught up. I spun around and decked him. It took every ounce of self-restraint I possessed not to beat the living daylights out of him. He was the reason Jade didn't feel safe. He was the reason she left. Okay, part of the reason, but still, a big fucking part.

"He hurt her, numbnuts," I spat. "Scott used to knock her around. He tried to kill her. She barely survived."

He looked up at me with both hands in front of his face, protecting his ugly mug from my retaliatory anger. "That's not what I heard. Didn't you read the paper? She must have been involved in some shady shit. Scott tracked her to a motel and got gunned down by some asshole she was meeting."

"If you really believe that, who's to say I'm not the asshole?" I stared at him. "If I'd kill a cop, I don't see any reason why I'd bat an eye before killing you."

Danny swallowed. For a tough guy, he'd just lost his nerve. But crazy trumped tough every day of the week.

"How long were you following her?" I asked.

"Just that one day. I spotted her at the café where she used to work."

I glowered at him, wondering how long it would take the police to respond to a report of gunfire in the area. Five minutes? Seven? "What were you going to do?"

"I wanted to confront her about what went down with Scott, about the trap she lured him into."

I didn't argue, though every cell in my body desperately wanted to. "You stayed camped outside my apartment all night."

"Most of the night. I fell asleep, and when I woke up, I decided it wasn't worth it and left."

"If I ever see you again, I'll kill you. If you go near Jade again, I'll kill you. Do you understand?"

He let out a grunt, his eyes still on the barrel of my gun. "Yeah."

"Good." I thought about all the strange circumstances. Was anyone following me? "Where were you tonight?"

"What?"

"Answer the fucking question."

"At work."

"Where do you work?"

"I'm not telling you. You're crazy."

I cleared my throat. I could find out easily enough. "Someone close to me was attacked tonight. If you had anything to do with that, tell me now."

"No way. It wasn't me."

He didn't appear to be lying, but I wasn't sure. I wasn't sure about anything at this point. "Are you sure? I'll go easier on you if you tell me the truth. You don't want to know what happens if I find out you're lying."

"I'm not. I swear."

Narrowing my eyes, I asked one final question. "What about Trey Knox?"

"Who?"

Without wasting any more of my time or energy, I turned and headed back to my car, listening for the sound of his footfalls behind me. But he didn't try to jump me. When I got to my car, I turned to see him creeping back inside the apartment building.

Once inside my car, I locked the doors, placed my gun on the seat, and filled my lungs with air. I was so angry, I was shaking. Justin had been right. The last time I'd been this on edge was before I blew up everything around me. This time, I'd do things differently. I had to.

Eight minutes later, a patrol car turned down the street. He double-parked behind me, flashed his lights, and hit the siren once so it'd make that obnoxious sound. I took my gun off the seat and stuck it in the glove box while grabbing my registration. By the time I straightened, he and his partner had stepped out of the vehicle. They approached from opposite sides, with one hand on their service pieces and the other near their belts. The officer who'd been driving rapped against my window, gesturing that I roll it down.

"Evening," I said, holding out my identification and credentials.

He read my name. The "oh shit" registering a moment later. "Mr. Cross, we received a report that you brandished a firearm and threatened a man."

I nodded at the cards in his hand. "That's my carry permit."

"You're not going to deny it?"

"I have a weapon. As you can see, it is not on me at the moment." I kept my hands on the steering wheel. Cops were jumpy. It was best not to give them reasons to freak out. "As far as threatening a man, I believe that might have been a misunderstanding. The asshole in question, Danny Foster, admitted to stalking me. He attempted to intimidate Jade McNamara and scared the poor woman into fleeing the city. He's a menace. If he wants to press charges, I'd like to do the same."

The cop handed back my credentials and rubbed his neck. "Mr. Cross, no one is pressing any charges, but it'd be best if you head home."

"I agree."

The cop gave me a final look. "Drive safe."

"Yep." I rolled up my window, watching as the officers walked back to their car. They didn't leave until I pulled away.

TWENTY

I didn't go home. Instead, I went back to the office. My hands were still shaking when I turned the key in the lock and pushed my way inside. This had to stop. Forcing a few breaths into my lungs, I checked the computer. Facial rec continued searching for the assholes who attacked Freddy.

So far, I'd threatened two men due to the SUV, and I still had no idea if anyone had been following me. Grabbing a notepad, I tried to recall events in the proper order. My timeline had some holes, but until Jade said she'd been followed, presumably by Danny Foster, I hadn't noticed anyone tailing me. And ever since then, I'd been hypervigilant at observing all vehicles within my vicinity.

Grabbing my computer, I did a quick check to see if I could connect any dots between Danny Foster and Scott Renwin. It didn't take more than a few minutes to find Scott's name in Danny's list. I checked the memorial page which remained, ignoring all the sickening posts celebrating what a wonderful man Scott was. *Lies*, I thought.

Danny had donated to the charitable organization Scott's mother had chosen. At least the bastard told me the truth. Frankly, I didn't care how Danny connected to Scott. He hadn't been there for his friend when his life unraveled. He hadn't been there to stop him from raising a hand to Jade or threatening her life. As far as I was concerned, I had no use for Danny.

The familiar twinge in my back reminded me being too tense wasn't healthy, but no matter what I did, I couldn't force myself to relax. So I dug deeper.

Danny worked until after midnight, just like he claimed. However, since two other men attacked Freddy, I pulled a few more strings and analyzed Danny's phone records. From what I could tell, he didn't hire anyone or phone his buddies to beat up Freddy or deliver a message to me. This was a dead end. I had to let it go.

"Enough." Pushing away from the computer, I stared up at the clock. It was almost six. An hour to go. If I didn't do something for the next sixty minutes, I'd go insane.

The one bright light about this cramped office was the shower I had installed in the bathroom. Justin and Gloria thought I was crazy when I cut out half the vanity and stuck a tiny square stall in the already too small bathroom, but I thought it might come in handy.

After showering and changing clothes, I felt like a new man, calmer and more rational. My brain had finally given up on the possibility I'd been followed, which meant the goons who attacked Freddy had done so because of the questions he'd asked. Everyone knew Freddy didn't procure items for himself, so somehow, the attackers deduced the collector's ring was for me.

Who had Freddy contacted? He always kept his connections private, but I needed to know. I'd asked him numerous times, but he wouldn't budge, even after having the snot kicked out of him.

I considered all the ways I could find Freddy's contacts, but he was careful. He used unregistered phones that changed weekly, possibly daily. He kept one number for his clients to use to contact him, but he never used that line to procure items. It was smart. Law enforcement agencies would have trouble pinning him down, should his actions prove illegal. So how was I supposed to track him?

His internet activity was hidden behind a VPN and other ingenious protections. At this rate, I should probably hire him to work for me. Freddy had a car, but he rarely used it. His location always changed. At the moment, he was housesitting. Before that he had rented a condo, and before that it had been a hotel room.

Since I was unsure how to track Freddy's movements, I couldn't help but wonder how his attackers had found him. He didn't broadcast his address, except to clients and friends. That made me pause. How did they find him? Did they track Freddy? Or did they track me?

"Shit." I ran a hand through my hair before realizing what I was doing and forcing myself to stop. That was one tell I had to eliminate. "And you've come full circle." Letting out a frustrated sigh, I picked up the phone and dialed Knox.

"Hello?" Knox sounded tired.

6:45, that was close enough. "Morning, Mr. Knox. This is Lucien Cross."

"What's going on?"

"What isn't?" I fought to keep the annoyance out of my voice. "I'm e-mailing you a photo now. Tell me who these men are." I sent a copy of the still taken from the surveillance footage to Knox and waited.

Knox's phone emitted several clicks before he said, "Um...I'm not sure."

"Have you seen them before?"

"Um...maybe."

"And around and around we go." Again, we were playing the same game. The longer this went on, the more I wanted to get off this carousel. "Do you know either of them?"

"I'm not sure. The one on the left, with the darker hair and the scar on his cheek, I think I've seen him before."

"Where?"

"Um..."

"Help me out here. Could it have been at work?"

"No, I don't think so."

"At one of the auction houses or trade shows?"

"They're sports collectors conventions," Knox corrected. "But to answer your question, no it wasn't there."

"Then where?"

"A bar maybe."

"Okay, which one?"

"Um..."

Luckily, the call was on speaker or I would have thrown the phone in frustration. While Knox thought about it, I pulled up a copy of his credit card statement and checked to see which bars he'd been to recently.

"It might have been McGinty's, but I can't be certain. He might work there. I feel like I've seen that scar on a bouncer or something."

"Does McGinty's have bouncers?" Sports bars usually didn't, but bar fights were common enough, especially in establishments where betting occurred.

"The dishwasher or busboy or whatever doubles as security, I think."

"Fine. I'll check it out."

"Is that necessary?"

I stopped. "Why wouldn't it be necessary?"

"I thought you said you had a lead on getting back the ring and my other stuff. What does that have to do with these two guys in the photo?"

"Possibly everything."

"Are you sure?" Knox asked. "Like I said, I'm not even sure if I recognize that one. It just seems like a lot of extra trouble to go to for no reason."

"You hired me to do a job for you. That's what I'm doing."

"Yeah, okay. Sorry." He hung up.

Was it me? I shook the thought away. McGinty's closed a few hours ago. They wouldn't open again until after four. That meant I couldn't see if the man who attacked Freddy was the same one who worked in the sports bar. What else could I do?

Getting up, I circled my desk a few times, made coffee, and drank it while staring out the window. When I knew what I was doing, work kept me busy, focused. I could push everything else out of my mind and do what had to be done. But ever since Jade told me she was coming back to town, my mind had been elsewhere. That had never happened before, and I didn't like it. So I tried to bury myself deeper into Knox's case, but I didn't know how to proceed.

I didn't give a shit about Knox's stolen property, but I cared a great deal about my contact getting attacked and even more about Jade being followed. The two didn't appear connected. Intellectually, I knew they weren't. It was bad timing. A coincidence. But my mind had latched onto a pattern that didn't exist, and I couldn't shake it.

"Breathe." Inhaling slowly through my nose, I held my breath for four seconds before letting out a lengthy exhale. I repeated this twenty times until my thoughts cleared. While I waited for Gloria to arrive at the office and the rest of my day to get underway, I dissected the Knox file and my notes, separating out what wasn't relevant or related.

Before I finished my project, the computer dinged. Facial recognition identified the man on the right, the one without the scar. His name was Alexei Balakin. He had several assault charges on his record. From what I could tell, he was hired muscle. He got paid to beat people up, which is what he'd done the previous night, but he didn't work for one guy. He floated around. This wasn't helpful.

I ran a list of his known associates, but I didn't find the man with the scar. From what I gathered, Alexei was a hitter who typically worked alone. He'd flitted from loan shark to loan shark, taking a cut of the money he recovered.

Trey Knox gambled online. We saw the charges on his bank statement. I'd also seen a few withdrawals from ATMs near his preferred sports bar, but I couldn't be sure that was to pay a bookie. The amounts were always a couple hundred, which could have covered a business dinner or just a night out with friends. For someone to hire a hitter like Alexei, the debt would have to be at least several grand.

It was still early, especially for Freddy, but I sent him a text to see if he was awake. When he didn't reply, I assumed he was sleeping off the ordeal and most of the morning, per his usual. What did he say to me last night? The thieves took the cocaine and cash as payment for the additional trouble, meaning what? Had Alexei already been hired to recover a debt? It had to be Knox's.

Since I'd been a money guy, I combed through Knox's financial statements, searching for the discrepancy. But I didn't see anything to indicate he had an outstanding gambling debt. He hadn't paid off his credit cards or house, but he had money in the bank. He received a steady paycheck. Part of it went into his 401K. People who owed loan sharks money didn't behave like that. They didn't invest in a future. Their first priority was usually to keep their kneecaps.

I called Knox again. "Mr. Knox, do you have a gambling addiction?"

"What?"

"Humor me."

"No."

"What about outstanding debts?"

"My credit card companies might think so."

"Anyone else?"

He didn't answer immediately. "No, and I don't appreciate your tone. If you're worried about receiving payment for your services, you should know I'd be more than happy to drop off a check to cover whatever expenses you've already incurred."

"That won't be necessary."

"It sounds like you're trying to nickel and dime me. Did you run my credit report? You'll see my credit is fine."

It was passable, but I didn't want to quibble or admit to having checked into the client. That would be bad for business, so I backed off. "I'm just trying to figure out why someone would steal your collection. Since you are such an avid fan who participates in fantasy leagues and online sportsbooks, I'd be remiss not to consider the possibility the theft was revenge."

"Well, it isn't." He sounded indignant. "Let me ask you a question. Is this how you conduct business with all of your clients? Traumatizing victims and blaming them is not the way to go. It's bad enough when actual law enforcement does it and a travesty when lawyers in the courtroom or the media do the same thing. But I will not have a private investigator, someone I personally hired and paid, treat me like a criminal, like the theft was my fault. Do I make myself clear?"

"Yes, sir."

"Good. I suggest you remember this lesson when you deal with your future clients. I've put up with a lot of your off-the-wall questions and accusations. I'm not doing it anymore. If this continues, I'll take my business elsewhere and seek to sever our contract. Is that clear?"

"Yes," I said, forcing myself to remain professional.

"Very well."

The only thing I learned from that phone call was how much I disliked Trey Knox.

TWENTY-ONE

"At least you didn't stay here all night," Justin said when he showed up a little after ten.

"I should have."

"Uh-oh." He closed the door to my office. "Do I want to know?"

"Jade wasn't paranoid. She was right. Some asshole was stalking her."

"Is she okay?"

"She's fine. She's not here. He is. Problem solved, right?"

"Just to satisfy my own curiosity, did you have to make any late night calls to Mr. Almeada or, I don't know, buy a shovel in the middle of the night?"

"He's fine, probably better than I am."

"What about the two jerks who beat up Freddy? Is one of them the same guy who was stalking Jade?"

"No, but I thought he was. It turns out Freddy was attacked by hired muscle. I don't know who hired them or why." I pushed my chair back and put my feet up on the edge of my desk. "To be frank, I don't know anything." I rocked back as far as the seat would go without tipping over. "I don't even know the name of the hired muscle's accomplice."

"Have you spoken to Jade?"

"Why would I?"

"To tell her she isn't crazy, that she didn't imagine it."

"What good would that do? She doesn't feel safe. Telling her would only make it worse."

"Suit yourself." From his tone, I knew he disagreed with my thoughts on the matter. "Who was stalking her?"

"Danny Foster. He drives a silver SUV with a bike rack. That's how I found him. It was purely accidental. I was looking for the guys who attacked Freddy and robbed Knox's house." I scratched my head, finding that I despised Trey Knox.

"That means the kid you scared the other morning had nothing to do with anything, right?"

"I guess not." At the time, I thought he was lying. Maybe I didn't have a nose for this kind of work.

"All right, so what's your next play?"

I puffed out my cheeks and blew out a breath. "I get back to what matters. Cross Security needs to expand, possibly hire some additional investigators to deal with these types of issues." I rubbed my eyes. "What we need to do is find the ideal office space, get our new hires situated, and build our client list. As far as Knox goes, I can't do anything until the thieves try to fence the stolen merchandise. And as far as Freddy goes, I'm waiting to get an ID on the second perp before I do anything."

"That sounds sensible," Justin cocked an eyebrow at me, "which leads me to my next question."

"What?"

"Who are you and what did you do with Lucien Cross?"

"I've spent the entire night going over this, waiting for a lead on the intel, and even with it, I still can't make a move." I dropped my feet to the floor and climbed out of the chair. "I'm going home to take a nap. I'll be back in a couple of hours. Hold down the fort until then."

"You got it, boss."

Slipping into my jacket, I didn't bother checking facial rec again. I would have heard the ping. Instead, I left the office, went straight home, and dropped onto the bed without taking the time to even kick off my shoes.

My phone woke me. I opened my eyes and reached for the device. Freddy sent me a text message in response to the one I had sent him earlier. He'd spoken to every contact he could think of who specialized in rare collector's items. He didn't name names, so I did.

Alexei Balakin, do you know him? He and one of his buddies attacked you last night, I wrote.

After sending the text, I got myself cleaned up and rummaged through the fridge. A few containers of leftover Chinese stared back at me. I grabbed a fork and ate while standing at the counter. I stared at the table, picturing Jade, with her legs tucked beneath her, animatedly gesturing with the chopsticks while eating the beef and broccoli. I had it bad, but I had to let it go. I had to let her go. It was done. Over.

I dropped the container into the trash and grabbed a bottle of juice from the fridge and drank out of it. Danny Foster was lucky to be alive.

My phone beeped. *Not personally. By reputation.*

Texting back and forth was ridiculous. I hit the speed dial and waited for Freddy to answer. "What do you mean by reputation?" I asked.

"Alexei's connected."

"Connected to whom?"

"C'mon, Luci, I'm not going to spell it out for you. He collects debts and makes sure everyone pays up. He's been known to make examples out of people."

"Who do you owe?"

"No one." His voice went up an octave. "I trade in favors. I don't leave outstanding debts for more than a few days, and that's only when a client takes his sweet time paying up."

"I left payment with you last night," I said.

"Not you." He sighed. "Thanks for paying off the doc. I appreciate that."

"Yeah, no problem." I hoped he'd get back on track, but the silence dragged. "I don't owe anyone either. But you said he and the other guy stole from you and said it was to make up for the added trouble. You also said this had to do with me. That I was supposed to have been there."

"About that," Freddy chuckled uncomfortably, "maybe I got it wrong. I'm not sure exactly what went down. A lot of it is fuzzy."

"You seemed clear last night."

"I was out of my mind last night."

"Freddy, tell me the truth. I can help."

"I don't know. Seriously, I don't. I've been making calls all afternoon, but I can't figure it out. None of my regulars have anything to do with loan sharks or the people Alexei usually works for."

"You must have spoken to someone new."

"The only new people were the ones I contacted about the ring. There could be overlap. Sports betting is big business."

"I know." Again, I thought about Trey Knox and possible motives for the break-in, but I didn't find anything solid to indicate he had a gambling problem. His behavior hadn't changed. He didn't appear erratic or unstable, at least not to any extreme. And he'd told me in no uncertain terms to back off of him. He'd been right. I wouldn't have questioned a corporate client like this.

"Look, Lucien, I like you. You know that. But I can't get your ring. I don't know if last night had anything to do with that, but it might. And I can't afford that kind of trouble again."

"I understand. I just wanted to know who you reached out to."

"The usual places. Local fences, the dark web, a few bookies I know who are dialed into the sports scene."

"Bookies." That had to be the connection. It fit, and Freddy knew it. "Just give me their names."

"I'm sorry."

"Freddy, I'll pay for the intel. I don't care."

"I'm sorry." He hung up before I could argue further.

That had to be the connection. Alexei worked for loan sharks which went hand in hand with bookies. Someone–a client, a bookie, the house–one of them must have heard about Knox's collection. Whether they orchestrated the theft or simply purchased the stolen goods was anyone's guess. But Knox wouldn't talk to me about any of this. He wouldn't even entertain the possibility. I'd pissed him off after he pissed me off, so I doubted he'd want to assist in the investigation.

"Justin," I said as soon as he answered, "I need you to sweet talk Knox and smooth things over." I explained the situation. "See what he'll tell you, just don't accuse him of gambling. That's a sensitive subject."

"All right, I'll try."

"Thanks. I'm on my way back." I glanced at my fridge. "I'll grab some Chinese food for dinner."

*   *   *

As predicted, Knox didn't offer up any helpful details. Alexei's accomplice was a nobody. He didn't have a criminal record, at least none the local police knew about, and he didn't work at McGinty's. I thought about running the photo through the larger national and international criminal databases, but I had access and time constraints to consider.

Instead, I spent the next few days focused on interviews, signing new corporate clients, and working through the security reviews and having upgrades installed as quickly as possible for Mr. Rathbone and two other clients. I left the Knox case on the backburner.

I was getting itchy and had to find an outlet for the pent-up energy. Working on what I could control and the things I knew how to do helped, like a release valve siphoning off the excess pressure. Almost an entire week passed without incident.

I'd just finished an assessment and had placed a call in to King Realty to check on their progress when the alert sounded on my phone. One of the GPS trackers had been activated. I'd gotten two of these alerts in the last few days, both of which had been false alarms, so I waited to see where the yellow dot would travel.

After five minutes, I was certain it was headed for Pauley's Pawn. "Justin, I gotta go." I didn't bother with instructions. Instead, I raced out of the office and down the stairs. Hitting the unlock as I jogged to my car, I got inside, gunned the engine, and peeled out of the space. With one eye on the road and the other on my phone, I wondered if I'd make it to the pawn shop in time.

When I arrived, the yellow dot was still two streets away. The moving van was coming from the opposite direction, so I did my best to find a parking space with a decent vantage point. But with limited time, I couldn't dawdle.

Leaving my car in the first empty spot I found, I walked down the street, scanning for somewhere to hide. When I couldn't come up with anything, I stopped at the end of the line near a food truck and stared at my phone. The yellow dot turned onto the street. I tucked my phone away the moment the white panel van came into view.

The driver parked in a loading zone near the pawn shop. The parking signs warned it was five minute parking and unauthorized vehicles would be towed at the owner's expense. The driver's side door opened and a man in jeans and a green sweatshirt stepped out. He wore a baseball cap with the bill pulled down. Specks of scruff stuck out on his chin and down his neck, but it wasn't quite a beard. At least not yet.

Removing my phone, I moved as the line did, snapping shots of the man while blending in with the crowd. Baseball Cap went to the side of the van, slid open the door, and grabbed a duffel bag out of the back. He slung it over his shoulder, closed the door, and knocked on the side door to the pawn shop.

As soon as he went inside, I dashed across the street. No one else was inside the van. When he'd opened the doors, I didn't see anything in the back, but I couldn't be sure. I checked all the doors, but they were locked. Quickly, I wrote down the van's details. I'd need that in order to figure out who rented this particular van and if they also rented a storage unit and which one.

Then I went back to my car, started the engine, and crept slowly toward the van, searching for spots along the way. A Jeep was in the midst of pulling out of a space, so I put on my blinker and waited. The vehicle had out-of-state plates, and from the way the driver edged forward and back in the tight space, I didn't think he had much experience parallel parking. While the guy proceeded to attempt what appeared to be a seven hundred point turn, the van driver exited the pawn shop with an empty duffel bag. He climbed behind the wheel and pulled out. I waited a few seconds before turning off my blinker and swerving around the Jeep.

I tailed the van back to the self-storage facility, but I didn't dare enter the gates. Instead, I continued past the facility, keeping an eye on things from outside the fence. The rows of buildings concealed me from the van but also concealed the van from me. This wouldn't do. At the first break between buildings, I turned the nose of my car inward and pushed forward as far as possible, brushing up against the fence. This wasn't a parking spot, but it'd do.

Creeping around the fence, I hoped to see where the van had gone. The driver parked it in the middle of the row with the rest of the rentable vehicles. He carried the duffel in one hand. I edged around the outside of the fence, hoping to see where he was going. He wasn't heading toward the front gate.

If the fence wasn't so tall, I would have climbed it. Instead, I jogged along the outside, past a long row of self-storage units until I happened upon another break. I couldn't see much, but Baseball Cap had opened one of the units. Grabbing my phone, I tried to zoom in on the number, but even the lens on the camera wasn't good enough to pick up the old, faded numbers at this angle and distance.

Deciding this wasn't going to work, I ran around the perimeter, sliding to a stop near the limited number of parking spaces. One of these vehicles had to belong to Baseball Cap. I was about to snap photos of each of the license plates when the gate squeaked open and the man emerged.

On instinct, I dove behind a dumpster brimming with cardboard pieces and dismantled boxes. The man who drove the van didn't get into any of the vehicles. By the time I realized my mistake and peered around the dumpster, he'd disappeared around the corner. I dashed to the edge of the property and scanned the sidewalk in both directions, but he'd vanished.

TWENTY-TWO

I walked up and down the rows of storage units, twirling my key ring around my finger. I knew roughly where he'd been standing. That narrowed it down to three possible units. Each one had a heavy duty lock. Eeny, meeny, miney, moe. I could break it or try to pick it.

The sound of tires on gravel caught my attention. I stepped to the side, reversing course and heading for my own unit. A woman and two young children got out of the car and went to one of the storage units across from where I'd been standing.

"You can pick two things to take with you. That's it. You know we don't have a lot of room at your aunt's house," the woman said.

"Mommy," the boy tugged on her arm, "can I unlock the door?"

"Go ahead, babe." She handed him the key, and he raced toward one of the units. His sister waited for their mom, who was trying to wrestle a second large box out of the back seat.

"I can help," the little girl said.

"That's okay, sweetie. This is too heavy for you." The woman groaned and dropped the box onto the sidewalk.

"Go help your brother with the door."

"Excuse me." I crossed to her. "You look like you could use some help."

She gave me a look as she tried to stack one box on top of the other but couldn't quite get them off the ground. "You could say that."

"Here." I bent over, careful to lift with my legs. She grabbed the top box, lightening the load, and I followed her toward the storage unit.

"Thank you. I'm sorry that's so heavy."

"What do you have in here? Bricks?" I teased.

"Dumbbells."

"I guess that means I can skip lifting at the gym today."

She laughed. "You can just put it down right here." She pointed to an empty spot on the floor. "No one's ever offered to help me before."

"It's my pleasure." I backed out of the unit, hesitant to ask about the units directly across from hers. "You wouldn't happen to know the guy who rents that unit, would you?" I pointed behind me.

"Sorry, I don't."

I gave her my friendliest smile. "No problem. I found a set of keys on the ground near there and thought they might belong to whoever rents that unit." I held up my own key ring. "I was just on my way to turn them in at the office."

"You're just an all-around good Samaritan."

"I'm trying."

I made my way back to the front gate and pushed the button to let myself out. Just like my last visit, the office wasn't busy. The same guy was behind the desk, reading a textbook. This time it was on post-modernism.

"Can I help you?" he asked, his eyes still on the page.

"I was wondering if you have a bathroom I could use."

He looked up at me, vague recognition crossed his face. "Not for the public, but I guess it'd be okay to let you use it this once." He pointed to a door off to the side.

I went around the desk and pulled open the door. It led directly into a bathroom which made the one in my office look huge. I pressed up against the sink in order to close the door. Closing the toilet seat lid, I stepped on top of it and slid one of the ceiling tiles out of the way. With the light from my phone, I peered around inside the ceiling until I found a few thick cable wires. They must connect to the router or modem.

Stepping down from the toilet, I checked my pockets for something to cut the cords, but I didn't have a knife with me. The best I could do was a bottle opener on my keychain. I'd have to be better prepared in the future.

After far too long, I managed to fray and sever one of the cables. Since I didn't get electrocuted in the process, I hoped I cut the right one. With the internet on the fritz, the office security system should be offline. I could come back after close and get the intel I needed.

After flushing the toilet and washing my hands, I made sure the ceiling tile was back in place and I wasn't covered in dust. Then I let myself out of the bathroom and went back around the counter. "Thanks."

"Sure. Have a good one."

I returned to my office to dig up everything I could on the self-storage facility. My initial assessment had been correct. The office security system required a network connection. Without it, the security system wouldn't send a notification that someone was lurking out front or report a breach from the sensors that surrounded the door. Thank you, wireless network.

From what I'd seen, the facility's computer was outdated, along with the software. Payment took a few seconds longer to process than most other places, which made me think customer information, including rental agreements and schedule information, was contained on the hard drive. Databases and spreadsheets, I knew how to work the indexing options. Figuring in a slow boot-up and shutdown process, I should be in and out in ten minutes.

"Need anything else, boss?" Justin asked.

"Did Mr. Almeada approve the drafts we sent him on contract proposals?"

"A courier dropped them off while you were out." He picked the manila envelope out of the intake box and held it out to me. "How many more hires do you want to take on?"

"As many as we can." I glanced up. "I should be here first thing in the morning, but if for some reason I'm delayed, you have a copy of the questions and the minimum requirements I set for new hires."

"Why would you be delayed?"

"Who knows?" I turned my attention back to the computer. "But I trust your judgment."

"Uh-huh. Sure." He didn't believe me, but he didn't waste his breath on an interrogation. In most cases, the less he knew, the better for both of us.

After he left, I uploaded the photos I'd taken of Baseball Cap and tried to clean them up, but I couldn't get anything usable. The computer extrapolated a few details and spit them out. 5'8 to 6', 170-200 pounds. That didn't do much for me. Based on what little I could see of his face and skin tone, I assumed I was looking for a white guy with dark hair. None of those facts were particularly helpful.

I could go to Pauley's and ask, but that didn't seem like a good idea. Instead, I switched gears, reviewed the employment contracts to make sure we didn't miss any typos, and poured myself a drink. The impending break-in had made me jittery. A little something to calm the nerves wouldn't hurt.

When I finished doing everything in the office that I could possibly think of, including dusting the furniture, I locked up and headed home to change. Comfortable, dark clothing and good shoes were a must. After that, I filled my pockets with lock picking gear, a Swiss army knife, wire cutters, a set of miniature screwdrivers, and an external hard drive.

Once I was sure I had all my bases covered, I headed back to the self-storage facility. The cameras posted around the perimeter had probably caught sight of me earlier. I hadn't done anything illegal, so it didn't matter. But if my break-in was detected, the police would have questions.

Making a mental note to delete the footage, I parked my car in a garage a few blocks away, cognizant of the cameras as I exited with my face down and my collar up. I didn't want to put a hood on or wear a mask in the garage. That would look suspicious as hell. I'd wait until I was closer to do that.

My heartbeat quickened the closer I got to the facility. The few parking spaces out front were empty. The lights were off in the office. As far as I could tell, no one was around. Still, it was a twenty-four hour self-serve facility. That didn't mean someone wouldn't show up. It was fairly early, a little after nine. I didn't want to wait too long. Police patrols picked up at night. It'd be safer to do this now.

Ducking behind the dumpsters, I pulled a ski mask on over my face and left my outer jacket, a dark parka, beside the dumpster. Hopefully, it'd still be there by the time I returned. Having altered my appearance enough to argue the person seen breaking in to the office couldn't have been me, I sidled up to the door.

In a moment, I'd know if I cut the correct wire on my earlier visit. I'd also learn if my assumption was correct about the security system not functioning without an internet connection. For all I knew, it could have a contingency figured in using phone lines, but I didn't think so.

My lock picks worked the tumblers with ease, and the door popped open in twenty seconds. Definitely not the best lock. When all was said and done, perhaps I should drop a Cross Security advertisement beneath the door. Snickering at the hubris such an act would require, along with a heavy dose of dumbassery, I held my breath and crept inside.

No alarms sounded. I scanned the corners of the room for blinking red lights but found none. Shutting the door, I flipped the lock and made my way around the desk. So far, so good.

The computer came to life and asked for my user name and password. Bypassing it would take extra time. After another quick glance out the door, I put the flashlight in my teeth and searched the desk for any notes. Beneath the desk pad calendar, I found a tattered sticky note. Bingo.

I keyed in the information and waited. The computer seemed uncertain about the entry, as if it didn't believe I was the user in question. Then it let out a welcoming chime, and the room brightened as the light blue background filled the screen.

Taking a seat, I searched the hard drive, unsure what naming conventions the management might have chosen. Within a minute, I'd found a customer database for the unit rentals. Now I just had to find the van rentals and link the two.

The van rental information was contained in a separate file labeled *Moving Additions*. I nearly overlooked it, but as soon as I found out who rented the van earlier today, I got the customer's name. Eric Beaufort.

Beaufort paid cash in advance for a one year rental. He had another four months left on the lease. I wrote down the unit number and shut down the computer.

Unlocking the door, I peered out the window, making sure no one had arrived. The lot remained empty, so I stepped out and relocked the door using my lock picks. That took longer, but it was done. Just as I was about to turn around, a car pulled up.

I stuffed the picks into my pocket. I had nowhere to go. As I turned around, I slid the mask up on my face, so it looked more like a watch cap instead of a ski mask. A guy rolled down his window to enter the code to unlock the gate.

"They close at nine," he said.

"Oh, yeah. I just saw the sign." I stuffed my hands in my pockets and walked away. That was close. Too close. I couldn't risk checking out the storage unit now, so I ducked back behind the dumpster and waited.

As it grew later, it got colder. I put my parka back on and headed for the street. I was just a guy taking a stroll. No reason for anyone to think otherwise. Two blocks away was a bus stop, so I took a seat on the bench and waited. Forty minutes later, the car drove away.

By then, my legs were stiff and my ass was numb from sitting on the cold, hard bench. More than anything, I wanted to get this over with. I just didn't know if opening Eric Beaufort's unit would reveal Knox's stolen items or if this would be another dead end.

Ditching my jacket again, I entered the code at the automatic gate. It opened, and I went through. I went to the unit and made fast work of the lock. The unit was twelve by thirty. From floor to ceiling, every inch was filled with shelves and boxes.

I let out a sigh and closed the door. This would take me all night.

TWENTY-THREE

I had no idea who Eric Beaufort was, but I was positive of one thing. He was a criminal.

The boxes on the shelves appeared to be organized chronologically. The ones nearest to the door contained the stolen items from Trey Knox's house. I didn't find any cash, but I found his tablet, watches, and most of his sports collection. The items had been divided into three large moving boxes. At the bottom of the last box, I found the championship ring in a Lucite box, seated on a velvet pillow.

Tucking the ring into my pocket, I looked down the rows of other boxes, wondering how many thefts Eric and his accomplices committed. They probably all had access to the storage unit. And from the looks of it, they'd been quite busy. How long had this been going on?

I did a quick count of the boxes, stopping when I hit a hundred. Several wooden crates were situated in the back corner of the room. They had international markings all over them. *Art*, I thought, *or artifacts*.

Picking up a pry bar that had been resting against a cabinet along the back wall, I opened one of the crates. The crinkled, hay-colored packing material filled most of the box. Beneath that I found a dozen assault rifles.

"Shit."

Without thinking, I popped open the box beside it. More automatic assault weapons, a few grenades, and some knives. The team of thieves could be smugglers. It'd explain why most of Knox's items hadn't been pawned. The buyers were probably overseas. But why was the World Series pennant available for sale at a local pawn shop?

Sifting through the materials in a third crate, I removed a false top layer which held various ceramic pots and found fifty or so bricks of what I could only assume was cocaine. Thoughts of the men who attacked Freddy came to mind. They took his coke. That could be a coincidence, but it didn't feel like one.

I stepped away from the crates and stared at the shelves of boxes. On a whim, I opened a random box from somewhere in the middle. It contained jewelry, likely stolen. The voice in my head reminded me this wasn't my problem. All I had to do was grab Knox's stuff and call it a job well done. He only really wanted the ring. I could walk off with that, leave the rest undisturbed, and get away scot-free.

I didn't owe the police anything. Officer Gallo said the detective in charge of the investigation was zeroing in on the culprits, but he thought the culprits were a bunch of bored, rich kids. Whoever burglarized Knox's house wasn't a bored, rich kid.

It's not your problem, I reminded myself, but the guns and drugs nagged at me. They had international labels, indicating they'd recently arrived in this country. They weren't getting shipped out. They had just come in, which meant they'd be hitting the streets soon. And while I didn't have the moral high ground when it came to recreational substances, the addition of automatic assault weapons left a bad taste in my mouth and a sinking feeling in my gut. Gang wars, it was the only thing I could come up with. No one should be slaughtered on my watch.

I might despise the police and bash their actions and inactions. I also claimed to want to privatize policing, to make things better, so I had to do something. But what?

I gave the boxes containing Knox's possessions another look. I couldn't carry out all three boxes without someone noticing, and I definitely didn't want Eric Beaufort or his unknown accomplices spotting me. Knox only really wanted the ring. I could return that and tip off the authorities about the rest of it. Knox would eventually get the rest of his collection back. It would just take time. Deciding that was the safest play, I headed for the door, but another thought struck me.

Was the storage unit under surveillance? If I had this kind of hardware and contraband hidden away, I'd keep an eye on it. "Dammit." As quickly and carefully as possible, I scanned the room. I didn't see any obvious cameras, but pinhole cameras were hard to detect, and that was only the tip of the iceberg. It'd be best to get out of here as quickly as possible.

With nothing but the championship ring in hand, I left the unit unlocked and the door open. When I made it back to my car, I put my mask, coat, and tools in the hidden compartment beneath my spare tire. Then I called Officer Gallo using a burner phone I'd taken from the office and gave him the address and unit number.

"You need to send officers to check it out. I saw a man lugging crates of guns inside."

"Who is this?" Gallo asked.

"That doesn't matter."

"How'd you get this number?"

"Just get your ass to the storage facility."

"Not until you tell me why I should believe you."

"I'm a friend."

"A friend, huh?" He sounded skeptical. "What else did you see besides guys toting in crates of guns?"

"A bunch of stolen stuff from open cases. You need to get down there ASAP. They could move it out at any moment." I hung up, pulled out of the garage, and found a better vantage point.

Twenty minutes later, a patrol car arrived on scene. I'd given Gallo the code for the gate, and the cruiser pulled through. Legally, I wondered if that was allowed. A few minutes later, more cruisers arrived. They remained outside. An unmarked pulled up, followed by another one. An evidence collection van arrived an hour later.

Satisfied that I'd done my part, I headed across town to Knox's house. He answered the door still dressed for work despite the late hour. "The police have found your collection. You'll be hearing from them soon. They should have recovered most of it. I didn't take an inventory, so I can't be sure everything was there. Some of the pieces might have been sold off."

"Okay." Knox raised an eyebrow. "How did they find my stuff? And why did they call you with the news?"

"That's not exactly what happened." I took the ring out of my pocket. "Here. They might have questions for you. You can tell them whatever you want, but I'd suggest you leave me out of this. Their case should be solid, even with this missing piece of evidence. Just don't make any false insurance claims. That's not the business I'm in, and I wouldn't appreciate you using my services for that. Do I make myself clear?"

"I would never."

"Good." I took a step back. "Our business is concluded. Your bill's in the mail."

I was halfway to my car when Knox called out, "Thanks."

*   *   *

Assisting the police left a bad taste in my mouth, but it had to be done. At least I could wash my hands of Trey Knox. He probably wasn't a bad man, but his story never sat right with me. I probably should have passed on the case, but I didn't. Next time, I'd know better.

I spent most of the next day conducting interviews. By the time night had fallen, I was ready to relax. Before I left, I stuck a stamp on Knox's invoice and dropped it in the mailbox. Now I was free.

But the itchy feeling didn't go away. If anything, it grew stronger. After checking the time, I headed to KC's. As usual, the cop bar was crowded with regulars. I ordered a beer and spun around on the stool to survey the room.

"Now what are you doing here?" Jim asked as he wiped the bar behind me. He'd missed my entrance, and I had hoped he wasn't working tonight.

"Getting drunk or trying to."

"Based on the condensation on that glass, you're not doing it right. Turn around. Drink. Order another. And drink that. We'll keep going until you can't stand up straight. Then I'll take your keys and toss you into a cab. Doesn't that sound like fun?"

"Not particularly." I glanced over my shoulder at him. "You planning on getting handsy when you toss me in the cab? That might be fun."

"I should wash your mouth out with soap."

"Will that help get rid of the taste of this cheap beer?"

"You don't like it, go somewhere else. Anywhere else." Jim's eyes twinkled. He enjoyed the ribbing and argument, even if I wasn't entirely sure either of us was kidding.

"In a sec. I'm waiting for someone."

"Who?"

"Joe Gallo."

Jim narrowed his eyes as he scanned the smoky room. "He's not here." He looked at the clock on the wall over our heads. "Give him an hour."

"Okay." I turned back around and sipped my beer.

Jim continued to refill drinks and wipe down the bar, all the while eyeing me. "This is just pathetic. I can't let you sit there looking like that." He sighed dramatically. "The least you could have done is dress down. T-shirt and jeans. None of this fancy suit shit. Someone's going to think the IRS is auditing me."

"They don't dress this nicely."

"My point exactly. They'll probably think you're trying to sell me insurance."

I took another sip of beer. "Deal with it."

Jim muttered to himself and pulled out a worn deck of cards and a bowl of pretzels. "You still play poker?"

"Not as much as I used to. My weekly game kicked me out."

"It must have been your personality." He shuffled the cards. "How 'bout gin?"

"Is that supposed to be funny?"

He snorted and dealt the cards. "Why do you want to talk to Gallo?"

"I just wanted to see if he had a breakthrough on the case. A client hired me because his house was burglarized. Gallo was first on scene."

Jim didn't offer any snide remarks or comments, which meant he might have heard the other cops talking about last night's bust. He picked a card and discarded. I grabbed the ace of spades and put down a three of clubs. "What are we playing for?" Jim asked.

"How about rounds?"

"Fine. You win, you drink for free. You lose, you pay double. I don't drink on the job."

"That would make one of us."

He laughed. "It's probably a good thing you're not a cop."

"You know what, you're probably right." I toasted in his direction and took another sip.

Three beers later, Gallo showed up. I finished the hand and told Jim to let Gallo drink on my tab.

"Are you bribing an officer?" Gallo asked.

"Nope." I waited for him to settle on the stool beside me. "I just wondered if you've made any progress on Knox's case."

"In fact, an anonymous tip came in late last night." He glanced at me. "But I'm sure you don't know anything about that."

"If I did, why would I waste my breath asking you about it?"

Gallo shrugged. "From what I heard, most of Knox's collection was recovered. It's being held as evidence for the time being. Several other stolen items were also discovered in the same location, as well as contraband. The detectives are still working on narrowing down the leads."

"Where was this found?" I asked.

"A storage unit. Damnedest thing, really."

"Was anyone arrested?"

"Not yet. The person who rented the unit used a fake name and ID. We spoke to the facility's management. They don't recall much, or they're just not talking. But that's not my problem. I'm not in charge of investigations. That's above my paygrade." He turned to me. "Why the sudden interest?"

"I just wanted to make sure Knox was squared away. I've grown tired of his case."

"I bet your clients love to hear that."

"You've met Knox. What do you think of him?"

Gallo gave me a funny look. "Nothing indicates he's involved in whatever's going on inside that storage unit, if that's what you're asking."

"It wasn't." But it might have been. "I just wanted to make sure the city's finest have everything under control before I get back to private security matters."

"We got it."

"Great." I tapped the bar to get Jim's attention. "Night."

"Don't come back," Jim warned.

I smiled. "I won't."

TWENTY-FOUR

After I left KC's, I went to a club. I was no stranger to partying all night and working all day. I hadn't in a while, but maybe that's what I needed. Something to distract me from the whispers in my ear.

Olympus was loud and crowded. I ordered bottle service for a table and homed in on a group of attractive women on the dance floor. Eventually, they felt my stare. I smiled. The leggy blonde smiled back. She turned to her two girlfriends, jerked her head in my direction, and the three of them laughed. *Fish in a barrel.*

I poured a shot of vodka into my glass, raised it in their direction, and swallowed it down. Two minutes later, the three of them had clustered around the cushioned, semi-circle of a couch.

"Do you mind if we join you?" the blonde asked.

"Not at all." I sunk back into the seat and nodded at the shot glasses and vodka. "Help yourselves."

"I'm Candace," the blonde said. She picked up a shot glass, teetering on her spike heels as she brushed against my leg and practically sat on top of my thigh. "That's Helena and Barbie." She indicated the other two women.

"Barbie, really?"

"Barbara." The brunette glared at Candace. "Candi's just

being a bitch."

"I'm Lucien," I said.

We made small talk, which consisted of shouting pointless things to one another while we drank. When the bottle was empty, they dragged me onto the dance floor. Someone else caught Helena's eye, but Barbara and Candace didn't mind using me as the meat in their sandwich. I didn't mind either.

"Do you want to get out of here?" Candace asked, her eyes and hands making her intentions obvious while Barbara blew in my ear. "We could go back to your place."

If it hadn't been for the words *my place*, I would have said yes. "How 'bout somewhere else? My place is a mess."

"I'm sure it's fine," Barbara insisted. She turned my head to face her and kissed me, her fingers digging into my shoulders. My nerve endings lit up, the pain sobering me.

Blinking, I pulled back. "Sorry, ladies. I'm game for anywhere but there."

Barbara and Candace exchanged a look. "Hotel?"

I spotted a hotel key in Candace's hand. My sluggish thoughts snapped to attention. This wasn't random. I thought I'd zeroed in on them, but they might have zeroed in on me. Turning, I checked to see what happened to Helena, who was now dragging some guy by the collar out the side door.

"How much?" I asked, hoping I'd get slapped for asking the question. It'd be easier to apologize than face the alternative.

"For all night with the both of us?" Barbara asked.

"Jesus." I rubbed a hand down my face and took a step away from them, needing some distance. I should have realized from their sparkly mini dresses what this was, but in places like this, it was hard to tell sex workers from working women.

"I'm sure you can afford it." Candace's eyes had dropped to my watch.

"Sorry for the confusion, ladies, but I'm not interested."

"Are you sure?" Candace ran her hand along the front of my slacks. "From what I can tell, you seem very interested."

"Good night, ladies." I stepped away with the undeniable urge to gargle with something a hundred proof.

When did I become such a prude? I never would have reacted like this before. Though, I'd also vowed I'd never pay for sex, even when the rest of the guys in the office paid through the nose for their preferred stripper to take a more hands-on approach. But I never crossed that line for tons of reasons, some of which actually involved morals and ethics. So this made no sense.

Twice in the last two weeks I'd been propositioned by hookers. What the hell was wrong with me? Was I exuding desperation and loneliness after Jade's departure? Could they smell it on me? Cringing at the notion, I left the club and took a cab home.

The next day, I told Justin the story, hoping he'd have some insight to offer. Instead, he enjoyed quite the laugh at my expense. But the hookers just made me edgier. The nagging itch in my brain continued to grow. Maybe I was seeing patterns that didn't exist.

The first time, the police had been in the midst of a sting operation. Perhaps the same thing happened last night. After all, Danny Foster had been close friends with a cop. I bet he knew plenty more cops. Since Foster was willing to stalk Jade, why wouldn't the police want to arrest me on some humiliating charges? Getting the story of my arrest blasted across the front of the paper would hurt my business. That could be just the kind of revenge they wanted since the settlement made me otherwise untouchable.

So the next night, I went to a different club. A few women talked to me, but no one offered to service me or take me home. That should have been a win, but it made me feel as if I was off my game. It also made me wonder if I actually wanted a companion for the evening. The thought held some appeal but not as much as it should. Perhaps I was a little heartbroken.

"Did you run into any more sex workers last night?" Justin asked the next day.

"No."

"I'm sorry?" He shrugged. "I'm not sorry? I don't know.

What kinds of places do you go to drink that you run into these ladies of the night?"

"Mostly high-end bars and clubs."

"Shouldn't the management keep them out?"

"How many politicians, businessmen, and celebrities make the news because they had sex with professionals?"

"A lot. Is that how you plan to compete in the big leagues?"

"No." I found the conversation vexing. "My point is establishments that cater to those individuals allow them to entertain plenty of vices."

"That sounds risky."

"It is."

"Should I worry what kinds of vices our clients hire you to cover up?"

"We're not fixers. That's not our business."

"It seems like a fine line."

"We'll see." I shook my head. "So what's on the agenda for today?"

"You have a couple of calls on the schedule. You also have a meeting with Unbreakable, that security equipment firm that wants to woo you. You're supposed to be meeting one of their reps for lunch."

"That's right."

"They're sending a car for you. Do you think they'll hire hookers?"

"You're not funny. But it is a nice change of pace, being wooed instead of doing the wooing." If nothing else, I might pick up a few tips on signing clients.

"Oh, and King Realty called. They found a few properties that might be of interest."

"See if they can show them to me after work today. Our days are too busy."

Justin reached for the phone. "I'll do my best."

The phone calls I had to make didn't take long. Corporate clients wanted progress reports and explanations on the work I'd already done and the changes and suggestions I'd made. When that was finished, I read my e-mail. King Realty had sent me photos and estimated costs of a few of the properties in question. I made a list of the priority locations, figuring my time was valuable.

Tapping the intercom button, I leaned closer to the speaker. "Justin, what did King Realty say?"

"Guinevere Harris can take you to see the properties after five tonight. She's one of the junior real estate agents they assigned to you."

"Guinevere?"

"Yeah, boss. Is that a problem?"

"Nope." While I grabbed my tablet and a portfolio of projections that I'd need for my lunch meeting, I wondered if Guinevere was her real name. It fit in perfectly with King Arthur and his Knights, which would be a great gimmick for King Realty. "Where am I meeting her?"

"She said she'd meet you here," Justin said as I stepped out of my office. "Seriously, Lucien?" He rolled his eyes and let out a disgruntled grunt. "You make me talk to you over the damn intercom and you aren't even in your office to hear my response."

"But I still heard you."

"Which is the entire reason why I don't think we need an intercom."

I clapped him on the back and headed for the door. "Gloria, see if you can explain the system to him while I'm out."

She looked up from her spot. "Mr. Cross enjoys irritating you. The intercom is the best way to do it."

"See," I winked at Justin, "she gets it. Why don't you?"

"Ugh." He glared at me and went back to work.

A chauffeured, black SUV sat in front of the building. Hesitantly, I approached. The driver got out, asked if I was Lucien Cross, and opened the door. I slid into the back, surprised to find a woman waiting for me. Thankfully, she wasn't a hooker.

"Hi, Mr. Cross. I'm Dani Heller." She held out her hand, and we shook. She had a firm grip and looked me in the eye. Her business suit was professional but feminine. She wore a black skirt with a modest slit in the side that I noticed when she crossed her legs. "I represent Unbreakable. We specialize in security equipment and systems."

"I'm aware."

"Wonderful." She nodded to the driver, and he pulled into traffic. "Let me be blunt. Cross Security and Investigations has caught our attention. I realize you install systems and customize upgrades. May I ask if you have a supplier?"

"A few." I knew this game. Unbreakable wanted to offer me a partnership of sorts. I'd install their systems and use their products, and for my trouble, I'd receive compensation. "I'm not entirely knowledgeable on your specs or what you're offering."

"We'll get to that." She kept her eyes on me. "But before I launch into the whole song and dance, will you tell me if I should save my breath? I believe working together would be beneficial for us both, but I'm perfectly happy writing this meeting off and enjoying a fabulous lunch with a brilliant man. Either way, I win."

I conducted business in a similar fashion, and I appreciated the tactic. Compliments always helped in negotiations. "I'm open to the possibility of a partnership. But I want to know how Unbreakable envisions this going. I won't put my name or reputation on something I'm not one hundred percent sure about."

She reached into the leather bag at her feet and pulled out a binder and handed it to me. "I find it's easier to have hard copies and printouts available. It makes it easier to flip back and forth and make notes." While I skimmed the tabs of the binder, she tapped on her phone. "I also e-mailed you the same information, in case you prefer it that way."

I flipped pages, eyeing the sensors, cameras, locks, and mechanisms Unbreakable produced. "Let's talk numbers."

"That's music to my ears."

The ride to the restaurant flew by, and we spent hours inside, going over projected costs, what Cross Security would gain out of it, and the role Unbreakable would play. I wasn't willing to sign on the dotted line until I personally vetted every piece of equipment I planned to use, but if the specs and tests proved accurate, I didn't see any reason why I couldn't use Unbreakable as a supplier when suggesting physical upgrades to my corporate clients' security systems. Unbreakable had everything from motion sensors to cameras to biometric scanners. With my knowledge, know-how, and the right software to operate the system, I could make a building more secure than Fort Knox.

Ms. Heller paid the tab and gave me a ride back to my office. "Let's schedule a follow-up meeting. My boss will want to speak to you directly. I'm sure he'll be able to answer all those questions that I couldn't." That was an embellishment. Heller had answers for almost everything, except how much my cut would be or how much of a deduction they'd take off the price that I'd make up for when charging my clients. I also wanted to know if they'd reciprocate our relationship by suggesting my firm conduct the security assessments and overhauls to their existing client base. "How is Tuesday at ten?"

Pulling out my phone, I checked the calendar. "I'm busy at ten."

"Not a problem." She tapped on her screen. "One?"

"Can you make it 1:30?"

"Absolutely." She marked it in the calendar. "I'll send a car to pick you up."

"That's okay. I have another meeting that day. Will it be at your headquarters?"

"Yes." She hit a few more keys, and my phone chimed. "I sent you the address and details. Is there anything else I can do for you, Mr. Cross?" She uncrossed her legs and crossed them the other way.

"No, this looks promising. I hope our next meeting will be just as productive."

She hit another few buttons, and my phone chimed again. "That's my private line, in case you think of anything else you might need."

"Thanks." I stepped out of the car. Sex appeal sells. I knew this. It's why plenty of pharmaceutical reps were attractive young men and women. It's also why PanAm and other airlines had such rigid standards back in the day. I'd hoped we'd made progress since then as a society, but I wasn't sure we had. But since I was on the beneficial side of things and rather enjoyed the potential perks that came with it, I didn't want to complain, which probably meant I hadn't evolved much from the Neanderthal days. No wonder I'd been arrested for practically clubbing someone to death.

While musing on the lack of societal and personal evolution and contemplating the overlap of the sex industry from every other industry, I went inside and took the elevator up to the proper floor. When I got into the office, Guinevere Harris was waiting for me. I hadn't realized my lunch had lasted five hours.

"I'm sorry to keep you waiting," I said to the woman. "I'll be right with you. I just need ten minutes." I opened my office door. "Justin, can I see you in private?"

My assistant stepped into the office, closing the door behind him. I gave him the binder and updated him on the situation.

"I'll review everything myself to make sure the hardware is sound, but let's have a third-party conduct a test to make sure we aren't getting into bed with a company that has unreliable or unprogrammable hardware."

"I'm on it. Anything else?"

"Just make the call and go home."

"Hey, Lucien, don't forget, I want my own office. Prioritize that when you view these new properties."

TWENTY-FIVE

"What are your long-term plans, Mr. Cross?" Guinevere or Winnie, as I was told to call her, asked.

"Please, call me Lucien." It seemed only fair. "Honestly, the sky's the limit."

She whistled, a smile on her face. "How often do you plan to upgrade your office suite?"

"I'd like that to be a one and done, if at all possible. Frankly, I don't know what I'll need aside from that list I already gave you."

"You need room to expand. Are you sure you don't want to buy your own building?"

"Unfortunately, that's not in my price range. Cross Security is still in its infancy."

"You could buy an office building and rent out the other floors. It's a nice side hustle."

I hadn't considered that until now. Despite the dollar signs dancing in front of my eyeballs, I knew it'd be a bigger headache than it was worth. "That would make me responsible to all the tenants. I'd have to provide building security, deal with plumbing, and the window washers." The list could go on forever. "I'm not ready to tackle that just yet."

"Not a problem." She parked in the garage beneath a forty-story office building that was still undergoing the final stages of construction. "As you can see, parking is available for you and all your employees. Several floors are currently available." She rattled off the square footage. "The contractors can create whatever you want. Offices, conference rooms, et cetera."

"The floors are available for purchase, not just rent?"

"The space is available for purchase. However much you need would be carved out. It's also available for rent, but you made it clear you didn't want to risk losing your office space or come under pressure with rent increases." She cocked her head at me as we waited for the elevator. "Although, you don't seem to want to deal with plumbing issues either. Owning makes you responsible. The building's super won't fix it for you."

"I know that." I also didn't want any unauthorized personnel snooping through sensitive materials.

We toured the building. Several of the lower levels had already been filled with accountants, investment bankers, and lawyers. This would be a professional building with professionals working inside. These were the types of people I wouldn't mind my clients bumping into in the elevator.

Winnie arranged for an architect and contractor to meet with us, and I went over the lab specifications with them. They promised they could do it. Everything was feasible. I'd want a training area, gym, and other equipment. I didn't know if I could have a shooting range in the building, but it wasn't beyond the realm of possibility. Nothing was.

When we left, I felt good about the location. "Let's make an offer. I'll need at least three floors. That should give me enough room to expand." Worst case, I could buy out my neighbors above or below. Who knows, there might be a point where the entire building would become Cross Security. The thought made me giddy.

She tried to hold back the smile, but she was just as excited as I was. We went back to my office to discuss matters in private, and I ordered dinner for us to celebrate.

After deciding on a reasonable offer, Winnie went back to King Realty to get started on the paperwork and I called Almeada to warn him we might have upcoming real estate issues to address.

"Congrats, Cross," he said.

"Thanks."

"I'm taking you out to celebrate."

"You?"

"Yeah, why not? Aren't we friends?"

"I'm not sure. Would you hang out with me if I didn't pay your retainer?"

"Good point." Almeada laughed. "But you do, so we are. I'll pick you up in fifteen minutes."

Almeada took me to a private club he'd recently discovered. The main area was like a nonstop rave with strobing lights and pulsing tones. I glanced at Almeada, never expecting my attorney to have much of a life, let alone one this crazy. He caught my eye and gestured with his hand. I followed him to the bar. He leaned over, speaking to the bartender. A moment later, a door beside the bar unlocked, and Almeada pulled it open.

I followed him inside. Once the door closed, the room was nearly soundproofed. I could barely hear the rumble of the music. "What is this place?"

"It's great, isn't it?" He took a seat in one of the chairs and reached for the humidor. "A lawyer from my firm turned me on to this place. I don't know how he found it, but I suspect a client recommended it." Everything was leather and mahogany. No wonder lawyers liked this place; it looked like most law offices I'd seen.

They had an array of cigars, large humidors, and expensive liquors. Scotch, whiskey, bourbon, brandy. The golden hues blended in nicely with the rest of the décor. The room smelled like fine spirits, good cigars, and leather. I took a seat across from him.

A moment later, a waitress came through the door with an order pad. The service was excellent. This was the perfect place to make deals, meet clients, or think. Closing my eyes, I let my head rest against the backrest. I couldn't remember the last time I wasn't doing something productive. Even in my sleep, I suspected I was making lists and perfecting client pitches.

"Has business picked up?" he asked.

"Somewhat."

"I figured it'd be booming with all those new hires."

"I'll need them." And just like that, my mind was back on work. Something was bothering me. I just couldn't figure out what. Maybe that's why I'd been going out most nights. Okay, every night. Well, that and Jade told me I had to move on, so I wanted to tell her I'd made an honest attempt. That might make her more willing to accept that we could be together, no strings, every once in a while. A trip here, a vacation there, it wouldn't be bad. And during the interim we could date around and live our lives. It was the only solution I could see to our dilemma, aside from never seeing one another again, which I didn't want to think about.

"Lucien," Almeada puffed on his cigar, "are you having that 'oh shit, I just made an offer on three floors of a brand new office building' moment?"

"No, smart ass." I told him about my recent encounters with the prostitutes and the run-in I had with Danny Foster.

"It could be the police keeping tabs. Foster didn't press charges, but since he and Sgt. Renwin were so close, they might have other friends in common."

"Yeah, other cop friends."

"What does Foster do?"

"He works construction."

"Before that?"

"He was a paramedic and before that active military."

"So he was a first responder. That's probably how he and Renwin became acquainted." Almeada let out a sigh and reached for his snifter of brandy. "The police can't go near you for anything related to Renwin per the terms of the settlement. That didn't necessarily encompass Jade or your involvement with her, but they wouldn't want to risk muddying the waters by bringing you in on an assault or stalking charge that had to do with Jade."

"He was the one stalking her," I growled.

"I know. But if they could get you on something unrelated, even something minor, the less informed could use that as an opportunity to make their point or even make an example out of you. You need to be careful."

"Is that your professional opinion?"

"Don't break the law and don't give them any reason to arrest you." He pointed at me. "That's my professional opinion."

"Easier said than done. Given my line of work, we cross paths."

"Avoid police cases, especially ones that could result in obstruction or tampering charges. No murder cases. Other than that, just pick and choose."

"I need to pick my clients more carefully. The last one was a real pain in my ass."

"I have clients like that." The lawyer grinned at me.

"Zip it. I don't lie to you."

"Sometimes, I wish you would."

"Let me know when I should."

"I'll try to remember that." He finished his brandy and cigar. "Okay, I'm calling it a night. You coming? We can split a cab."

"Not yet."

"Suit yourself."

After he left, I went back into the main room of the club and sat at the bar. The bartender brought me a gin and tonic, and I watched the reflection of the strobing lights in the glass. I didn't see any security, but no one seemed interested in starting a fight or getting into an altercation. The club was private, but from the line out the door when we arrived, I wasn't sure just how exclusive it was.

"Hey," I said to the bartender, "how does one go about becoming a member?"

"Member?" He looked confused. "Oh, you mean access to the private rooms and all that." He reached beneath the bar and pulled out a clipboard. "Just fill this out. We need to keep a credit card on file to run your tab. And that's about it."

"How much for the room?"

"Planning a bachelor party or corporate event?"

"No, maybe just some quiet time."

The bartender laughed. "We have several private areas available. For parties, we normally need advanced notice. For intimate meetings, we'll add the charge to your tab. It requires bottle service. That's about it."

"Nice." Although from the aged spirits on display and the bar's marked up prices, bottle service would run a few hundred easy. Good thing I had the money because this seemed like the perfect place to unwind.

TWENTY-SIX

I'd been showing up at the club regularly. I'd drink, flirt a little, and ignore the warning voice in the back of my head. The cops weren't allowed in private venues like this, not without being invited in by the management, and I didn't see that happening. So I should have nothing to worry about.

"The usual?" the bartender asked when I took a seat in the corner.

"Sure."

He filled a glass and placed it on a napkin in front of me. The woman I'd been flirting with for the last week and a half spotted me and came over. She eased onto the stool beside mine. "Come here often, stranger?"

"It sure feels like it."

"I know what you mean. I like the vibe. Chill, laidback, no one pawing at me, or fights breaking out." She picked up her martini and took a sip. "But it's far from quiet. I don't like boring."

"Who does?"

She spun on the stool to study me. "You never told me what you do for a living. Let me guess. International spy."

"You got me." I chuckled, picking up my own glass. "I'm

guessing only a spy would recognize another spy."

"Oh no, you've figured me out." She put her hand on my forearm and leaned in closer. "Are you my contact?"

"The bird flies at midnight." It was stupid, but it kept her entertained.

She laughed in delight. "The morning sun knows no flame."

"What?"

"I don't know. Isn't that a spy-like thing to say?"

"It is."

"Good." She sat up straight and fidgeted with her napkin.

We'd had exchanges like these several times in the last ten days. I always spotted her when she came in around 8:30. She'd grab a drink from the bar, wander toward one of the high-top tables, finish her drink, and dance. It never mattered if she was alone or with a couple of friends. She always found partners to dance with. After almost an hour, she'd wander back to the bar, take a seat, and talk to me. I liked our routine.

"Are you ever going to ask me to dance?" she inquired.

"I don't dance."

"Liar. I've seen you out there." She finished her drink, and I gestured to the bartender to bring us each another. The second always went on my tab. "Men don't come to clubs to drink alone at the bar. They come to dance. To meet people."

"I met you."

"You don't even know my name."

"We're spies. We don't exchange names."

"That's right. I almost forgot." She picked up the fresh martini. "So aside from whatever spy game you might be playing, why do you come here every night if you don't want to dance?"

"I like to watch."

"Oh?"

"Not like that."

"Sure," she teased. "Whatever you say, Mr. Mystery Man."

Screw it. "Do you want to grab a drink somewhere a

little quieter and we can get to know one another better?"

"That has to be the worst pickup line I've ever heard."

"It's not a line." I jerked my head toward the thick door just to the side, indicating the private room. "If you decide I'm a jerk, you can walk right out, and your night isn't ruined. What do you say?"

"Give me an hour on the dance floor first."

"Go ahead. I'll be here."

She tugged on my hand. "No, silly. You're going to dance with me, and the private room is my treat."

After we were hot, sweaty, and a little out of breath, she dragged me across the club. She nodded to a different bartender, one I didn't recall seeing before, and he tossed her a key to a different private room. Obviously, I wasn't the only regular around here.

She unlocked the door and tugged on the handle. The heavy door opened, and she pulled me inside. The door hadn't even fully shut when she kissed me.

"What's that?" she asked, her hands had found their way beneath my jacket to the bulge behind my back. "Shouldn't the hard thing be in front?" For the first time since we started talking, I noticed she had a slight accent. She reached for my gun, but I caught her hand.

"Hardware," I took it out and placed it on one of the tables, "for the spy trade."

The gun didn't freak her out, which it probably should have. "Are you really a spy?"

"No, I'm a security consultant."

"What does that mean?"

"I work private security."

"Like a bodyguard?"

"A little higher up the chain than that."

"It sounds dangerous."

"Sometimes."

She grinned. "I can be dangerous too." She pushed me down onto a leather couch and straddled me. Her lips found mine, and whatever thoughts about what was happening trickled out of my mind.

The rear door opened, and she crawled off my lap. A cruel laugh left her lips. "You were right. He had no idea."

"Excellent," a man with a thick Russian accent said. "You did well."

"That makes us even, no?" she asked, the accent even more pronounced now.

"Almost." He reached into his pocket. "Let me give you what you are owed."

Despite the thick tapestries and plush furnishings, the gunshot boomed in the enclosed room. I scrambled off the couch, but it was already too late. She was dead.

"Don't be stupid," the Russian warned, aiming at me.

Blood and tissue dripped from my once white shirt. I took a step back, hands raised. "Who the hell are you?" I stared down at her body, horrified. "Why would you do that?"

My eyes burned. A suffocating cloud of gunpowder had replaced the pungent haze of cigar smoke and fine spirits. I inched toward the table where I'd placed my nine millimeter. If only I could reach it.

"I wouldn't recommend it." The Russian toed the woman's body out of the way, clearing a path to the oversized leather armchair which squeaked in protest under his massive frame.

"What would you recommend? I'd suggest Jenny Craig." *Not the time, Cross*, my internal voice warned.

"Do you think that's funny?" he asked.

"A little." But nothing was funny. I wanted to kill him. "Who are you?"

"Vasili Petrov."

His face meant nothing, but his name did. He was a Russian gangster. *The* Russian gangster.

Vasili reached into the box for a cigar. He put his gun down and trimmed the tip of the Cuban. "Have you ever seen what one of these can do to loosen a man's lips?" He held up the single blade guillotine, a wicked grin on his face.

"Can't say that I have." Nor did I want to. I had to escape, but Vasili had brought two of his enforcers along for the ride. They blocked the only exits. I needed a weapon, but getting my hands on one would be tough. And taking out all three Russians without getting my brains splattered against the wall would be damn near impossible.

I couldn't count on help to arrive. The back room of the club was private. Soundproofed. But even if it wasn't, the pounding beats beyond the door would easily drown out weapons' fire. No one would interfere, except maybe the waitstaff, and they'd end up gunned down in the process. I couldn't let that happen. Why had I been so stupid to ignore the nagging itch that told me something was wrong?

How did I end up in this nightmare? None of this made sense. What was going on? Why was Vasili after me? Stray thoughts entered and left my mind as my synapses misfired. I'd made a mistake somewhere along the line. But where?

He smiled, knowing he could take his time. He didn't have to worry about the noise, which was exactly what he wanted. He examined the end of his cigar, put the cutter down, and struck a match. He rotated the Cuban, puffing slowly until the end glowed red. "Have a seat, so we can discuss your options, Mr. Cross."

What options? This wasn't a discussion. It was an execution, possibly a double-execution. I thought back, trying to clear my mind. What had I done to piss him off? Suddenly, a single possibility came to mind. *Shit.*

"You should have called my office and made an appointment." My gaze drifted to the dead woman. I didn't even know her name. Guilt and sadness flooded over me, but I held my emotions at bay. There would be time to mourn later, if there was a later. "You could have saved on the dramatics and bloodshed. We're both businessmen. We should behave as such. Killing was unnecessary. Ruthless." Rage boiled inside of me. Could I take him out before he killed me? The two enforcers standing at either end of the room made me think otherwise.

"I wanted you to understand how serious this is and the peril you face." He jerked his chin at the couch. "Sit."

I stared into the woman's lifeless eyes and silently vowed Vasili would pay for this. "What do you want from me?"

"Cross Security interfered with one of my shipments and turned it over to the police. You have twenty-four hours to get it back."

"That's not possible."

"You will make it possible or unfortunate things will befall you and everyone you know." Vasili flicked the ashes off his cigar, letting them fall onto the dead woman's thigh. He lifted my gun off the table, aimed, and fired a few rounds into her body. Then he unloaded the weapon and tossed it to me. "In case you were thinking of calling the police, don't, unless you want to explain why you shot and killed Svetlana."

I noted the gloves on his hands. He had come prepared. He set this up. He even knew her name. "She was one of yours," I said, the realization coming too late. "Why did you kill her?"

"She stole from me. People shouldn't take what doesn't belong to them. I thought you could use the object lesson, right, comrade?"

"I'm not your comrade."

"Fine. Have it your way, Mr. Cross. All that matters is you return my shipment. If not, I will destroy you. Piece by piece." He puffed on the cigar.

"You should kill me now."

"Who said anything about killing you? I need you alive. Dead men aren't good at following instructions." His gaze dropped to Svetlana. "There are plenty of other ways to hurt you besides death. An anonymous call to the police for starters. They have an axe to grind, no? How about I give them evidence of a homicide?"

"You can't seriously believe you'll get away with this." Scanning the room, I memorized the details in case I had to prove my innocence, but the facts were against me.

"Get away with what? That's your gun. Those are your bullets in her body. You're the murderer. No one will believe otherwise. Now retrieve what belongs to me. Meet me at pier nineteen at this time tomorrow. Don't be late." The big Russian nodded to his men, and they yanked me off the couch, dragged me to the door, and tossed me into the crowded club.

I stumbled backward, pinwheeling my arms to regain my balance. I didn't go down. Instead, I knocked into several people on the dance floor. A couple turned to give me the evil eye. The annoyance on their faces quickly morphed into revulsion and fear at the sight of the dripping blood.

"It's okay," I said, even though it wasn't. I had to get out of here before Vasili opened fire on a few innocent bystanders or one of them decided to report me to the police. Ducking away from them, I removed my bloodied shirt and wrapped it around my unloaded weapon before tucking the bundle against my stomach and hurrying to the exit. Leaving the scene of a crime wasn't advisable, but I didn't think I had a choice.

Vasili wouldn't call the cops. Not yet. But the gangster had gone to a lot of trouble to make sure I wouldn't either. He had a plan. For all I knew, everyone and everything was part of it, from Svetlana spotting me to the unknown bartender who tossed her the key. It'd been a setup from the start. A slow burn. How far back did it go? Was Almeada involved? No, that wasn't possible. He was my lawyer. We'd been through hell, but someone introduced him to the club. A coworker's client. Which one? How far down the rabbit hole did this go? When did it start? What about the prostitutes who'd approached me in the other clubs? Had they been on Vasili's payroll too? I didn't know what to think. All I knew was I had to get out of here.

As I pushed my way out the front door, I cautioned one final look behind me. Thankfully, the couple I'd bumped into seemed to have forgotten all about me and had gone back to dancing and drinking. That bought me some time, but Vasili had put me on a clock.

Setting a timer on my phone, I slid into a waiting cab and gave the driver my office address. Then I dialed the only person I truly trusted. "Justin, I need you back at work. We have a problem." I didn't wait for a reply before hanging up. The specks of blood and fluid clinging to my undershirt distracted me from proper phone etiquette. I picked at a piece of brain matter as a wave of nausea rolled through me. "Don't get sick." I swallowed down the bile and let my forehead rest against the cold window. "You'll figure it out. It'll be okay."

"Long night?" the cabbie asked, curious as to why I was mumbling to myself.

"You could say that." I shook out the tremors in my hands.

The cabbie alternated his gaze from the road to the rearview mirror. "You feeling okay, buddy? If you gotta hurl, let me know, so I can pull over."

"I'm fine."

I forced my thoughts away from the sticky dampness I held in my lap. For the rest of the ride, I contemplated calling the police, but Vasili was right. They did have an axe to grind, and given the evidence, I doubted they'd believe me.

Thoughts of exactly what linked me to that club ran through my mind. Credit card receipts and my nightly chats with Svetlana worked against me. The cops would think I'd made a move, she refused my advances, and things went south. That's what I'd assume.

What about security footage? I couldn't remember where the security cameras were hidden in the club, but it could exonerate me. It'd prove Vasili entered the private room and shot Svetlana. I had to find out if such footage existed. I wasn't sure I'd be able to clear my name otherwise, and even that might not be enough. "Who owns the club?"

"Hmm?" the driver asked, eyeing me through the rearview mirror.

"Nothing."

The taxi came to a stop. "Here we are."

I tossed the money into the front seat and stepped out of the cab. So many thoughts cascaded through my mind. I had to focus on one thing at a time. The problem was I didn't know where to begin. After all, I'd never been framed for murder before.

TWENTY-SEVEN

Unlocking the door, I went straight to the bathroom and stripped down, desperate to wash her blood off my body. Was this destroying evidence? Would the police think I'd done this intentionally to conceal my crime?

Flashes came as I showered. This time, I couldn't contain the bile that burned the back of my throat. Gagging, I hoped this was a nightmare, that I'd wake up, but that didn't happen. Once I had my faculties in order, I rinsed my mouth and remained under the spray for a few minutes longer, compartmentalizing the facts. I had to pull it together and get to work.

I dried off and dressed from the waist down. Then I shoved my bloody clothes into a zippered plastic bag and wiped my prints off the gun. That wouldn't solve anything. The weapon was registered to me, but it might slow down the police, should they come knocking. I washed my hands again, trying to recall everything I knew about gunshot residue.

"Lucien?" Justin tapped on the bathroom door. "Are you okay?"

"I'm glad you're here. Find out what kind of security system Club Nova has. We have to gain access to their footage, and monitor the police frequencies. Listen for any calls pertaining to a homicide, female victim, blonde, mid-twenties."

"Right away."

I checked the countdown timer and turned to grab a fresh shirt, catching a glimpse of the angel of death tattoo in the mirror. I didn't get into this business to deal with death, quite the opposite actually, but death always found me. Thank goodness Jade was safe.

I went into the outer office. "Justin, when you get a chance, get Almeada on the phone. It's about time my attorney answers a few questions."

"Yes, sir." He glanced at the bag in my hand. "Do you want to tell me what's going on?"

"No." I opened the top drawer in the cabinet. "Where's the Knox file?"

"Look under pending."

"Got it." I took the folder and settled in behind my desk, scanning the contract we signed. Nothing in the research indicated Knox's case involved anything other than recovering stolen property. It should have been simple. So what went wrong?

It had to be Knox's gambling that had led to all of this. The hired muscle, Alexei Balakin, was Russian. Surely, he worked for Vasili. That's the only way any of this fit together. The Russians must have stolen from Knox in order to make him pay his debt or to take his prized possessions as collateral. That would explain the professional break-in and the storage unit I found. But what if I was wrong?

After turning on the computer, I poured a shot of bourbon, needing something to calm my nerves. My fingers flew over the keys. None of my other cases or clients had any connection to organized crime. It had to be Knox. How could I have missed his connection to a Russian gangster? Why hadn't I done a better job performing my due diligence?

I knew the answer. I just wasn't ready to admit that I'd let Jade's visit derail me this much.

The intercom beeped. "Lucien, Mr. Almeada's on line

one."

I grabbed the handset. "Hello?"

"Do you have any idea what time it is?" Almeada asked.

"This is an emergency."

"It better be. Tell me you aren't under arrest."

"Not yet. I have to ask you about the club you took me to. How long have you been a member?"

"I'm not. Not really. I've been there a couple of times. It's quiet."

"Sure." I snorted. "Who told you about it?"

"What is this about?"

"Answer the question."

"Lucien, what happened?"

I bit my lip. Almeada had been my attorney for years. He'd started out working contracts for me, but when I'd gotten into that scrape with my previous boss and the assault charges, he'd handled it, just like he'd handled the settlement negotiation involving the fatal shooting of Sgt. Scott Renwin. I could trust him. If I couldn't, I'd already be dead. "May we speak in hypotheticals?"

"I'm your lawyer. This conversation is privileged. You know that."

"Hypothetically," I ignored his declaration, "a man goes to a club, meets a beautiful woman, and takes her into the private back room to get to know her better."

"I've heard this story before. Guy gets too rough, and the girl ends up dead. What does that have to do with you?"

"Different story, same ending. You left out the twist. The girl worked for a gangster, who killed her to emphasize his point. And then he shot her four more times with the other man's gun."

"Your gun," Almeada surmised. So much for hypotheticals. "This happened inside Club Nova?"

"An hour ago."

"Shit."

"Does Vasili Petrov own the club?"

"I don't think so. I don't know. I never looked into it. I had no reason."

"What do I do now?"

"You realize I'm a lawyer, not a fixer, right?"

"Then bill me twice, or find someone who can deal with this. You're the reason I was even there in the first place."

"You're right. I'm sorry. Do the police know?"

I peered into the outer office, but Justin hadn't notified me of any radio chatter. "Not yet."

"Where's her body?"

"I don't know. Probably still in the back room."

"And your gun?"

"Here, along with my clothing."

"Any physical evidence placing you at the scene?"

"Plenty."

"How about your DNA on her body?"

"Things didn't progress that far."

"All right. I can work with that. Fingerprints, fibers, we can explain those away. Bullets, not so much. Hopefully, the ME can determine which shot proved fatal. Ballistics will identify two guns, indicative of two shooters. It won't exactly clear you, but it should take murder off the table. The DA would have a hell of a time getting a conviction under those conditions, but they might still try. Your history works against you."

"I know." I sipped the bourbon, my focus divided between the conversation and the information on the screen. "How do I proceed?"

Almeada weighed his words carefully. "As an officer of the court, I feel an obligation to tell you to trust in the law. You should report this to the police, turn everything over, and explain the situation. Things are likely to resolve in your favor."

"That's bullshit, and you know it."

"You could go to your father. Tell him what happened and let him handle it."

"No."

"Christ, Lucien, he's the police commissioner. Let him help you."

"Help me? He'd be first in line to arrest me. What's option three?"

"Life isn't always multiple choice, my friend."

"Find me a third option. That's why I'm paying you."

He mulled over the facts. Finally, he said, "The Russians

wouldn't want the attention either. We're talking about the ones who operate out of Brighton Beach, right? Little Odessa? They have their own clean-up crew, or so I hear. Are you sure the cops will even find her body?"

"Maybe not. It depends on how willing I am to cooperate. Vasili has a gun to my head. I have to find a way to remove the bullets."

"We are talking in metaphors, right?"

"Yes."

"All right. Good." He exhaled. "Are you sure you have your gun? Maybe it was stolen."

"Maybe." I knew what I had to do, but at this point, it was probably too little, too late.

"That changes things. Make sure you report it missing first thing in the morning. The less evidence hanging around, the better off you'll be. An alibi might also come in handy in case her body surfaces, but it has to be airtight. Lies, if discovered, will only make you look guiltier. Are you sure the Russians will move her out of the club?"

"I'm not sure of anything. I don't even know how they got inside. I have to figure out if there's video footage and what it shows. After that, I'll figure out how to proceed." An image of Svetlana flashed behind my eyes. "I should have realized she was a prostitute, but she didn't dress the part. And she certainly didn't approach me in typical fashion. Vasili must have coached her, planted her, and killed her."

"Do you think your other recent run-ins with pros was his doing?"

"Possibly." I thought back to the SUV I thought had been tailing me. What if there had been two? Foster and someone else, someone more sinister? "I don't know anything right now."

"Focus on damage control. We'll deal with the rest as it comes," Almeada promised.

But I couldn't do that. I had to be proactive. Waiting would get me killed or arrested. Vasili wanted his shipment back. I wasn't sure what that meant, but I didn't think he was referencing a bunch of stolen DVDs and laptops. He wanted the drugs and guns returned to him, and if I couldn't get them, all hell would break loose. The only problem was I had no idea what he'd do once he had what he wanted.

"Lucien, are you still there?"

"The police won't find her body unless Vasili tells them where to look. I should be in the clear as long as I give him what he wants."

"That sounds like wishful thinking." Almeada hesitated. "What does he want?"

"It's best if you don't know."

"Isn't it a little late for that?"

"Regardless, I won't be able to get him what he wants if I'm under arrest, so the police won't find her body. Not right away. He'll have to move her. But in case I'm wrong, I need you to hold on to a package for me for a few days. Let's call it an insurance policy."

"I don't like the sound of that."

"Neither do I, but you introduced me to the club. You owe me."

"Fine. I know I can't talk you out of this, so I'll save my breath. Send the package to the office, just make sure it's sealed and contains explicit instructions. Label it for my eyes only. The last thing either of us needs is a legal assistant opening it. Then we're both screwed. I don't want my license revoked because of this shit you've gotten involved in with the Russians."

"Thanks."

"And Lucien, try not to get yourself killed. I can't afford to lose your retainer and all the billable hours."

I snickered. "I'm glad my life means so much to you."

"Seriously, I am sorry."

"Save it." I sighed. "But for the record, so am I."

After disconnecting, I stuffed my clothing and gun into a large bubble mailer, wrote detailed instructions and a personal account of what happened, and brought the package out to Justin's desk. "Have the courier deliver this to Mr. Almeada. Make sure you use our regular guy. I don't trust anyone else."

"No problem, boss."

"Where are we on figuring out the club's security system?"

"Surveillance footage is stored on the cloud. We should be able to access it remotely, but I haven't had any luck getting past the firewall."

"Let me do it." Even though I wasn't a hacker, I had been a computer science major and a decent programmer before shifting my knowledge of the tech industry into making money on Wall Street. That was before everything went to hell and I turned to private security. Oddly enough, that's when I made friends with a few elite hackers and picked up a couple of useful tricks. But I couldn't get anyone else involved in this when the ramifications could prove fatal. "Remind me we need to get a computer expert on the payroll sooner rather than later."

"Have you thought about taking your checkbook into the FBI training facility and offering an entire class of recruits a job in the private sector?" Justin asked.

"I have. But by then, it's already too late. They're brainwashed. Indoctrinated with all those oaths, rules, and regulations. I can't work with people like that. I don't want idealists. I want realists. Life isn't black and white. It's messy, just like this situation."

I held my breath, waiting for the cursor to stop spinning. Bingo. I was in. Quickly, I scanned the database for the footage from an hour ago. Clicking on a video file, I watched the events play out on the screen. The club's back room didn't have cameras. But the main areas did. Plenty of footage had been captured of me with Svetlana, including our disappearance into the private room and my reemergence a few minutes later covered in her blood.

"Lucien, what happened in there?"

"You don't want to know."

I backed up the footage, scanning the front door and main areas of the club for signs of Vasili or his enforcers. At certain points, the footage blacked out. Obviously, he had gotten to the cameras first and deleted anything damning.

The back hallway, which the waitstaff used to enter and leave the private rooms, didn't have any security cameras posted. I couldn't prove anything. Vasili had covered his tracks and painted me as the only possible suspect in

Svetlana's murder.

"Come on you bastard, where are you?" I checked the current feed but saw nothing but a blank screen. Vasili must have deactivated the cameras. He had to in order to move her body to the service exit and conceal his involvement. "Are the video files saved on the premises?"

"I don't believe so," Justin said. "Everything goes straight to the cloud."

If I had more time, I'd do a full workup on Svetlana, if that was even her real name, and run backgrounds on every one of Club Nova's employees. But I didn't have that kind of time. That would have to wait until later. Right now, I had to run interference or damage control as Almeada put it. Forcing the warning voice in my head to quiet, I pressed delete, replacing one fear with another. "You didn't see that."

"No, sir."

One problem solved. Plenty more to go. "Get started on a business profile for Club Nova. I want to know everything about it, the owner, and every single person who's ever stepped foot inside."

"How?"

"Find a way."

"I'll do my best."

"Thanks."

Closing myself in my office, I called the members of the security detail who hadn't been assigned to guard Miranda. At this point, I only trusted the original hires. Everyone else would have to be reevaluated if I was still alive and walking around free. But that wasn't a priority. Having teams guard Justin and Gloria were.

TWENTY-EIGHT

"When did you first notice it was missing?" the cop asked.

"I don't know. It's not something I pay attention to."

He looked up from the computer screen. "Your best guess." From his tone, I knew he didn't approve of my answer. Admittedly, it was a terrible answer, but it was better to appear incompetent and reckless rather than guilty.

"Um...I know I had it last week."

He gave me a look. "Where was it?"

"In the glove box of my car."

"Do you keep your car locked?"

I shrugged.

"Does anyone else have access to your vehicle?" he asked.

"No."

"Did you notice signs of a break-in?"

I sighed, as if these questions were nothing more than an irritation. I was a busy man who had a busy day ahead. "Maybe. I noticed one of my windows was rolled down, but I didn't think much of it at the time. Now, I'm not so sure."

"All right." He hit print. "I need you to sign this."

Grabbing a pen from the cup on the counter, I signed

the report, alleging the facts presented were true to the best of my knowledge. If Vasili called in the tip or Svetlana's body surfaced, the lie would be the least of my problems. "Anything else?"

"Yeah." He gave me his hardened cop stare. "You have two other weapons registered to you. Keep an eye on them."

"Absolutely, Officer."

He scowled at me. "We'll let you know if we find it, but if I were you, I wouldn't hold my breath. If we do find it, the circumstances won't be pleasant."

"Got it." I took my copy of the report, stuffed it in my pocket, and headed for the door.

Before I made it out of the precinct, Sara turned a corner in her freshly pressed sergeant's uniform. She'd just arrived for her shift, early as usual. "Lucien, what are you doing here? Is everything okay?"

"Fine."

"Are you sure?" She took a step closer and peered into my eyes. "You don't look like you've slept."

I shrugged noncommittally.

"Are you here to see Officer Gallo? I don't know if he's working. He could be getting off or coming on. Hang on." She called to a rookie to find Gallo before I could even answer her question.

"I spoke to him last week. I don't need to see him again."

"You sure?"

"Yeah." A thought came to mind. "What happened to all the evidence that got collected?"

"Oh, your client wants to know when he'll get his stuff back. Most of the boxes are being held in the evidence locker. Everything's been catalogued, but since it's an open case, well, you know how it works."

"Gallo mentioned contraband—drugs, guns, other nasty stuff. Any idea who it might belong to?"

"No one's looking at Mr. Knox as the owner. Tell him not to worry."

"Okay, I will." That didn't answer my question, but if I asked too many questions, Sara would get suspicious. And

I didn't want that. "I'm on my way to see him now. I'll be sure to tell him the good news." I gave her a quick hug. "Take care."

She gave me an odd look. "Get some sleep."

"No rest for the wicked." I continued past her, glad to get out of there before Gallo appeared. At least now I knew the evidence had been processed. That meant it was downtown in the off-site storage facility. That tidbit was crucial if I planned to meet Vasili's demands. I just wasn't sure breaking into a secure police facility and stealing evidence was the best way to deal with this situation. Unfortunately, it might be the only way.

I had to figure out a better plan. Any plan. At this point, I was open to suggestions, except there weren't many people I could ask.

Once inside my car, I took a fresh burner phone out of the packaging, plugged the charger into the outlet, and called Freddy G. He didn't answer, but Freddy didn't exactly do mornings. The only reason he'd be awake now was if he hadn't gone to bed. Usually, he'd answer if he thought the call was from a client. However, he wouldn't know this number, so he wouldn't bother picking up.

I sent him a text, *Answer your phone*, waited ten seconds, and called again. He still didn't pick up. If I wasn't on a time crunch, I would have paid him a visit, but I had to prioritize. As far as I knew, Freddy didn't cater to crime bosses. He stayed away from the questionable crowd as much as possible, so I didn't think Vasili had found me because of Freddy. Everything linked back to Trey Knox, or so I suspected.

Putting the car in gear, I headed for Knox's neighborhood. It was early enough that I could catch him before he went to work. Today, I wasn't putting up with his petulance, accusations, and hollow threats. He was going to tell me who he owed and why men had broken into his house and stolen his stuff, or else he'd have a very bad day. Not as bad as mine, but close. I'd make sure of it.

The gated community was difficult to enter without the proper credentials or standing invitation, and I didn't feel like trying to pay off the guards again. So I parked on a nearby street and found a coffee cart. Caffeine would keep me going, especially now that some of the shock and fear from last night had worn off.

While I waited in line, I turned to stare back at the gate. Knox would probably drive right past me. I couldn't let that happen, so I called him.

"I'm a block from your place. Meet me for breakfast," I said.

"I don't have time, Lucien."

"Make time. This is important. I have valuable information about your collection and getting the rest of it back. There's a coffee cart set up right near your neighborhood. It's a short walk. It won't take more than a couple of minutes."

"Fine. I'll be there as soon as I can, but I only have a few minutes."

Tucking the phone into my pocket, I ordered a cup of dark roast and paced the sidewalk beside the gate. The steam rose from the top of my cup, and I blew on it before taking a sip. The air was crisp. In a few hours, the sun would burn away the early morning haze, leaving a clear sky and nothing but the brutal cold.

I shifted from one leg to the other, wiggling my toes to regain feeling in them. Had I planned better, I would have grabbed my wool overcoat and thermal socks. Vasili really knew how to inconvenience a guy.

Come on, I thought, *I haven't got all day.* I resisted the urge to check the time. No more than five minutes had passed since the last time I looked. Where was Knox? At this rate, the man would be late for work. Well, later, since I had every intention of detaining him until he answered a few important questions to my satisfaction.

The gate opened. *Finally.* I bounced on the balls of my feet, preparing to intercept him the moment he stepped foot on the sidewalk. But he didn't walk through the gate. Instead, a grey-haired woman and her bearded schnauzer did.

The schnauzer strained against the leash, eager to go on his morning walk. But once he made it to the curb, he stopped. His ears perked up, and he stood as still as a statue. A deep growl emanated from within his taut body, and he bared his teeth.

"Buddy, you stop that right now." She whacked the pooch on the backside with the newspaper. "Where are your manners?" She offered me an apologetic smile. "He never does that. I don't know what's gotten into him."

"It's quite all right. Dogs usually like me." I crouched down for the dog to sniff my hand.

But Buddy didn't budge. His ears flattened against his skull, and his sharp eyes zeroed in on something in the distance. He let out a deep, warning bark.

"Quiet, Buddy." The lady tugged on the leash, but the dog didn't move. She scooped him into her arms and carried him past me. The dog's eyes remained on a fixed point as he continued to growl.

I turned to see what had caused the animal's unease. At first, I didn't see anything. The morning mist mixed with plumes of exhaust limited visibility, but as the icy vapor dissipated, I spotted two men in dark overcoats at the bus stop. One of them carried a shiny metal briefcase, and the other had what appeared to be a golf club inside a sealed duffel bag. At least I hoped it was a golf club. The only other option was a long gun, possibly a sniper rifle, which didn't bode well for my client or me.

Taking another careful sip of the nearly scalding liquid, I returned to the coffee cart and pretended to study the menu while keeping one eye on the two men. I recognized them from the club last night. They were Vasili's enforcers. Did they follow me?

I hadn't noticed anyone outside the police station, but that didn't mean anything. I'd missed a lot lately. Trusting my instincts and skills had failed me, resulting in Svetlana becoming an unnecessary casualty.

Part of me wanted nothing more than to go over there and even the score, but that would be stupid. Right now, I had to be smart. Everything from their cold weather gear to the bags they carried told me they were already here when I arrived.

"Are you gonna stand around all day and stare, or are you actually gonna order something else, mister?" the guy at the coffee cart asked. "I got other customers in case you haven't noticed."

"Right. Sorry. Give me a number six." I pocketed a few napkins, watching as the bus rumbled down the street. The man held the brown paper bag in front of my face, shaking it for emphasis. I grabbed it and handed him a twenty. "Keep the change."

The airbrakes exhaled, and the bus lurched to a stop in front of the Plexiglas structure. The doors opened, and a cluster of waiting passengers formed a line. The Russians remained seated, their noses and cheeks rosy pink. I was right. They'd been here a while and had no intention of leaving. The only question remaining was if they were sent to keep an eye on me or Knox.

Several people exited from the rear of the bus, blocking my view, so I headed toward a nearby trashcan. I couldn't lose sight of them. Doing so would be detrimental to someone's health, probably mine.

The crowd moved past. The line for those boarding continued to grow, but neither of the enforcers made any attempt to join the early morning commuters. I decided it'd be best to wait them out, at least for now. I'd make a move only if they made one first.

With nothing else to do, I pulled my sesame bagel out of the bag and took a bite. The toasty exterior was perfectly offset by the cool chunk of cream cheese sandwiched in the middle. I swallowed and wiped my mouth, barely remembering to chew. Damn, I was hungry.

My attention remained split between the Russians across the street and the metal gate behind me. Where was Knox? Perhaps, under these circumstances, it'd be best if I went to him.

For a moment, I was distracted by thoughts of classic cartoons I'd watched as a kid. This must have been how the moose and squirrel felt watching the two spies, except these Russians weren't watching me back. As far as I could tell, they hadn't even noticed me. That meant they had to be here for Knox. I just didn't know why.

Tossing the brown paper bag into the trash, I searched for a better vantage point to stake out Trey Knox's house, away from the prying eyes of Vasili's men. I had to spot Knox before they did, and if I could do it without them noticing me, that would make things even better.

I was mid-dial, hoping Knox would answer and invite me in, when the gate slid open and he emerged with a leather attaché case in one hand and a cell phone in the other. I peered around the thick trunk of the tree, feeling even more like I was trapped in an old cartoon. *Surely, this can't be happening*, I thought, but it was. "Knox, go back inside," I hissed.

"What? Why?" He looked utterly bewildered. "You said you wanted to meet." Just then, his phone rang. He held up a finger, indicating I should wait, and answered.

The moment the Russians spotted Knox, they split up. I lost sight of the one carrying the suspicious duffel, but the other headed directly for us. I had to act, but the gate had closed.

Knox had already trudged down the sidewalk to meet me near the coffee cart. Oblivious to the danger, he didn't notice the enforcer heading his way. The Russian brought the briefcase up to chest height, held it flat, and popped it open with his thumbs. In a flash, he removed a hidden gun, knocked the lid closed with his forearm, and slipped his hand inside his jacket to conceal the weapon.

"Mr. Knox, we need to go. Now." I grabbed his elbow, spun him around, and led him in the opposite direction.

"Lucien, I don't have time for this. I'm already late. You said we'd get coffee at the cart and talk. I told you it had to be brief."

"Change of plans."

He tried to tug his arm free. "Let go of me."

"You don't want me to do that." I squeezed his elbow harder, using his arm to steer him away from danger. He cautioned a glance over his shoulder. The man with the briefcase continued to follow us. "Last night, Vasili Petrov paid me a visit. Care to explain why?"

"What? Why?"

"You tell me."

"Why would I know anything about that?" Knox stiffened, stopping short. "I'll call you back," he said to the person on the other end of the line and stuffed his cell phone into his pocket.

"Oh, I don't know. Do you have any unpaid debts you forgot to mention?" I pushed against his back to keep him moving.

"Debts?"

"Gambling, loan sharks, that sort of thing. Alexei Balakin attacked a friend of mine a couple of weeks ago and took his cash and drugs to make up for the trouble you caused. Do you want to guess who Alexei was working for at the time?"

Knox's face went white as a sheet. "I don't know."

"If you're going to lie, at least make it believable. Now keep moving, and keep your eyes facing forward."

"Why? What's going on? Where are you taking me?"

The light at the crosswalk turned red, halting our escape. I spotted the man with the duffel bag waiting on the other side. Vasili's men knew what they were doing. They intentionally herded us in this direction. They wanted to box us in.

"Come on. We can't stay here." I jerked Knox away from the crosswalk. Since we couldn't move forward, we'd have to move laterally.

"Whoa." He yanked his arm free, swinging his attaché case wildly. "Are you crazy? Are you trying to get me splattered across someone's windshield?"

"No, but Vasili's men are about to splatter your brains all over the sidewalk. We're out of options." Traffic wasn't moving that fast. We could make it, if we hurried. "It's just like *Frogger*."

"What does that mean?"

"It'll be fun."

"Fun?" His eyes grew to the size of saucers.

"Well, more fun than a cigar cutter to the genitals or a gunshot to the noggin'." Again, I flashed back to the club, feeling her blood spraying my face. The bagel had been a bad idea. I swallowed and shoved him into the street.

The man who was tailing us removed the gun from inside his jacket and held it down by his thigh. Vasili must have instructed his men to handle this quietly. Two silenced shots wouldn't be noticed, not on a busy street like this. If done correctly, Knox's body could be left on a bench or propped against a doorway, ensuring the Russians were long gone before the authorities arrived.

"Good news," I grabbed the attaché case from Knox's hand, "it doesn't appear Vasili has any intention of torturing you. He just wants to kill you." As for me, the jury was still out. But Vasili needed me. I didn't think the kill team he sent would harm me unless I interfered or the gangster had changed his mind.

Knox opened his mouth to speak, but I pushed him across the first lane, propelling him forward with a hand between his shoulder blades. The man with the gun paced up and down the sidewalk, hoping to follow us across the street, but a sudden influx of cars stopped him. We darted through traffic, amidst a sea of honking horns, squealing brakes, and shouted profanities.

Knox tripped over the curb, skinning his palms on the pavement. I grabbed him underneath the arm and hauled him to his feet. We had to keep moving. My car was parked a block away. If we could get to it, we'd be safe.

"Lucien," he winced, rubbing his hands together, "you gotta get me outta here. I don't wanna die."

"Are you ready to tell me the truth?"

"Yes, anything, just get me out of here."

"I'm working on it." I turned to see where the shooter was, but I didn't spot him across the street. The man with the duffel remained at the crosswalk, waiting for the walk sign to illuminate. Hopefully, his comrade was doing the same. "Stay close."

We only made it a few steps before the shooter hopped directly into our path from behind a parked car. The sun glinted off the silver suppressor. I reacted, swinging the confiscated attaché case against the Russian's extended arm. The gun went off. The shot impacted with a tree, causing the birds in the branches to scatter.

Pivoting on my left foot, I followed through with a hook. It connected squarely with the Russian's jaw. The enforcer stumbled backward, dazed by the unexpected hit. I grabbed for the gun, and we banged into the parked car.

He lifted the weapon, and again, I batted it away with the attaché case.

The force of the strike caused the handles to slip from my hand. The momentum of the clunky leather bag tugged the suppressed weapon from the Russian's grip, and the gun skittered into the street and clanged against a sewer grate. The shooter cursed and headbutted me.

Pain erupted where he hit me, from my teeth to my forehead. Something snapped. I heard it at the same moment I felt it. I was temporarily blinded by the tears that sprang to my eyes.

I swung blindly. My jab connected with his ribcage. He grunted, and I hit him again and again. I couldn't see, but I could hear and feel. From the grunts he emitted, I knew my punches were connecting.

"Shoot him," Knox urged as he dashed around the bench to grab the papers flying in the air. One of the compartments of his attaché case had fallen open, spewing his work materials across the sidewalk and into the street. Passersby had taken notice. Most gawked from a safe distance, but a few had come to assist, only to find me in the midst of a brawl.

"Great suggestion," I growled, aware of the blood dripping into my mouth. I swung again before taking a moment to wipe my eyes. The enforcer threw an uppercut which sent me reeling backward. Everything spun. I teetered but stayed on my feet.

A woman called 9-1-1 while several men shouted at us to stop fighting. The Russian turned, and I delivered one final blow before shoving him against the side of the car. Leaning in close, I said, "Tell Vasili I'll get him what he wants, but Knox is off limits. Got it?"

He expelled a hot puff of acrid air into my face and smiled, his teeth tinged red with blood. He cursed at me in his native tongue and laughed.

"Got it?" I asked again, but someone pulled me away before he could answer.

A group of men surrounded me while several others clustered around the now unarmed Russian, checking his injuries and asking if he was okay. A few guys got in my face.

"Are you okay, man? You're bleeding."

"No shit." I pressed a napkin to my nose and spun around, expecting to come face to face with the other Russian, but the second enforcer wasn't in the crowd. Pushing my way through the group of men, I searched for Knox. "Trey?"

"Here," he said.

The same guy who pointed out I was bleeding grabbed my arm. I spun, ready for another attack.

He held up his palms and stepped back. "Cool it, man. You're already in enough trouble. The cops are on the way."

"Wonderful." I wiped my watering eyes again, catching the briefest glimpse of the oddly shaped duffel moving down the sidewalk in the opposite direction. It was suddenly too hot for the Russians to carry out the execution, which meant it was too hot for me to stick around.

I pushed my way through the throng and grabbed Knox, who was reaching for a folder that had fallen beneath the bench. "Leave it. We have to go."

TWENTY-NINE

"Are you okay?" Knox asked.

"Do I look okay?" I used one hand to hold a napkin to my nose while I drove with the other.

"No." He exhaled, his left leg jittering up and down. "Maybe you should pull over. Can you even see to drive?"

I turned my head, feeling the bruise along my jaw. "Think of it this way, if we die in a fiery car crash, Vasili's men can't kill you."

"You don't have to be so mean."

I cursed, slapping my palm against the steering wheel, which reverberated through my knuckles. I'd forgotten what it felt like to be in a street fight. Granted, it had only happened a handful of times before, but if memory served, I'd be feeling it for the next few days. Hell, I was already feeling it.

"Where are we going?" he asked. "We just passed a police station."

"We're not going to the police."

"Okay." He fidgeted with the seatbelt, taking it off and untwisting the strap. "Why not?"

"Are you prepared to explain to them what's going on?"

He didn't say anything, confirming what I already

suspected. Knox must have been involved in some sort of illegal activity. I just didn't know what, and he wasn't talking. "Are you sure you're okay to drive?"

"Jesus." I switched lanes without looking and headed for Freddy G's place. I had to make sure Alexei or more of Vasili's men hadn't gone back to the penthouse to finish what they started. "Why didn't you go to the police in the first place?"

"I couldn't."

"Why not?"

"It's complicated."

"Not really. You screwed Vasili Petrov, so he's going to kill you." I glanced at him. "How did you cross paths with him?"

"Gambling, I guess."

"You guess?" I squeezed the steering wheel harder, attempting to keep my anger in check. "How much do you owe?"

"Before interest, thirty grand." He swallowed. "I was good for it. I just needed to put some things together, but I had it."

"You didn't pay on time."

"When I went back with the money, he told me it was now sixty."

"Did you give him what you had?"

"No. I told him he couldn't do that, and I wouldn't give him back a dime."

"And Vasili just let you walk away?"

"Not exactly. I didn't meet with Vasili. The man I owed was a nobody bookie. I doubted he would do much. That whole kneecap thing only happens in movies, and everyone knows you can't kill someone who welches on his debt or you'll never get paid."

"Vasili found a workaround."

"Yeah, I guess. I didn't realize that's who my bookie reported to, not at first anyway. I didn't know they emptied my house."

"What did the message on your bathroom mirror say?"

Knox stared at me, shocked that I knew about that. "How?"

"Officer Gallo told me about the spray paint. What did it say?"

"It said next time I'd pay in blood."

"And you didn't think to mention this to me?" I slammed on the brakes, causing Knox to fall face first into the dashboard. Satisfied, I backed into a spot and cut the engine. "How could you have known what it said since the glass was shattered? Did you break the mirror?"

"I just...I didn't know it was him. I panicked. I read the message, and it freaked me out. I had to get rid of it."

"How could you not know who wrote it?" None of this made any sense. "Who else wants to kill you?"

Again, he shrugged. "Lots of people."

"Really? If we lump Vasili and his goons together, I can only think of one other person who wants you dead, and he's sitting beside you. Who else am I missing?"

"Seriously?"

I snorted, which sent a wave of pain through my nose. Annoyed, I opened my door. "Stay here. I'll be back in a few minutes."

"You're just going to leave me here alone?"

"You're right. That could be dangerous." I pulled a pair of handcuffs from my inner jacket pocket. "Give me your hands. I don't want you going anywhere without me." I gave him my most threatening stare. "It's not safe."

Once he was cuffed to the steering wheel, I climbed out of the car. "I'll be back in a minute. Don't do anything stupid while I'm gone."

I went inside and upstairs to the penthouse suite. After a solid minute of knocking, Freddy G answered. From the leopard print pajama pants he wore, I assumed he'd been in bed.

"Luci, what happened to you?"

"It'd be easier if you asked what hasn't." I entered his apartment. "Do you have company?"

"No, my head's still foggy from the attack. It messes with my performance."

I eyed a few pill bottles on the kitchen table and went over to examine them. "Did the doc prescribe these?"

"I believe in self-medicating."

At the moment, so did I. I picked up a bottle of Vicodin. "You mind?"

"Help yourself."

I swallowed one down and tucked the bottle into my pocket. "Can I pay you next time?"

"Don't worry about it."

"I appreciate it." I took a seat at the counter while Freddy went to the fridge and came out with an ice pack.

"Tilt your head back." He cringed, examining my nose. "That looks bad. You're gonna need someone to reset it for you." He went into the bathroom and came back with a first aid kit and some tissues. "You might want to pop another pill."

"Can't. I gotta drive."

"Still." Without warning, he gave my nose a sharp tug. My eyes watered again, but the pain eased. Freddy went to the sink to wash his hands.

After I shoved some rolled up tissues in each of my nostrils to stop the bleeding, I wrapped my knuckles in the bandages and held the ice pack to my chin. "I didn't come here to get patched up."

"I didn't think you did, but you might as well. I'm nothing if not full service." He poured himself a glass of orange juice and added a hefty splash of vodka to it. He held it out to me, but I waved it away. Pills and liquor didn't mix, especially when I had to remain alert and coherent. "Were you the unknown call and text I got earlier?" he asked.

"Yeah." I adjusted the ice pack, suddenly exhausted. I'd been up all night, facing one trauma after another. "I have some questions. What can you tell me about Vasili Petrov?"

"You don't want to cross him. He's one evil son of a bitch. He'll kill his own people for looking at him wrong, and those are his friends. You don't want to know what he does to his enemies."

"You ever work for him?"

"Hello, I like to breathe."

"Do you know if Alexei works for him?"

"Possibly. I wouldn't doubt it. The Russians tend to cluster together. Between trafficking and bookmaking, they all run in the same circles."

"Not that we're profiling."

He laughed. "Not at all." He swallowed half of the screwdriver in one gulp. "So the two guys who broke in here and knocked me around, Vasili sent them?"

"It looks that way."

Freddy finished his drink and made another one. "Well, shit, I guess it's a good thing they didn't come here for me."

"What do you mean?"

"If Vasili Petrov sent guys here because of something I did, I'd be dead." He stared out the window. "I make it a point to avoid anyone with a rep for being a backstabber or just a nasty, ruthless bastard. I don't do business with the Russians, and I don't do business with anyone who does, which means this is all because of that damn ring you wanted me to find."

"I didn't know Vasili had it."

Freddy nodded. "Are you gonna be okay? I'm guessing the reason you look like that is because Vasili sent one of his boys to have a chat with you."

"Something like that." I put the ice pack down and got off the stool. "I'm sorry I dragged you into this."

"You didn't know." He continued to stare out the window. "The thing is, when assholes like that come into my house and take my stuff, I have a real problem with it. I'm no pushover. I got this desire to push back, which is stupid, but it's there. And it isn't going away."

"Neither are they."

"Yeah, that's what I figured. This won't stop unless someone makes it stop. Whatever you did kicked the hornet's nest, and now these fuckers are swarming around. It's been almost two weeks since they paid me a visit. Now you." He sucked in his bottom lip and stared out the window.

"I'll take care of it. I just wanted to make sure you were okay." I just wasn't sure how to get off Vasili's radar now that I was on it.

"I'm fine. I can take care of myself, but it won't be that easy for you. He doesn't let people screw him over. Whenever Vasili's done playing with you, he's going to kill you."

"Yeah, I know. That's why I have to take care of it."

Freddy gave me another look. "I'll help in any way I can."

"Freddy—"

"No, he pissed me off. Now he's gonna get the horns. Tell me what you need me to do."

"Nothing."

"Bullshit."

I knew from Freddy's tone, he was serious. "I have to find out who Vasili's in business with and why he's made such a bold threat with such a short deadline. He must owe someone, or a deal's about to go down. One way or the other, I have to know about it." I didn't necessarily have those kinds of contacts, but I knew some people who knew people. That had been one perk of growing up around cops.

"I don't run in those circles, but I know some people who do."

"He can't know I'm asking. It'll jeopardize everything." I met Freddy's eyes. "Don't go out on a limb. Only people you trust or no one at all, okay?"

"Whatever you want, Luci baby. You know me. I'm all about satisfying my clients." He jerked his chin at my face. "By the way, you probably want to get a professional to look at that schnoz. I'd suggest a plastic surgeon. You don't want to end up like one of those ugly boxers with all that scar tissue and a deviated septum. Then the ladies will only be attracted to you for your money, and you don't want that."

"I'll keep it in mind." I went to the door. "Thanks for the ice and the pills."

THIRTY

Thankfully, Knox remained quiet until we arrived at my office. That gave me time to think, but I still hadn't come up with a solution. Men like Vasili Petrov didn't just let bygones be bygones. Even if I gave him precisely what he wanted, he'd shoot me and spit on my grave. I had to find a way to neutralize the threat. Perhaps blackmail would work. But I'd already turned over the storage unit. Either the police had enough to make a case, or they didn't. Considering it had been over a week and no charges had been filed, I didn't have much faith in their evidence.

As I waited for the elevator to open on my floor, I looked at my watch. With a little over sixteen hours to go, I doubted I could come up with solid, irrefutable proof of Vasili's illegal enterprises in time to leverage that for my life. Pauley's Pawn and the self-storage facility could be fronts. Maybe I'd have to hedge my bets and bluff my ass off. It could work; I had a great poker face.

"Come on," I said when the doors opened.

Knox followed me down the hall. I noticed the stenciling on the door as I opened it. *Cross Security and Investigations*. The writing wasn't very large, just like the office, but it was something I didn't want to lose.

Gloria came around the desk, gently taking my face in her hands. "What happened?"

"I got in an accident."

"You poor thing. Are you okay?"

"I'm fine," I gave her a reassuring smile, which made me wince, "just a little banged up."

"Boss?" Justin eyed me from his spot on the opposite side of the room.

"When you get a chance, get a few recommendations for plastic surgeons and schedule a consultation for me."

"Are you going to change your face and disappear?" Knox whispered.

"No." But come to think of it, that might not be a bad idea. I made a mental note to consider that as a last resort. "I'd like to come out of this no worse than when I went in."

"I'll get on that," Justin said.

"Thanks." I turned to the receptionist. "Gloria, could you clear the schedule for today?"

"No problem."

I led Knox into the break room, closed the door, folded my arms over my chest, and stared at him. "Take a seat."

Obediently, he sat. "I'm really sorry about this."

"That makes two of us." I opened a cabinet, moving the liquor bottles out of the way while I searched for medical supplies. Once I found the first aid kit, I disinfected the cut on my nose and smoothed a bandage over it. That'd have to suffice for now. "Start at the beginning."

"You already know everything. I placed some bets that didn't pan out. They broke into my house and took everything to cover my debts, I guess. I wasn't sure that's what had happened. I didn't think that could happen."

"And you didn't bother mentioning this could be a possibility even after I asked you point blank if you had debts. Instead, you turned it around on me. You're an asshole." Reaching into my pocket, I took out the pill bottle, shook a few into my palm, and swallowed them dry. At least my eyes had finally stopped watering. Though, that was the least of my problems.

"What do you want me to do?"

"There's nothing you can do. It's up to me now." I wondered if I handed Knox over to Vasili on a silver platter if that would make us even, but I didn't think so. "Do you think your collection even comes close to covering your debts and whatever additional interest you accrued?"

"I don't know. My bookie basically doubled the amount I owed him. Who knows what he's decided my debt is or was? Did Vasili ask you for more money? Is that why they tried to kill me? They figure you'll pay up on my behalf."

"You pissed Vasili off. That's why he wants you dead. It's simple."

"But how? What did I do?"

"You hired me to steal your shit back. That was dumb." And I was the moron who took the case.

"Is that why he came to you?"

It was time I fess up. "Vasili wants me to get his shipment out of police custody. Do you have any idea the kind of hell that will rain down if I do or the pain Vasili's prepared to inflict if I don't?"

"Shit."

"My thoughts exactly."

"Lucien, you gotta believe me. I didn't know this would happen. I needed the money. I didn't know he'd come to collect. I didn't realize he was behind the break-in. If I did, I never would have asked you to track down my stolen sports memorabilia. That championship ring alone is worth well into five figures."

"I know what it's worth. So does Vasili. That's why he stole it. You should have told me the truth from the beginning."

"Would you have taken my case if I had?"

Probably not. "At least I would have known what was at stake. You didn't keep up with your payments. You didn't even try to make good on your debt. That's why he took the ring."

Knox jittered his leg up and down, causing the floor to vibrate, something he'd been doing all morning. "All of this isn't because you just stole back the ring. I'm sure the rest of my collection would have covered most of my debt. Shit, you told me the ring was in a box. He wouldn't have even noticed it was missing if you hadn't called the cops. You did that. That's all on you. I said the only thing that mattered was the ring. I could have lived without getting the rest back, but you pushed. It's not my fault the police confiscated everything in the storage unit. It's not my fault Vasili's pissed at you. It's yours."

"Dammit, did you take a class on gaslighting? Because I'm not falling for your shit again." Perhaps Knox had a point, but I didn't see it that way. "You lied to me." I held up a hand before he could protest. "A lie of omission is still a lie. Is there anything else I should know? Anything at all? Now's the time." I had sixteen hours until deadline. And I still didn't know what I should do. Saving Knox's life and fighting off Vasili's enforcers hadn't earned me any favors with the gangster.

"No," Knox shook his head for emphasis, "that's it. I swear. Cross my heart and hope to die." He drew an x on his chest with his pointer finger.

"Do you owe anyone else money?"

"No." He reached for the bottle of Irish whiskey and poured it into a coffee cup with shaking hands. "I thought the matter was taken care of when I said I wouldn't pay. I was sure I'd be safe. Isn't it bad business to kill a debtor? That makes logical sense to me."

"Vasili's no longer worried about your outstanding debt. He wants revenge."

Knox took a swig directly from the bottle, capped it, and put it down beside the coffee cup. "Please don't hand me over to him."

"I should," I picked up the liquor bottle and moved it out of his reach, "but I won't."

"What are you going to do?"

"I wish I knew."

"Can I ask you a question? Why did you call the cops about the storage unit? According to everything I know about you, you despise the police. It's part of the reason I trusted you to get my stuff back. I figured you wouldn't ask questions and you wouldn't have any problem finding the thieves and stealing from them. Why didn't you leave the rest of it alone?"

That question had been on my mind since the moment Svetlana's blood splashed against my face. At first, I blamed myself for her death, but that wasn't my fault.

Vasili would have killed her anyway. She had to pay for her betrayal, and her murder gave the gangster the leverage he needed over me. It would only take one anonymous tip for the police to find her body, just like it took one call for them to raid the storage unit. Obviously, Vasili Petrov believed strongly in an eye for an eye.

Even if I was cleared of murdering the prostitute, the look of impropriety might be enough to deter future clients from hiring Cross Security and drive a larger wedge between my firm and local law enforcement. If my private investigator license was revoked, I'd be out of business. Vasili didn't have to kill me. He had plenty of other ways to make my life miserable, but he'd kill me. Freddy told me as much, and after what I'd witnessed in the last eight hours, I didn't doubt it.

"Lucien?" Knox waved a hand in front of my face. "You still with me? Why'd you involve the police?"

"Besides finding your ring, I also discovered several other interesting items."

"You thought the thieves had stolen from other people too?"

"I thought it was possible." The bricks of cocaine and crates of assault weapons had driven me over the edge. I had to call in the tip. I couldn't turn a blind eye to that kind of contraband.

My gut said the drugs and guns were what Vasili wanted back. He must have been in the midst of a deal, and with the merchandise gone, he could no longer deliver. His buyers would not be pleased. Maybe they threatened him. That would explain why he was anxious to get his shipment back and why he'd put me on such a tight deadline. I could work with that.

Grabbing the same burner phone I used earlier, I sent a message to Freddy and told him to let me know as soon as he found someone who could verify my theory. Hopefully, it'd pan out. I needed as many details as I could get if I wanted to stand a fighting chance.

"I guess it doesn't pay to do the right thing," Knox mused.

"How would you know? None of your actions have been

even remotely close to the right thing." I opened the freezer and took out an ice pack before glancing at my reflection in the mirror. I looked like a boxer who'd lost a fight. Maybe that would earn me some sympathy. "I'll take care of this. In the meantime, you need to stay here. Don't call anyone. Don't go out. Vasili wants you dead. He'll send more of his men to finish the job unless I can convince him otherwise."

"Yeah, okay. No problem."

I held out my hand. "Give me your phone. Vasili could be tracking it. Tracking you. It's for your safety. When this is over, you'll get it back."

"Sure." He fished it out of his pocket. "I owe you."

"Don't worry, I'll send you a bill. I suggest you pay it this time."

Stepping out of the tiny break room, I pulled the door closed behind me and scrolled through the call logs, text messages, and contacts on Knox's phone, but nothing stood out. I went into my office and plugged the device into my computer. While I ran reverse lookups on the numbers and read each and every message, Justin barged into my office.

"You have a consultation with the plastic surgeon on Wednesday," he said.

"Let's see if I'm still breathing by then. If not, I'll need you to cancel."

"Will do."

When the numbers didn't connect to any gangsters, con men, or bookies, I unhooked the phone from the computer and tossed it to Justin. "Hold on to this. I don't want Knox making any calls or contacting anyone. He's not the sharpest tool in the shed. He could compromise his safety and yours by doing something asinine."

"Okay. I'll keep an eye on him."

"Thanks." I climbed out of the chair, my shoulders and back stiff and sore. Crinkling my nose, I winced, which made my eyes water again. "Dammit." I grabbed a tissue from the box.

"Lucien," Justin dropped into one of my client chairs, "what's going on? How can I help?"

"It's best if you don't."

"You're probably right, but you need my help."

"No."

"C'mon, boss, we've been in scrapes together before."

"Not like this."

"Is this another Scott Renwin situation?"

"Worse."

He stared at me, slowing deflating in the chair. "You need to call your dad."

"I can't. This is basically a hostage situation."

"Who's being held?" My assistant seemed even more freaked out now than he had when he spotted my bloody clothing in the bag last night.

"My freedom. My livelihood. My life." I unlocked my bottom drawer and took out the emergency funds I kept there and a backup to my backup. "I appreciate everything you do around here, but I have to do this on my own."

"That didn't work out so well last time."

"This isn't like last time. Knox will be here with you. He'll be safe."

"That's why you have our security teams guarding Gloria and me, so we'll be safe?"

"They could use the practice." I swallowed. "If I don't come back, take Knox to the precinct, turn over our records, and call Almeada. That should be enough for Sara to piece everything together."

"Sgt. Rostokowski?"

"Yep."

"Are you sure you can handle this?"

"There's only one way to find out. But if this is it, you know what to do."

"Rename the business and order new stationery?"

I smiled. "Exactly."

THIRTY-ONE

"Hey, Sara." I kept my sunglasses on as I waited for her to step out for lunch. She always took her break at the same time each day, unless something pressing was going on inside. Luckily, today was a slow day for the city's finest.

"Jesus," she clutched her chest dramatically, "you know better than to sneak up on a cop." She peered at me. "What the hell happened to you? You didn't look like that a few hours ago."

"I got into a fight with my desk chair. It slid out from beneath me, and I hit my face right on the edge of my desk."

"Ouch." She didn't believe me, but that didn't matter. "Why are you back to pester me?"

"I need a favor."

"That'll cost you lunch."

"I don't have time for lunch, but I need to know if gangs, narcotics, or organized crime has any operations in the works."

She grabbed my arm and stopped dead in her tracks. "What are you doing? You know better than to mess with people like that. Drugs are bad. Don't you remember the egg in the frying pan?"

"I just need to know if any big exchanges are going down."

She pursed her lips and turned to stare at the people passing us on the sidewalk. "I work the desk."

"And everyone talks to you. You know more about what goes on inside the precinct than anyone else."

"Why do you want to know?"

"Morbid curiosity."

"Try again."

"Sara, please."

She looked the other way before looking back at me. "I heard something about the KXDs wanting to make a play for the big time. They're hoping to get into business with one of the syndicates to run drugs and girls."

"When?"

"I have no idea." Before I could open my mouth, she added, "And no, I can't find out."

"Anything else?"

"Whatever you're doing or thinking about doing, don't. You are private security, Lucien Cross. Organized crime and gang activity has absolutely nothing to do with you. That is a police matter. You interfere, and I'll personally throw your ass in jail."

"You'd arrest me? I thought you liked me. Don't you think of me like a nephew? What about all those times you babysat me?"

"You mean on the rare occasion your dad brought you to work and didn't have any idea what to do with you?"

"Yeah." I offered up a charming smile.

"That's precisely why I'll taser you and handcuff you to my desk. Arresting you would be a kindness, a necessity to save your life."

"I'm not doing anything."

"You better not." She thought about the way I hugged her this morning. "The last time you asked me for information, you nearly died. Don't you dare do that to me again."

"I won't. I promise."

*   *   *

After my visit to the precinct, I returned to the office and did some digging on the intel Sara had provided. I didn't know much about the local gangs or what they planned to do, so I asked around. Apparently, one of the gangs wanted to make a power play. They figured the easiest way to do that would be to convince the Russians to enter into a partnership. The gang would move product, take a cut, and hand the rest back to Vasili.

However, from what I'd been told, the rest of the Russian crime syndicate wasn't pleased with this arrangement. They wanted to keep things in house. Sourcing out drugs and girls to a gang was beneath them. It would harm their reputation and decrease the perceived power they held. But Vasili thought this would be a great opportunity to gain more power and expand into gang-controlled territories. He figured he'd use the gang to his benefit, just another pawn in his game. That meant everything had to go right, and I'd screwed that up by having his shipment intercepted by the police.

Why didn't the Russians just send for another shipment? I wondered. This wasn't making much sense, but they might have had transport issues or customs issues. More than likely, it was neither. Vasili still had his own territories to supply—the strip joints, the clubs, and the street corners he controlled. He needed back those fifty kilos and the guns to go with it.

I brought up blueprints on the evidence warehouse and dug into the police database, searching for info on protocols and procedures. The evidence warehouse was one of the most secure buildings in the city. It contained everything to make or break cases, convict offenders, and enough cash and contraband to finance someone's own private island and army.

Getting inside would be hard enough. Getting through the gate and into the locker would be even harder. This wasn't like the evidence room at the precinct. This was centralized for the entire city. I couldn't get in and out without detection, especially if I had to lug out two crates of assault weapons and fifty bricks of cocaine.

I'd need forklifts and diversions. "Stop it," I mumbled. My mind had gone to dark places, daydreaming about blowing up the side of the building and hauling off the loot. Truthfully, I had no desire to give any of these things back to Vasili. He'd put them on the street and people would die. It was that simple, and I wanted no part of it.

Plan B, it is. I just didn't know what that was. If I could con the gangster, I could buy some time. But even if I succeeded, that wouldn't solve my problem in the long-term. As soon as he found out I couldn't deliver, he'd kill me. So I had to deliver or make him believe I could. But then what?

He's going to kill you either way, the voice in my head reminded me.

My phone rang. I picked it up, staring at it a bit too long before figuring out what to do with it. Yep, that probably meant I needed to lay off the painkillers. They didn't help me think, but since I figured I was a dead man walking, I hadn't exactly refrained from making my remaining hours as pleasant as possible. And with a broken nose and a looming death threat, that wasn't an easy feat.

Sober up, Cross. You have too much riding on this. I answered the phone. "What did you find out?"

"Deal's supposed to go down at four a.m., right after the club closes. Vasili's supposed to make the exchange in the back room of one of his strip joints. He's unloading all the coke and the weapons," Freddy said.

"Same buyer?"

"As far as I know. I didn't ask too many questions. You said you didn't want this getting back to him."

"No, you're right. Thanks." If it hadn't been for Freddy's continued rambling, I might have hung up before he got to his second point. I made a few exaggerated blinks to focus my mind. It might not have been the pills. It could have been lack of sleep.

"I set up a meet between you and the Irish. They might know more about what's going on than you do. They definitely aren't fans of Mr. Petrov, so I think they'll help for a price."

"How much did you agree on?"

"Twelve. Guns aren't cheap, especially the ones you want."

"Thanks."

I hung up and counted the money I kept on hand for emergency use. Five grand. I could withdraw another seven from the bank. Cash was nearly untraceable, which would be good because I didn't want my name tied to organized crime or possible terrorist activity across the pond. This had to be the lesser of two evils, but I still didn't like it.

Hoping my gun problem was solved, I now had to deal with the drug problem. More importantly, I needed to figure out exactly what I was working with. I hadn't paid much attention before I tipped off the cops, so I'd have to pay more attention now. First stop, the bank, then the evidence warehouse. After that, the grocery store for supplies. I'd swing by and pick up the guns, and then I'd be set. Except that would only buy me a bit more time. I still had to figure out how to eliminate the threat, and aside from waging a one-man war against Vasili and his men, I was out of ideas.

"All right, I'm leaving." I looked around my office for what might be the final time. "I'll see you tomorrow." Maybe.

"You're not driving," Justin said, more of a statement than a question. "I'll call you a cab."

"You always watch out for me. That means a lot."

He gave me a look and picked up the phone. Luckily, Gloria had already gone home for the day, so I didn't have to deal with her concerned looks or questions. Her heart was in the right place, but I didn't want to drag her into any of this.

When the cab arrived, I went downstairs and climbed in. After giving the driver the address for the bank, I settled into the seat and closed my eyes. *Sleep when you can,* my mentor had said when I'd been shadowing him for those two hundred hours to get my license. He'd meant on stakeouts, when working with another investigator, but I'd been awake for the last thirty-something hours. Given the circumstances, I decided that meant it applied now. I just hoped Vasili didn't have men tailing me because I would never notice.

THIRTY-TWO

"We're here." The cabbie turned around, knocking his fist against the partition that separated us. "Wake up, mister. This is your stop."

Slowly, I opened my eyes and looked around. "Are you sure? It doesn't look like much."

"This is the address you gave me." He stared at me. "You want me to take you somewhere else instead?"

"Actually," I reached into my wallet, "would you mind keeping the meter running? This shouldn't take long." I passed him fifty dollars. The first cabbie, who'd driven me to the bank, had no interest in chauffeuring me around for the day and had taken off as soon as I got out of the car. I hoped my luck would improve with this second taxi driver. "I'll give you another hundred if you're still here when I get back."

The cabbie peered out the windshield. "Yeah, okay, but this better not be a drug deal."

"It's not. My drug dealer lives in a much nicer neighborhood."

He snorted, thinking it was a joke. "I'll be here."

"Great." Stumbling out of the cab, I regretted popping those painkillers when I'd returned to the office the first time. The benefits had worn off, leaving me a little dizzy, groggy, and nauseous. At least I'd listened to Justin and didn't drive myself. Heavy machinery and narcotics didn't mix. That's why the bottle came with a warning label.

I blinked a few times and stared bleary-eyed at the numbers above the door. This was the place. On my way inside, I unbuttoned my jacket. The police officer behind the desk barely glanced up when I walked into the evidence warehouse.

"Sign-in." He slid the clipboard through the opening in the cage. I picked up the pen, wondering what I should write. But this guy appeared to be bored. He'd do everything by the book. So I wrote my John Hancock neatly on the line and slowly reached into my jacket for my ID. He took the clipboard back and read what I had written. "Badge number?"

"I don't have one." I handed him my ID. "I just wanted to check on what was catalogued. My dad said it'd be okay."

"Who the hell's your dad?"

"Commissioner Cross."

"Seriously?" He exchanged a look with one of the cops posted on the outside of the cage.

"Call him up and ask. I'll wait. I'm sure he doesn't have anything better to do."

"What did you want to know?"

"I provided the department with a tip about a bust at a storage facility two weeks ago. Lots of stuff came in. I just wanted to know about the drugs and guns."

"Why?"

"You realize informants get rewarded based on a percentage of the bust. I wanted to know how many kilos and how many guns we're talking."

The officer stared at me. "What happened to your face?"

"I got in an accident."

"With someone's fist?"

"Yeah."

"Uh-huh." He pulled up the inventory list. "Fifty bricks, two dozen assault rifles, and six handguns."

"Make and model?"

"Why do you need to know that?"

"I just do."

"Knowledge like this isn't for public consumption."

"It'll be introduced into evidence at trial. Those records will be made public. I don't see what the big deal is if I find out then or I find out now."

"I just want to know why you want to know."

"Because Dad's worried about things going missing from here. I'm not supposed to say anything, but you seem like an upstanding guy and a decent cop. The DA's office has complained that evidence has disappeared a time or two." I stared at him for a moment before flicking my gaze over my shoulder at the other cops. "You know exactly what I'm talking about, don't you? That's why I was asked to check in. IA has their suspicions who's involved, but if they are wrong, they can't risk telling a dirty cop what they're doing."

"So they sent you? You're not even a cop."

"No, but I'm the commissioner's best kept secret." Actually, my father would probably do everything in his power to make my entire existence a secret if he could, but that was beside the point.

I didn't think the officer believed me, but since I didn't actually ask him to do anything illegal, he pushed away from the desk.

"Hang on a sec." He disappeared into the rows of shelves. When he returned, he had a few evidence bags in his hands. "You can see for yourself."

I stared at the assault rifles. Kalashnikovs. I'd remembered them correctly. At least I hadn't made plans to purchase incorrect assault weapons. "What are those, AK-12s?"

"Uh-huh."

Those weren't easy to find. No wonder the price was so high. "What about the handguns?"

"They're just Sigs. Nothing special." He held one up, and I analyzed the details and notations on the evidence bags.

"What about the coke?"

He held up a brick, which had been tested and carefully wrapped. Official police evidence tape covered the bottom portion. The lab results were marked on the form, along with the tech's initials, date tested, and date collected. "It's coke. What do you want with it?"

"Nothing." It hadn't been divided into little baggies, so that'd make my life easier. "I just wanted to make sure it was still here and sealed. None of the bricks have walked off, right?"

"Nope."

"Did you count them?"

"Give me a break." The cop jerked his chin toward the door, indicating it was time I leave. "Tell the commissioner everything's good, unless you think it'd be better if I call him and tell him myself."

I held up my palms and stepped back. "Nope. It looks like you have everything squared away," I squinted at his nameplate, "Officer DeLaine." I headed for the door. "Dad will be pleased."

When I got back into the waiting cab, I handed the driver the hundred dollars I promised him. "Now where do you want to go?" he asked.

"I need to get some groceries."

"Any store in particular?"

I gave him the address of one of the bigger supermarkets and eased deeper into the seat. Before I took another unintentional catnap, I sent a message to Freddy and gave him the updated list. He knew arms dealers. Supposedly, he never did direct business with them, but he claimed to be able to get anyone anything. And right now, I needed to make sure the Irish had two dozen Kalashnikovs and a few Sigs waiting for me.

Less than twenty seconds passed before he gave me an affirmative, along with a name, address, time, and place for the exchange. Reassured that Vasili would have no way of knowing what I was up to, I let my eyes close and thought about how costly this endeavor would be. Money wasn't important, I reminded myself, but I didn't completely believe it. However, in the grand scheme of things, I could always find ways to make more money. I couldn't exactly find a way to resurrect myself if Vasili Petrov shot me dead or the police decided to lock me away in a deep, dark hole and throw away the key.

Still, it would be cheaper and safer to take back Vasili's shipment from the police evidence locker. But the police department wouldn't agree, and if things went south, I didn't want Vasili to win. Returning the contraband wouldn't ensure my survival. If anything, it'd give him a reason to kill me faster.

"What a mess," I mumbled.

The cabbie cleared his throat, but he didn't speak. For the brief ride, I slept, wondering if today would be my final day on Earth. If it was, it was a really shitty day. I wanted a do-over somewhere warm with tropical drinks and skinny dipping with Jade. That'd be nice. Maybe she would agree to meet up for the occasional vacation, but I didn't know. Right now, I didn't even know if it'd ever be safe for her to be around me again. Everything rested on tonight.

THIRTY-THREE

"Are you sure you have everything you need?" Freddy G stared at the cases covering the counter and table of the penthouse. "This is insane."

"Yeah, so?"

He laughed. "I always knew there was a reason I liked you."

"I thought it's because I pay well and don't ask for anything too ridiculous."

"No elephants or tigers on a leash."

"Someone asked you for a tiger on a leash?"

"Not to keep, just to show up at a birthday party. A rented tiger on a leash."

"That doesn't make it better."

"Probably not for the tiger, but his trainer was pleased."

I shook my head, not wanting to think about the illegalities of the exotic animal trade. As it was, I already had plenty of other illegal ventures to think about. Breaking down another assault rifle, I made sure the weapon was unloaded and removed the firing pin. Then I reassembled it and tossed it in a box.

Freddy wandered toward the bricks of cocaine, which I'd wrapped in evidence tape and labeled just like the confiscated stuff, along with the forged test results and tech's initials. Hopefully, Vasili would believe it was legit, right out of lockup. The last thing I needed was for him to test it.

"What is this stuff?" Freddy held up one of the bricks. "Mind if I have a taste?"

"I do."

He put the brick down. "I thought you were opposed to giving him back the drugs."

"Those aren't drugs. They're baking supplies. Flour, cornstarch, sugar, that kind of thing." I chuckled. "The woman at the register asked if I owned a bakery."

"What did you tell her?"

"That I was participating in a bake sale to raise money for refugees."

"What'd she say?"

"She gave me five dollars."

Freddy laughed. "And the tape and official forms, where did you get those?"

"The tape I had from when I swiped it a few years ago to use at a Halloween party, and the forms came off my printer."

"If things don't pan out, you might want to go into forgeries. Start with passports. We'll both need a one-way ticket out of the country if Vasili finds out what you have in store for him."

Sucking in a breath, I forced myself to focus on disarming the weapons. I didn't want to think about what was to come. I'd sent an anonymous message to the head of the gang to tell him the Russians intended to double-cross him. I'd given vague details about a second buyer who offered more money for the product, which would explain any delay that might have occurred. I'd also alluded to the Russian's unwillingness to deal with non-Russians and the possibility that the product might not be as pure as expected.

Without knowing if he believed me, I didn't know what the gang leader would do. But he'd replied, and we had exchanged numbers. I told him I'd let him know as soon as I found out the time and place the Russians planned to meet with their other buyers. I'd been afraid to give too much away because I didn't know how reliable my intel was. The local gang and foreign gangster could already be in bed together, but I counted on a level of distrust between the two.

"All right." I finished removing the last firing pin. "Now I just have to load everything into the car."

"Your car?"

"Hell no. I got a rental that doesn't link back to me."

"When did you become some secret, ninja spy?"

"When you weren't looking." I grabbed one of the boxes and sealed the top. "Do you mind helping me carry these downstairs?"

He looked at his nails, as if about to say he'd just had a manicure, but thought better of it and picked up one of the other boxes. "I did offer to help any way I could. I guess this is me getting off easy." He laughed. "You know what, that sounds like a brilliant idea." As soon as we loaded up the back of the SUV, he pulled out his phone and texted the woman from the other night. "You want to stick around for a few minutes and go out with a bang? She has a friend."

"No, that's how I got into this mess."

*　　*　　*

I watched the reflected city lights dance across the water's surface. This was a bad idea. Possibly the worst one I ever had. I never thought of myself as a killer. So what was I doing here?

I had spent the day collecting everything I needed to pull this off, but I was starting to have doubts. With enough time and planning, I could have devised a scheme to steal what I needed from the evidence room, but that would have required days or weeks of planning. Vasili didn't give me that much time, and even if he had, he'd kill me. The tiny, naïve voice in my mind kept saying if I followed the rules and had been a good boy, he'd leave me alone. That voice sounded a lot like my father, but following the rules had never gotten me anywhere good. It had gotten me kicked out of the police academy and fired from my Wall

Street job. No, rules were meant to be broken, which is how I ended up devising plan B.

Except plan B required precise timing. Whenever Vasili showed up, I'd have to get things moving. I still had two hours until deadline, but I arrived early at the wharf and found a spot where I could keep an eye on pier nineteen.

Getting out to stretch my legs, I opened the rear hatch and moved the guns into an extra large rolling suitcase before filling a second suitcase with the white bricks. Vasili should be pleased. These would replace what the cops confiscated, more or less. But he'd never see this as a completed business transaction. He'd probably kill me on the spot, or he'd use me to get more drugs or guns. Believing I could get in and out of the evidence warehouse would open up a whole new world to him. If he let me live, he'd never let me go free.

That thought hadn't occurred to me until now. I slammed the trunk, more resolute in my decision, and got back behind the wheel. I looked down at the unregistered gun on the seat beside me. Killing Vasili held a certain appeal, but pulling the trigger would place an even greater target on my back. His family would want revenge, and this would never end.

I flexed my gloved fingers, comforted by the familiar creaking of the leather. Then I checked to make sure the gun was loaded; something I'd already done a hundred times. Even though I didn't plan to shoot him, I'd do it if I ran out of options.

"You're losing it," I muttered, tucking the gun into my holster. My hands weren't nearly as steady as they should be on account of the caffeine and adrenaline, but on the bright side, I was finally awake and alert. When this was over, I'd go home, pop a few more pills, and sleep for days. Or I'd die on the pier and sleep for all eternity. Either way, I'd get my rest.

Headlights bounced off the pavement, but the car kept going. I glanced at the neon display on the dash. It was too early. He shouldn't be here yet.

Again, I considered phoning the authorities. But that's how I got into this mess. Plus, power and money spoke volumes. Vasili would walk. I knew it in my gut, and once he was a free man, I'd be right back here or in worse shape.

My mind wandered to thoughts of Jade. Her gorgeous eyes and fiery red hair brought a smile to my lips. For the first time since she left the city and left me, I felt relief. Vasili didn't know about her. He'd never find her. She was safe. No matter what happened tonight, she would be okay. That consoling thought bolstered my confidence. I could do this. I had to do this.

Settling deeper into the seat, I checked the time again and reached for the burner phone. Instead of messaging Freddy, I sent another anonymous message to the gang leader with the place and time of Vasili's alleged double-cross, a.k.a. his meeting with me.

The seconds ticked by faster and faster. I could feel the end getting closer, the air electrifying. Surprisingly, I wasn't afraid. Okay, maybe a little, but I was also exhilarated by the adrenaline high. Any minute now.

As if on cue, an Escalade parked in front of the pier. Two men got out. Even in the dim lighting, I could see the machine pistols hanging at their sides. The one on the right opened the rear door, and Vasili Petrov stepped out.

I typed another text message, put the rental in gear, and drove the few yards to the pier. Parking at an angle with the rear corner facing the waiting Russians, I took a deep breath and opened the car door. It was game time.

"Mr. Cross," Vasili smiled, his accent more pronounced, "what happened to your face?"

"You should know." I glanced at his men but didn't recognize either of them. "Where are Boris and Natasha?"

"Who?" he asked.

"Never mind."

"Do you have my shipment?"

"Did you get my message? Trey Knox is off limits. You don't touch him. His debt is forgiven. Understand?"

"That matter doesn't concern you."

"Consider me concerned. How much does he owe you?"

"You mean before all the additional trouble he caused?"

"Yeah, before that."

"Seventy-five."

I whistled. "That's a lot of money. He didn't borrow that much."

"He also didn't pay. I have a business to run. Surely, a man of your nature can understand that."

"I can." But I didn't have that kind of cash, and neither did Knox. "I want you to be compensated for the initial loan." I tossed the MVP championship ring to Vasili. "Sports collectors will pay through the nose for that, possibly even double or triple what it's worth. Will that cover it?"

Vasili held the ring up, examining it beneath the dim lights. "Da. I have grown weary of Mr. Knox and his peculiarities." The Russian tucked the ring into his breast pocket. "I'll consider his debt paid in full if you delivered my shipment. If not, neither of you will enjoy what happens next."

"Don't get your panties in a twist. I got your drugs and guns. The rest of that crap wasn't worth the effort." I clicked the hatch release. The lights flashed, and the rear gate popped open. I took a step back and to the side, catching a glimpse of two approaching vehicles. Who knew gangs were this punctual?

Vasili said something in his native tongue, and the man on the left lifted the hatch and pulled one of the suitcases closer. He unzipped it and took out an assault rifle, examined it, put it to the side, inventoried the rest of the contents, and said something to Vasili.

"How'd you get them out of evidence?" Vasili asked.

"You know who I am. You know who my father is. How do you think I got them?"

He chuckled. "You said it couldn't be done. This just proves anything can be done with the proper incentive." He said something to his men, and the one exploring the cargo hold checked the rifle and offered a response. Vasili frowned. "The guns are empty. Where are the bullets?"

"Bottom of the bag."

The enforcer peered inside again, finding what he was looking for and loading the rifle he had placed to the side. The last thing I needed was for him to test fire it. I needed more time. Just a few more minutes for the gang to get here and break up this little shindig. Another thought came to mind. Would I die in the crossfire or by gang bullets since I was an alleged interloper? My brilliant plan didn't seem as brilliant as it had ten minutes ago.

"Whoa there, cowboy," I said to the man holding the rifle. "Don't you want to see what's behind door number two first?"

"Ivan, not yet." Vasili shook his head, and the man lowered the gun. "Open the other bag."

Ivan unzipped the suitcase and held it open for Vasili to see. The white powder bricks practically glowed in the dark. The Russian licked his lips and eyed the police evidence labels, complete with case number and initials. He believed this was their stash.

"All right, comrade. You've impressed me. Knox is forgiven," Vasili said. "I'll let him live out the rest of his worthless life. He'll probably die old and pathetic."

Ivan zipped the second suitcase, hefted it out of the trunk, and rolled it to Vasili's vehicle. He secured it in the back seat and shut the door. Then he returned to the rental and picked up the rifle.

"What are you doing?" I asked as Ivan pointed the rifle at me. My gaze darted to the two vehicles. By now, they had parked a hundred yards away. I thumbed the phone in my pocket, hoping to hit the right button to send the pre-typed text. That was one of the few benefits to flip phones, besides the price and disposable nature. "I thought we were square."

"You interfered in my business. You stole from me. No one steals from me, Mr. Cross. Not even you."

Ivan squeezed the trigger, confused when it failed to fire.

"Did I mention I removed the firing pins?" I couldn't wait any longer. I pulled my gun, an untraceable piece my new Irish pals had included in our deal, and shot Ivan before he could switch to the machine pistol hanging at his side. The Russian stumbled backward. He didn't even hit the ground before Vasili and the second enforcer opened fire.

I darted around the side of the SUV, running in a

crouch. Bullets impacted all around me, leaving deep pockmarks in the metal shell. Skidding to a stop in front of the vehicle, I gripped the brush guard with my free hand and peered around the side. My breath came in ragged gasps.

"Don't make this more difficult," Vasili warned. "Accept your fate and die like a man."

"You first."

I fired blindly in Vasili's direction. The Russians returned fire. Three sets of bullets rang out. Obviously, the man I shot had worn a vest, or this gun was a piece of crap. Another barrage blasted in my direction, shattering the side mirror and taking out the turn signal. That was close. Too close. I moved toward the middle of the SUV. Gunfire broke the rear window and burst through the front windshield, showering me in glass fragments.

Based on the footsteps, the two enforcers were coming around the side. I couldn't stay here. Help wasn't arriving. The gang leader, who I thought might save me, appeared to be taking his sweet time enjoying the crisp, night air.

"Stay back." I slid to one side, firing blindly around the front tire before lunging to the other side and firing a few more shots. I heard a grunt, which I hoped meant I'd hit someone.

I'd lost track of Vasili. He probably went back to the car to stay warm. It was cold out, not that I'd noticed much of anything with the glass and bullets flying in my direction. All right, it was time to move on to plan C.

Across the parking lot were freight containers and some warehouses. A good fifty yards stood between me and the nearest structure. I couldn't escape that way without getting a few more holes in my back. Considering my options were to stay here and die or make a run for it, I had to at least try to survive. Run in a zigzag. Don't look back. Don't stop moving no matter what. If I did that, I might survive.

Getting into position, I placed one hand on the ground in a runner's lunge. *Three. Two.* Gunfire erupted behind me, and Vasili let out a surprised scream. I didn't understand Russian, but from the gangster's frantic tone, I knew the ambush worked. Vasili's buyers, the gang, hadn't been pleased by the delay. And they were even less pleased to learn Vasili had lied to them and decided to sell to a competitor for a higher price. The late night exchange and the bag of unidentified powder safely tucked in the back of the Escalade proved it. Vasili had double-crossed them. Plan B had worked.

But before I could celebrate this small win, I realized this left me with one big problem. When the gang finished dealing with the Russians, they'd want to knock off the competition. I had to get out of here.

More shots pinged against the rental, popping the rear tires with a sudden whoosh. Despite the crossfire, Vasili remained determined to kill me. Ivan had retreated, but the other enforcer continued to fire potshots along the driver's side. I'd never make it across the parking lot, and with two busted tires and bullets flying, I couldn't drive away. That left only one clear path down the pier. It was a long, narrow, straight line with no cover. By the time I made it far enough to board a boat, I'd be dead.

Fuck it. I edged along the front of the vehicle until I was positioned behind the passenger's side tire. Inhaling a deep breath, I let it out, sucked in another one, and burst into a run, firing at Vasili and the gang as I ran. I took two steps onto the rickety wooden pier and dove into the water.

The freezing cold assaulted my senses and instantly cramped my muscles, but I forced my limbs to obey and swam underwater beneath the dark pier until I reached the end. Surfacing, I gripped the wood piling and waited.

My teeth chattered, and I wondered if I'd freeze to death. My hands and feet were numb, and my legs were already tingling. I wouldn't last in the frigid water much longer. Gunfire continued. A few shots nicked the wood above me, but the majority weren't concentrated at the pier. A pained scream rang out, followed by another gurgling cry. That was the sound of men dying.

Soon, the gunfire abated. I listened, straining to hear over the lapping waves and the blood rushing in my ears. Was it over? I didn't dare move. I waited, knowing I couldn't wait too long. The firefight would attract attention. I had to disappear, possibly forever. *No, don't think like that.* Again, I found myself annoyed by the optimistic voice in my head, and for the thousandth time today, I questioned my own sanity.

Finally, I dragged myself onto the pier. The two foreign vehicles had vanished, leaving no trace of the gang's presence, except for the Russians dead in the street. The back door of Vasili's Escalade remained open.

As I approached, I recognized it as the white Escalade I'd seen parked outside Olympus. I hadn't imagined it. Vasili had been keeping tabs on me. That's how he knew which club I started going to and how to tell one of his working girls to approach me. He'd been observing, but for how long? Had he been watching me since I took Trey Knox's case? He must have known what I was up to. But why? How?

I didn't have time to think about it now. The cops were on the way. The suitcase with the fake drugs was gone, but the bag of assault rifles remained. At least those would be off the street, even if I'd paid a hefty price to get them here, a price that might fund the IRA or whatever Irish resistance group currently existed. But I'd have to find a way to make peace with that. It had been the lesser of two evils, or so I hoped.

I'd been extremely careful. None of this connected to me. The gun, the phone, the car, they'd all been untraceable and disposable. For the first time in twenty-four hours, I didn't have to look over my shoulder. Only one thing could connect me to this scene, and I sure as hell wasn't going to leave without it.

"I win, asshole." I looked down at Vasili. The large man had been struck at least six times. I reached into his breast pocket and removed the ring. That was the only damning piece of evidence. And now it was gone.

Sirens grew louder in the distance. The police could clean up the mess. Secure in knowing I was finally safe, I wrapped my arms around my shivering body and set out for the nearest bus stop. From there, I called a cab and went home.

Once I was dry and warm, I phoned Justin. "I just

wanted to make sure you didn't order new letterheads yet."

"Not yet. Is everything okay?"

"I hope so. Tell Knox he can go home. I'll stop by and see him tomorrow, but Vasili won't bother him again."

"Will do."

I yawned, wanting nothing more than to climb under the covers. "Thanks, Justin. Get some sleep. You've earned it."

"A raise would be nice too."

"You already own shares in the company. What more could you possibly want?"

"I'll make a list."

"Fine. Give it to my assistant, and tell him to take care of it."

He laughed. "I'll see you tomorrow, boss."

"Actually, aside from paying Knox a visit, I'm taking the day off."

THIRTY-FOUR

I slept in the next morning, something I hadn't done since recovering from surgery. Despite getting plenty of rest, I felt like I'd been hit by a truck. Both of my eyes were black. My nose was swollen to the point where I had to breathe out of my mouth, and my jaw hurt as I chewed my cereal. The rest of me didn't feel much better either. My back had started spasming in the middle of the night and had yet to stop, and my limbs were sore and achy.

Somehow, I thought I'd feel better today, relieved or just lighter. But I didn't. I felt like shit and looked just as bad. The local papers had articles about last night's shooting at the docks. The police were still investigating. A reward was offered to anyone with knowledge of what happened, but I wasn't worried about eyewitnesses. No one else had been there except the gang, and they wouldn't turn themselves in.

The article mentioned a prominent figure in the Russian mafia had been murdered. The police feared it might be the start of war between the Russians and whoever killed Vasili. Organized crime and gangs would have a field day with this one. I didn't know if the Russians would retaliate, but I didn't think Vasili had shared his blunder concerning

Knox and my involvement with his comrades. If he did, someone would probably pay me a visit shortly. I'd just have to wait and see.

Picking up the phone, I called Sgt. Rostokowski. She didn't answer, which meant she was busy doling out assignments and keeping the officers on task with the investigation, so I left her a message saying I was just calling to check-in and that I was fine. She wouldn't connect me to last night's mess. She'd never think I was stupid enough to get involved in something like that, and even if she did, she'd never share her suspicions with anyone.

The only thing left for me to do was get rid of the ring. I'd give it back to Knox and call it a day. After slipping into casual clothes, I headed over to Knox's house. He'd told the security guards at the gate that I'd be stopping by, so they waved me through.

I didn't see Knox's car parked out front. Considering the time, he might have gone to work. After yesterday, he had to come up with some excuse to give his boss. Food poisoning or a stomach virus were always good reasons to avoid the office, but Knox might not have thought of that. Knowing him, he probably went to work first thing this morning to make up for lost time.

When I knocked on the front door, it squeaked open. That wasn't good. Unholstering my gun, I edged toward the open door. "Mr. Knox?" I called. "Trey? Are you here?"

I listened, but I didn't hear any movement. The security guards at the gate hadn't noticed anything amiss. Was it possible Knox had been in such a rush to get to the office he forgot to lock his door?

"Knox?" I called again, stepping inside. His security system was deactivated. The sensors and cameras remained offline. Had he deactivated them? From a glance, the system didn't appear tampered with, but that didn't mean anything. "Hello?"

The foyer didn't show any signs of a struggle. Neither did the living room or kitchen. I didn't see Knox's phone, keys, or attaché case anywhere. If he went out, he would have taken them with him. Maybe he really had left the door unlocked, but my gut said otherwise.

"Is anyone here?" I continued through the house, checking each room as I went. Nothing appeared disturbed, no broken glass or missing items. Wouldn't the guards at the gate have told me Knox wasn't home when I arrived? Did they even pay attention? The neighborhood consisted of a dozen homes, spread in a line, on a dead end street. It was supposed to be the ideal gated community. So where was Knox?

Scuff marks on the floor halted my search. I crouched down, keeping one eye on my surroundings. Black, rubbery streaks marred the hardwood. The two narrow skids were roughly eight inches apart. It looked like someone had been dragged. Beside the scuff marks were a few elliptical drops of what had to be blood.

Carefully, I made my way into the bedroom. The bed was unmade, but the covers remained tucked in on two sides. No blood or other substances covered the exposed sheets, so I didn't think Knox had been attacked while asleep. I didn't spend too long analyzing the bedding, but I didn't notice any long hairs or other indications he'd had company last night.

I checked the closet. No one was hiding inside, and nothing appeared missing. Taking a breath, I nudged open the bathroom door. The first thing I saw was my reflection in Knox's new mirror. Luckily, I didn't shoot the rough-looking guy staring back at me.

The bathroom literally sparkled in the morning sun. The entire floor was covered in glass. I didn't know where it came from until I peered into the shower. The glass door had been decimated so entirely not a single shard hung from the metal frame. A few drops of blood dotted the tiles.

Now what do I do? I crouched down to get a better look at the shower drain. Using the tip of my pocket knife, I pried up the flimsy metal catcher. A dark red ring lined the edge of the drain. More blood. Possibly a lot more blood. I had no idea how much might have washed away.

First things first, I sucked in some air and called Knox. After five rings, the call went to voicemail. I tried his office, but his assistant said he hadn't shown up for work in the last two days.

"Did he call in sick?" I asked.

"No, we haven't heard from him since yesterday morning. He said something came up and he'd be a little late, but he never showed."

"Has anyone else called asking for him today?"

"No," she considered the question for a moment, "why would you ask that?"

"Just wondering." I hung up before she could ask any more questions.

Before replacing the hair catcher, I grabbed one of the cotton swabs from the container on the vanity and collected a sample of blood from inside the drain and swiped Knox's toothbrush from the holder. I wasn't sure why I did that. I hadn't even figured out if Knox had been attacked or taken, but someone had bled in the bathroom. I had to find out who.

I went into the kitchen and searched the cabinets until I found some sandwich bags. I put the cotton swab in one and the toothbrush in the other. That would have to suffice for DNA analysis. It should be that simple. TV made it seem that simple. I didn't know, and I didn't want to waste time calling Amir to ask what he'd need. He'd just have to make do with what I brought him.

Before leaving the house, I went into Knox's study and checked the security system. Assuming the blood drops weren't caused by tripping in the tub and crashing through the shower door, which at this moment seemed just as plausible as anything else, I wanted to see what the security system showed. When I tried to check the logs, I realized the hard drives were gone.

Someone did this. Knox could be alive or dead. He could be anywhere, and even though I told myself that as soon as I dropped the ring off I could wash my hands of this mess, I had to find out what happened to him because the same fate could be waiting for me.

Now what do I do? My mind raced. After last night, my instincts were to erase my presence and disappear, but that was stupid. Or was it? The guy at the gate buzzed me in. He knew I was supposed to see Knox. When Knox's employer or someone else called the police to report him missing, my name would come up in the course of the investigation.

If the Russians had retaliated, they'd come for me next. Svetlana's body might have already surfaced. A tip could have been called in hours ago. The police could be getting a warrant for my arrest. If I called to report whatever this was, they'd find me without any muss or fuss.

I looked around the house. I'd gone through all the rooms, but I hadn't touched anything with my bare hands. The cold weather had forced me to wear my gloves, and I hadn't taken them off. That was a plus. I took the ring out of my pocket, carefully wiped it clean, and placed it in a drawer in Knox's study. The last thing I needed were the cops to find it at my place or the office.

"Think, Cross. Think." I had used my cell phone to call Knox. At least I'd been smart enough to ditch the burner on my way home last night, not that it mattered. Well, it might. I didn't know. Jeez, I was paranoid. Guilty was more accurate.

Unsure how to proceed, I called Mr. Almeada. Who better than a lawyer to advise me in this situation? The woman who answered said he was in a client meeting.

"This is an emergency. I just need to speak to him for two minutes."

"He'll call you back." She hung up before I could resort to begging.

I couldn't just wait around. I had to do something. I dialed the office. "Justin, have you heard from Mr. Knox today?"

"No. What's wrong?"

I cleared my throat. "Has anyone been by the office asking for me?"

"Just Winnie from King Realty. She wanted to let you know the offer you made was officially accepted and everything's been signed."

"No one else?"

"No."

"All right, I need you to see if you can locate Knox. Try pinging his phone. If that doesn't work, pull his vehicle records, get his VIN, and check to see if he has an anti-theft system installed, roadside assistance, or a GPS system. I don't care what. I have to know where he is."

While I waited for Justin to work some magic, I left Knox's house and went to speak to the guys at the gate. The rent-a-cop security guards were sitting inside the little shack, sipping coffee and eating bagels. They were watching a game show and bickering over if the showcase was worth more or less than the last contestant's bid.

"Mr. Knox isn't home," I said, interrupting them.

The one in navy blue turned in the booth to look at Knox's house. "Hey, you're right. His car's not there."

No shit. "What time did he leave?"

The one in navy exchanged a look with the one in light blue. "Did you see him leave, Pete?"

Pete rolled in front of the control panel. "His fob activated the gate at 8:02, but I don't remember seeing him."

"Do you mind if I ask what happened? He knew I was coming. I just wondered if he had any unexpected guests or an emergency that caused him to rush out early this morning." Resting my forearms on the edge of the window to their booth, I tried to appear as nonthreatening and concerned as possible.

"Let me see." The one in navy checked the logs. "Only a few delivery drivers came into the neighborhood this morning. Everyone else lives here, except you."

"And Mr. Knox didn't leave any messages for me or anything?"

"Did you try calling him? He might have forgotten," Pete said.

"He's not answering."

"He's probably at work. You should check there."

Before I could ask any more questions, my phone rang. I looked down at the display. *Almeada.* "Sorry to have bothered you." I held up my phone. "I'll try back later." As soon as I was safely inside my car and halfway through the gate, I answered the call.

"Lucien, what's wrong? Give me the short version."

"My client's missing. His front door's open, and I found a broken shower door and some drops of blood in his bathroom. What should I do?"

"I'm going to need a little more than that."

"Knox is gone. I don't know where. The Russians tried to kill him yesterday. You know which Russians. He was fine, and today, he's gone."

"Aren't those the ones I read about in the paper?"

"Yes."

"The same one who—"

"Yeah."

"Do you think they've taken him?"

"I don't know what's going on. He was supposed to be safe. This was supposed to be over."

"Okay, calm down."

"How can I calm down? A kill squad could be on their way to find me, or the police could be waiting at my house or office to arrest me for something I didn't do." How ironic, since I didn't think they'd ever find enough proof to arrest me for what I actually did.

Almeada cursed quietly. "I'm in the middle of something here, but I'll get someone to make a few calls and find out if any warrants have been issued or are in the works. In the meantime, get your ass to my office. We'll discuss the rest in person and figure out your next move."

"So I just leave the crime scene? What if the Russians try to pin this on me too? Shouldn't I call it in?"

"There's no body. No obvious signs of an attack or an abduction. Despite what you think you know, can you say for certain a crime was even committed?"

"No." Without a body, there was no crime. My thoughts went to Svetlana who'd been killed only thirty-six hours ago and then shot with my gun. What about her body? Where was that? With Vasili gone, would it surface? Why hadn't I thought about this yesterday before the shit hit the fan? "Oh god."

"Get over here. We'll figure this out," he promised.

If nothing else, the law office might serve as a temporary sanctuary or a purgatory until I was sent to hell. At least they had good coffee and plenty of booze. "I'm on my way."

THIRTY-FIVE

"You stole his toothbrush?" Almeada stared wide-eyed at me.

"I want to make sure the blood is Knox's. It made sense when I did it." Frankly, it still made sense.

"That's tampering with evidence."

"So don't tell anyone." I took a breath, forcing myself to focus. "Explain to me how a toothbrush is evidence. At worst, I tampered with a crime scene, not evidence. And I thought we agreed Knox's house is not the scene of a crime unless additional facts to the contrary surface." Should the cops raid my office and discover the item, I'd say Knox was obsessed with dental hygiene and must have forgotten it after visiting our bathroom.

"I'm glad you were paying attention." The attorney circled the room, absently straightening the framed degrees hanging on the wall. "Any idea where Knox is?"

"I'm looking into it. His phone's in airplane mode, so we can't get a location. As far as the whereabouts of his car, it was left in the parking garage at his office."

Almeada turned around to face me. "So he went to work?"

"It appears that way. Except when I spoke to his

assistant, she said no one has heard from him since yesterday morning. And with the broken shower door and the blood, I'm not sure he's even alive."

"So you were the last person to see him?"

"No, Justin was." I gently picked at the edge of the tape covering my nose. It had started to curl.

"You already caught me up on the fight in the street. Is there anything else I need to know?"

"Vasili Petrov's dead. I thought that would solve everything. But now Knox is missing, and I have no idea what became of the dead hooker's body."

"The DA's office hasn't heard anything on the subject of the Russians. No warrant requests have come in. The police are still piecing everything together."

"Last night's shooting didn't have anything to do with me," I lied, figuring I should start practicing now.

"Yeah, well, if the hooker's body surfaced, the DA's office would have heard about it. They didn't."

"You asked?"

"Give me some credit. I know how to get answers without asking questions. That's my job."

"So what do I do now?"

"Sit tight. You haven't done anything wrong. You're jumping to conclusions, which arguably could be a hazard of working private security and growing up in a law enforcement family." But we both knew that wasn't the cause of my anxiety. "If the police suspect Knox's sudden disappearance is the result of foul play, they'll have questions. Don't speak to anyone without me there. I'll tell you when to avoid answering, but there's no reason not to be truthful. You went to see your client about final payment. He was expecting you. You found it odd the front door was open, but thought he might have left it that way for you. When you couldn't find him, you searched the house, found the broken shower door, figured he slipped and had to go to the emergency room. You checked with the guards posted at the gate who had waved you into the neighborhood, and they told you they remembered him leaving. You called the office, but they hadn't seen him. That was it."

"Great." At least I had my story straight. Now I just had to find out what actually happened to Trey Knox.

"As far as your other worries, I don't know what to tell you. Now that Vasili's dead, the others in his organizations might not have any problem implicating him, but the police would be less likely to pursue charges against you if they suspect a dead gangster is responsible for his own sex worker's death."

"Again with the optimism?"

"Don't you pay me for positive outcomes?"

"That I do." Groaning, I got out of the chair and rubbed my back. Had I not been facing a potential imminent arrest, I would have popped a few more pills, but being high wouldn't help matters, prescription or not.

"One final thing," Almeada said before I left his office, "if you can avoid the cops until your face heals, I'd suggest you do that. They might unfairly judge your appearance and arrest you for looking like a criminal."

With that cheery thought, I left the law firm and headed for Cross Security. Amir was meeting me there to collect the samples. He still had privileges at the lab where he previously worked, so he could perform a DNA comparison.

Logic dictated the blood belonged to Knox, but I held out hope it wouldn't match, that it'd belong to his abductor, who would turn out to be some other loan shark that had nothing to do with the Russians and nothing to do with me. Call it wishful thinking, not that it was particularly upbeat. But it was the best I could manage at the moment.

When I arrived at the office, Gloria was reading a magazine while Justin quietly typed away. She looked up as the door opened, a surprised but pleasant expression on her face.

"Good afternoon, Mr. Cross." She put the magazine down. "I thought you were taking the day off."

"Relax." I glanced around, half-expecting SWAT teams to be hiding in my office and the break room. "Is anything going on? Any meetings I should know about?"

She gave me an odd look. "No, sir. You asked me to

cancel everything yesterday, remember?" From the way she studied my expression, I wondered if she thought I was suffering from memory loss from the hits I'd taken.

"No, I remember, but it's never a dull moment around here." I pointed at her magazine. "Don't stop on my account. I don't mind. Actually, since we're set to move into a new location pretty soon, I'll probably need you to work overtime for a few weeks and the weekends. I know what an inconvenience that can be, so why don't you take the rest of this week and next week off while we prepare for the move? It'll be paid leave, of course. Just some vacation time to make up for all the extra work I'm about to throw your way."

"Are you sure?"

"Absolutely."

"What about the calendar and meetings?"

"I'll deal with juggling the calendar, but our schedule's pretty light. Just some follow-ups."

She scrunched her brows together. "It's more than that."

"It'll be fine. Please, Gloria, if anyone deserves a break, it's you."

Justin made a coughing noise, and I turned to look at him. "Don't worry, you'll get some time off too," I promised.

Gloria still didn't look convinced and glanced from me to Justin.

"Seriously, if Lucien's springing for extra paid vacation time, don't question it. Just go," Justin said. "You don't want him to change his mind."

"Okay," she said uncertainly. "At least let me order lunch for you guys before I go."

"Thanks." I smiled at her before heading toward the filing cabinets. I didn't need anything inside, but I wanted her to think that I would handle the schedule so she would leave. After lunch was ordered, she grabbed her things, told me to call if anything changed, and headed out the door. The security detail I had tailing her would remain until I was convinced there was no threat. Sending her home was supposed to mitigate that, but sending her home with armed guards was even better.

"You're not serious about handling the calendar, are you?" Justin asked. "Since the day we met, I've never seen you schedule your own meetings."

"The day we met was when you were hired as my assistant. That's when you took over."

He sighed dramatically. "Should I be worried?"

"We should all be worried. Knox is gone." I pulled the zippered bags out of my pocket. "Amir is on his way to collect these."

"Is that blood?"

"Most likely."

"Is Trey Knox dead?"

"I don't know."

"But you think he is."

"We don't know. His car is parked at work, and his phone is in airplane mode."

"I'll run his financials and see if there's been any activity recently."

He looked into it while I paced back and forth and tried to figure out what to do. Almeada made it clear that I should do nothing, but I had to know what happened. I had to be prepared. Getting blindsided by the police or some psycho hell-bent on revenge wouldn't end in my favor. The more I knew, the better and safer I'd be.

"Nothing," Justin said.

"I want to search his car, but I can't go near it."

"Do you want me to go?"

"No. The garage has cameras. This can't connect to me. For all I know, I could be getting framed for this too. You don't need to implicate yourself."

"So am I getting the next week and a half off too?"

"Not exactly." I cleared my throat. "I'm sorry. You can walk if you want. I'll understand, but I could use the help. I don't have anyone else I can ask."

"How can I walk when you say shit like that?"

"Don't be smart. It is up to you."

He rolled his eyes. "You know I got your back. Where do we begin?"

Before I could answer, Amir came through the door. He looked at the nearly empty office, one eyebrow lifting in

question. "You said you needed me to analyze something."
He put his bag down on Gloria's desk and took out some
papers. "I hope it's less complicated than your previous
request."

"I need to know if the blood belongs to the owner of this
toothbrush." I held out the sandwich bags.

Amir didn't even reach for them, his eyebrow arching
even higher. "Is this a test?"

"No, I'm serious."

"You just want to know if they match?"

"Yes."

Amir sighed and took the bags from my hand. "Okay, I
can do that. It shouldn't take more than a few hours,
possibly a day, to run the comparison. It'll depend on how
degraded the samples are." He examined the bristles of the
toothbrush through the plastic before tucking them inside
his bag. "Here." He held out a folder.

"What's this?" I asked.

"The last assignment you gave me. There's not a lot
here. I checked the data and came up with a list of cell
phone users in the area at the dates and times in question.
Just because those phones pinged those towers, it doesn't
mean they were in the van or even in the vicinity of the
pawn shop or self-storage facility. I just wanted you to
know I did what you asked."

I took the folder and flipped through the dozens of
pages. "There are a lot of names here."

"I told you it'd be pointless to do this."

I skimmed past the list to the rest of the information
Amir had dug up regarding the security system and
original break-in at Knox's house. "Maybe not."

"What is it?" Justin asked, intrigued by our
conversation. "Who's on the list?"

I stared at the cell data from Knox's neighborhood at the
time of the break-in. "You're sure Trey Knox's cell phone
was in the vicinity when his security system was
dismantled and his house was broken into?"

"The nearest towers pinged his phone. He even sent a
text message within ten minutes of the time and date you
gave me." Amir pointed to the data on the page. "He was

somewhere nearby."

"The bastard said he was at the office. He lied. Do you think he was at home when they broke in?" I asked.

"Like I said before, I can't narrow it down that precisely," Amir said. "He might have been on his way home or he could have been anywhere within the vicinity of these two cell towers."

"Why would he lie about where he was at the time of the break-in?" Justin asked.

"He didn't want the police to know what happened. After all, he didn't even want us to know who was responsible or why they targeted him. He's covering something up. I just don't know what."

"But if he was there when someone broke into his place, wouldn't they have hurt him?" Amir asked.

"Not necessarily." I wasn't sure why they wouldn't. Then again, Vasili didn't try to hurt me the first time we met, not physically. Perhaps, he'd made Knox a similar offer. "Get me the results of the DNA test as quickly as possible, and keep this between us."

"Whatever you want, Mr. Cross." Amir picked up the bag. "I'll call you as soon as I have the results."

THIRTY-SIX

The blood from the drain matched the DNA sample from the toothbrush. Since that was the only toothbrush in the bathroom and Trey Knox had told me he didn't like to entertain overnight guests, I had to believe it belonged to him. Amir had told me the sample was male, AB negative.

"Don't even think about it," Justin warned. "Hacking medical records is a million different kinds of wrong. There are other ways to find out if Knox is AB negative."

"I don't need to hack them. I know it's his blood," I said resolutely, "just like that's his toothbrush. What I don't know is what happened to him." Thoughts of the scuff marks on the hardwood floor came to mind. "Someone dragged him." Considering the lack of significant amounts of blood on the floor, Knox couldn't have been too severely injured, unless he'd been wrapped in some kind of plastic sheeting. Glass shower doors didn't have shower curtains. If it had been a regular shower with an empty shower rod, I would have thought Knox's abductor wrapped his body in the curtain and dragged him out, but that wouldn't explain the scuff marks.

"Your forehead's doing that prune thing."

I tore my eyes away from the DNA results. "I'll ask about Botox when I visit the plastic surgeon. Will that make you happy?" Pulling myself out of the chair, I stretched one leg, then the other. The frigid water and stress had done a number on my back. I might need a consultation or a few more sessions in physical therapy to get everything back in proper working order, assuming whoever took Knox didn't come for me next.

"You're only in your late twenties. You should wait until you hit thirty before getting work done. Or is it already too late for that? When's your birthday? Somehow, the date has slipped my mind."

I glanced up at him, confused why he was bothering me with this nonsense. And that's when I realized he was freaked out, just like I was. "Look, it's cool. I got this. Go home. Wash your hands of this mess. I'll take care of it."

"No. I'm staying." He watched as I shifted my hips from side to side, wincing as I moved. "I'll make an appointment with your doctor." He reached for the phone. "Were you shot again?"

"Not that I know of."

He snickered uncomfortably. "I'd think you'd know."

"Hopefully."

While he made the call, I examined the intel I'd gathered on Knox. Until the police started their own investigation, I shouldn't poke around. Mr. Almeada had advised against it.

But Knox had been taken. The lack of a substantial amount of blood probably meant he was alive. He must have been in the shower when he was attacked. That would explain the broken shower door and the blood I'd found in the drain and the few droplets on the bathroom floor. But since there hadn't been spatter, Knox's injuries must have been minor.

Given the parallel and nearly identical scuff marks, I had to assume Knox had been allowed to dress after the incident in the shower. He must have put on his shoes before the abductor dragged him out of the bedroom. But why drag a conscious man? Knox could have put up a fight and had to be subdued. But the drag marks stopped at the bedroom door. Did he stop fighting and walk out on his own volition at that point? Or did the abductor have a friend who helped carry Knox's body out of the house?

Someone grabbed the hard drives on the way out, which made the security system useless. The guards at the gate might know something, but they didn't remember seeing Knox drive away. Could they be in on it?

I was in the middle of running a background check on the guards I'd spoken to today, which was the second time I'd investigated them, when a couple of police detectives came knocking. Automatically, I hit the power button on the computer.

"Lucien Cross?" the older one asked. From the badge he held out, I knew he'd been on the force for a while.

"Sergeant," I said.

"Detective," he corrected, even though he had earned the rank of sergeant, "Moretti. This is Detective Renner." He indicated the younger, eager man standing beside him.

"Newbie?" I asked.

Moretti snorted, as if it were an inside joke just between us. "Do you have a few moments to spare, Mr. Cross?"

"Not particularly."

Moretti didn't pay attention to a word I said. "We'll make this brief. I just have a few questions concerning your whereabouts this morning."

"What about them?" I bit my tongue before I said something flippant about jaywalking or traffic violations.

"You stopped by Trey Knox's house around eleven."

"That's not a question."

"What happened to your face?" Renner asked.

I turned to him. "Kickboxing class."

He touched his own nose absently. "First lesson?"

"No."

"You might need a refresher on the basics, like not getting hit in the face," Renner said.

I kept my expression neutral, though I had some suggestions I would have loved to share with him.

Moretti sidestepped, so he could stand in front of Renner. It was practically the equivalent of locking a misbehaving puppy in another room. "When's the last time you saw Mr. Knox?"

"Yesterday. He came to the office to speak to me," I said.

"Concerning."

"A case. He hired me to find some stolen property."

"Did you?" Moretti asked.

"Find it?" I didn't want to answer. Gallo suspected I'd called in the tip, as did Sgt. Rostokowski. I just didn't know if these two detectives had the same inkling. "What division did you say you work for? Robbery should be all over it, or is it called burglary? I never keep those two straight. Someone has my information."

"Mr. Knox's property was recovered by the police due to an anonymous tip." Moretti stared at me with unyielding eyes. "What else did Knox want to discuss?"

"Our conversation's privileged."

"No privilege exists between security personnel and their clients," Moretti said.

"We could have an NDA."

Moretti chuckled. "I was warned you'd be a pain in the ass. Look, let's just cut to the chase. Trey Knox never showed up to work yesterday. He didn't return home until after midnight last night. The guards at the gate remember seeing him leave his house this morning, but he didn't go to work. His boss called and asked us to check on him."

"It sounds like he's playing hooky."

"Probably." Moretti stared at me. "Except, aside from automated gate logs and the guards glimpsing his car entering and leaving, no one's seen him except you."

"I'm sure that's not true."

"Did you see him?" Moretti turned to Justin who'd done his best to blend into the background.

"Yesterday, yeah. He was here," Justin said.

"When did he leave?" Moretti asked.

Justin shrugged. "I didn't notice the time."

"Ballpark estimate," Moretti said.

"It was after dark," I said. "I left the office around seven."

Renner jotted down a note while Moretti continued to stare at Justin.

"Is that right?" he asked.

"Sounds right," Justin said.

"I thought you were going to make this brief, Detective.

We might not look it, but we're very busy," I said.

Moretti smiled, as if we were old chums. "You're right. Sorry about that. I get distracted easily. ADHD or OCD or some other acronym for catching on to little things that don't make a lot of sense."

"I'm starting to feel harassed," I said. "Justin, are you feeling harassed?"

"Should I call Mr. Almeada, your attorney?" Justin asked.

"That won't be necessary," Moretti said. "No one's being harassed."

"How about harangued?" I asked.

"That's not a legal issue the last time I checked," Moretti said. "I just have a few quick questions about this morning, and then we'll get out of your hair. Did you go inside Knox's house this morning?"

"Yes," I said.

"Did you notice anything amiss?"

"Yeah, I noticed he wasn't there. I wouldn't have gone inside if I'd known, but the door was open. I thought he left it that way for me. When I couldn't find him, I looked around. The shower door was broken, so I left and spoke to the guards at the gate. I figured Trey had tripped and fell. They told me he didn't call for an ambulance, and that he'd driven away, so it couldn't have been that serious. I don't know any more than you do."

Moretti continued the stare for another five seconds before turning and glancing at Renner. He jerked his chin toward the door. "Let's go, kid." Renner looked confused, but he obediently went to the door. I might be new to private security, but this homicide detective was still wet behind the ears. He couldn't be any newer. At least that would work in my favor should anything damning turn up. Moretti turned back to me, a business card materializing in his hand. "Thanks for your time, Mr. Cross. If you hear from Mr. Knox, give me a call."

"Sure thing." I knew better than to ask, but I did anyway. "Is there any reason to think there's something wrong? That something might have happened to him?"

"It's probably nothing. Then again, your dad's the

commissioner. So you know the detective bureau doesn't normally get involved if it's nothing. Guess we'll just have to wait and see. You take care of yourself, and get a steak on those eyes."

THIRTY-SEVEN

After the police paid me a visit, I kept my own investigation to a minimum when it came to Knox's disappearance. That barred me from a lot of avenues I would have liked to explore. I couldn't risk asking questions or hacking surveillance cameras, not when a potential murder charge was hanging over my head. Svetlana's body could surface at any time, possibly with Knox.

Almeada warned me to stay as far from murder investigations as I could get, but I couldn't let forces beyond my control decide my fate. So I went back to my original leads and dug into the self-storage unit's records. Eric Beaufort, the phony identity that had rented the unit Vasili used to hold his contraband, traced back to the Russian mafia. In fact, so did Mr. Lenmere. He'd taken a hefty payout from someone closely associated with Vasili in exchange for putting his name on the paperwork while Vasili used Lenmere LLC and its holdings to move merchandise.

The moving vans from the self-storage facility routinely made trips to the docks to unload freight containers. Those shipments would then be kept inside storage units until they were disbursed directly to buyers or sold in Pauley's

Pawn or another pawn shop. Of course, I discovered all of this too late.

Club Nova wasn't part of Lenmere LLC. I dug and dug but couldn't directly link it to Vasili or the Russian mafia. Vasili had to control it, or he had people working there. A part of me regretted my hasty decision to delete the video footage. If I'd been thinking more clearly instead of reacting, I could have recovered some of the deleted sections and figured out what Vasili had done with Svetlana's body or had irrefutable proof he was the murderer. Instead, I spent hour upon hour hoping to get myself out of the hole I'd dug, which had only gotten deeper and darker since Knox's disappearance.

"I need to go back to Knox's house," I muttered. It'd been three days since the cops had stopped by. As far as I knew, Knox hadn't turned up. His credit cards had gone dormant. His phone battery had died. He'd simply vanished. Everything about his disappearance indicated he was dead, and I wanted to know who killed him.

Maybe the police had gotten distracted with other things. They had a gang war to worry about. They didn't have time to waste on Trey Knox. Without a body, there was no crime.

I headed over to his place, but I didn't want there to be any record of my return visit. Given the guard station and nature of the gated community, getting in wouldn't be easy. It took several hours of careful consideration and some climbing gear, but I found a way inside.

Creeping up to Knox's house, I wondered if the police were watching. If they were, they'd probably arrest me on sight. But I didn't see any cars around. Just as I was about to try my luck with one of the first floor windows, a police cruiser entered the gate.

Danger, danger, the voice in my head said, *abort mission*. Without waiting to see why the police had shown up, I dashed back to the breach point, went over the wall, and pulled the rope up and over behind me. I landed funny, my back twisting. It served me right for being so stupid. With Knox's house off limits, there was only one other place to check—his office.

I dropped my car off and took a cab to his office building. When I entered the lobby, I spotted the security cameras. It would be impossible to conceal my visit, but it didn't matter. Knox had been my client. The cops could check to see why I stopped by. My questions would be about Knox's last known whereabouts and nothing else. It wouldn't be suspicious. If anything, it'd be expected.

"Mr. Cross?" Margaret, Knox's assistant, looked up from the computer as I entered.

I smiled at her. "You remembered."

She stared at my face for a few moments but was too polite to inquire as to what happened. "I'm sorry, but Mr. Knox isn't here."

"When's the last time you spoke to him?"

"He hasn't been to work at all this week." Her eyes darted to the left, and she got distracted with something on the desk beside her.

"Do you know where he is?"

She shook her head. "The police stopped by. Mr. Stone called them when Trey didn't show up for work two days in a row. I told them the same thing I'm telling you."

Resting my palms against the desk, I turned up the charm. "They can be rather annoying and intrusive. They came to see me too. I thought it'd only be fair to check on him myself, seeing as how I'm a private investigator and all."

She glanced at me. "I'm sorry I can't help you."

My gut said she was lying. "It's weird, isn't it? Trey was really into this job. It's all he talked about. And you, you're obviously an amazing assistant. Brilliant, I think is what he said."

She blushed. "That's sweet."

"He said you'd do anything for him. I can't believe he'd just disappear without telling you he was taking off." She bit her lip, glancing at me before dropping her gaze back down. "He contacted you, didn't he?" I asked.

"No. Not since the first day he missed. He called, like I told the cops." She looked up at me. "Like I told you. He said he was running late, but he never showed."

"Did he ask you to do something?" I knew there was

more to the story. "You won't get in trouble. This can be our little secret."

"He asked me to have a courier send over the portfolio he kept in his desk drawer. He said he needed it to prepare for a meeting. I just figured he was running late. I didn't think he wouldn't come back."

"What was in it?"

"I don't know. It was a nice leather bound portfolio. I always teased him it was his diary because he had this little lock hooked around the clasps to keep it closed. He said it was just data sheets and projections."

"So why the lock?"

She shrugged. "I asked him about it once, and he said it was to make sure it stayed closed. He's a freak when it comes to organization."

"Do you mind if I look around his office?" I asked.

"The police already did that. They didn't find anything, and Mr. Stone wouldn't like it if I let some outsider snoop around."

"I don't blame him." I looked around but didn't spot anything obvious. "Did you tell the police about the portfolio?"

"No," she said quickly.

"May I ask why not?"

"I don't want to get in trouble. If that was proprietary info or something valuable to the company, I don't want Mr. Stone finding out I sent it over to Mr. Knox's house the day before he disappeared."

"Did he have to sign for it?" I asked. Knox had been holed up at Cross Security that day.

"No."

"One final question. Do you know if Mr. Knox's car is still parked in the garage?"

She shook her head. "Police impound."

"Did they find anything?"

Again the headshake. "Nothing, but that's good, right? It means wherever he is, he's okay."

"Let's hope so." But I doubted it. "Thanks for your time. If you hear from Mr. Knox or remember anything that might be helpful, I wouldn't mind a call."

"The police said the same thing," she said.

"Yes, but they aren't nearly as much fun as I am, now are they?"

As I left Knox's office, I couldn't help but wonder when he would have had time to make the call. I'd already checked his phone records. He could have contacted Margaret while I had him handcuffed to my steering wheel, assuming he had been able to get the phone out of his pocket or had used the voice dial feature instead. But why would he want that portfolio? And could that be the reason someone broke into his house and abducted him?

None of this made sense. The only thing I could determine was it had been a ledger of what he owed Vasili, and he didn't want anyone at work to find it in the event of his demise. But that didn't make a lot of sense either. Nothing did.

When I made it back to the office, I checked the phone records again and did a bit more digging into Knox's office phone records. With the police snooping through everything, I had to be careful. If they caught me, it wouldn't be good.

But the calls Knox made from his office phone prior to his disappearance were all work related. The portfolio might not have anything to do with anything. I was tired of going around in circles. I just wanted to know if a threat remained, and the only way I could figure that out was by figuring out what happened to Trey Knox.

"Lucien," Justin called from the outer office, "Jim Harrelson's on line one."

I could only think of two reasons why he'd call, and if my father were dead, my mom would have told me. "Thanks." I picked up the receiver and hit the button. "Jim?"

"A couple of detectives were just asking questions about you."

"Moretti and Renner?"

"Yeah."

"What do you know about them?" I asked.

"I wouldn't worry about the snow pea," that was his affectionate term for green detectives, "but Moretti knows his shit. He's got a nose for things, and he doesn't have a good feeling about you. He thinks you're hiding something."

"What'd he want to know?"

"He wanted to know about you and Trey Knox."

"What'd you tell him?"

"What do you think? I don't know Trey Knox, and I sure as shit don't know what dumbass thing you're in the middle of. He spoke to Gallo about the recovery and the anonymous tip the cops got."

"Uh-huh."

"He thinks you called it in."

"Is he going to send me a thank you card?"

"I don't know, but if you did something stupid, now's the time to be smart and fix it. Open your mouth, say whatever it is, and get it taken care of."

"Did he find Knox?" I asked.

Jim didn't say anything for a long moment. "You're actually concerned. You know, son, you would have made a good cop."

"I'm not your son."

He ignored it. "You care. That's good. I'm guessing whatever happened, you tried to do the right thing. Have you been looking for Knox?"

"I would never interfere in a police investigation."

I could almost hear Jim rolling his eyes. "Stop being stupid. If you know something or can help with this, you better. They think he's dead. You don't want to look like a suspect." He hung up before I could respond.

Blowing out a breath, I looked over the information I'd learned. One thing continued to bother me. Knox might have been at home when the original break-in occurred. That meant he watched Vasili's men take all of his belongings. I didn't know if that was true, but if it were, everything Knox said to me was a lie. That fit with the one thing I knew about Knox; he was a liar.

If Knox had been at home, Vasili would have given him an ultimatum. Vasili wanted something from Knox, something more than just cash, and if Knox didn't do it, Vasili would have punished him. The Russian had been big on consequences. I just didn't know what Vasili would have wanted Knox to do for him or who was collecting in Vasili's place.

After going over everything with a fine-tooth comb, I was no closer to figuring any of it out. No matter how I tried to tackle my problem, I ended up at a dead end. I had next to nothing on Svetlana, so I couldn't track her down or figure out if the police were looking for her. No Jane Does matching her description had shown up at the morgue. Almeada had a contact down there who checked. Freddy G had his ear to the ground and had spoken to his Irish pals. They didn't know much of what was going on, just that they didn't trust the Russians and kept their business separate.

I needed the cops to stop digging. Once they gave up the investigation, I could speak to Knox's coworkers, check his office computer, check the office security, go back to his house, dust and print everything, and speak to his neighbors and the security guards. But I couldn't do any of that without overlapping the cops and getting moved up on their radar. As it was, Det. Moretti already had a few suspicions about me. That's why he'd gone to Jim. They must have been tracking my movements. He probably spoke to Gallo who said we'd met up there. Maybe Moretti had gotten the tip about KC's bar from my father. I wouldn't put it past the bastard.

The intercom buzzed, and I gave it an odd look. Justin and I were the only two people in the office, and my door was open. Before I could ask what he wanted, Detective Snow Pea came into view.

I pressed the intercom button before Renner finished flashing his badge. "Send him in."

Justin swiveled in his chair and glanced back at me. I nodded, and Justin turned around. "Mr. Cross can see you now."

The man stepped into the room. He had to be around my age, possibly younger. Depending on when he got out of the academy, he might be one of the youngest cops to make detective. That should mean he was brilliant and talented, but I doubted it.

"Thanks for seeing me." Renner looked down at my client chair.

"Have a seat, Detective Renner."

"Thanks, sir."

"Seriously, man, how old are you?"

"Twenty-seven."

"Then don't call me sir. Save that for my father."

"The commissioner. Yes, sir."

I gave him a hard look.

"Right, sorry, Mr. Cross."

"Lucien." I didn't think it was an act. "Is this your first case since making detective?" He didn't say anything, but from the gentle flush of his cheeks, I knew it was. "That's why they stuck you with that hard ass."

Renner made a face.

"He's right outside, isn't he?" I asked.

"Yes, s—"

Oh well. After Moretti finished playing twenty questions with Justin, he stepped into my office. Divide and conquer was a good tactic, but Justin had vague down to a science. Moretti took a seat in the other empty chair and leaned back.

"Mr. Cross, I had a conversation earlier today with Jim Harrelson. He said you work hard and always do the right thing. He also said you're a lousy tipper."

"You aren't supposed to tip the proprietor."

Moretti pulled out his notepad. "I just wanted to touch base with you. For the last few days, we've looked under every rock. We've got no leads on Mr. Knox's whereabouts. He hasn't returned to his home or shown up at his place of business. He hasn't contacted any friends or family, and he hasn't visited any of his normal hangouts. Nothing indicates he didn't just decide to disappear, but we have to be thorough. Most men with homes and jobs don't vanish without a trace."

"There's always that one."

Moretti didn't appear amused. He was sharp. He'd seen a lot and knew there was more to this situation. It had something to do with the look in his eyes. "I've been informed you're a private investigator."

"That's no secret. It says so on the door."

"Have you looked into Knox's disappearance?"

"A little." I should have said no.

"What have you found?"

"Nothing."

"Tell me why Knox hired you. What did he tell you about the break-in?"

"Not much." I went over a few vague details, avoiding anything and everything that might trace back to Vasili. "Knox didn't know who broke in to his house. I asked if he had any vengeful exes or disgruntled coworkers. He said no, and I found nothing to the contrary."

"Yeah, he seemed like a great guy." Moretti tucked the notepad away. "Any idea where he might go if he decided to drop everything?"

"No idea."

"And you're sure he didn't have any problems? Work? Money? Family issues? Anything like that?"

"Nothing," I said.

"That's what we got," Renner said.

I almost smiled at his candidness. "Perhaps his assistant or one of his neighbors might be more helpful," I suggested.

"They weren't," Moretti said. "Knox kept to himself. No one knew much about him. We even canvassed the bars he went to and spoke to a few of his collector buddies. No one knows anything. We figured maybe he decided to follow the conventions."

"That sounds like him," I said.

Moretti nodded. "Well, anyway, we've done what we can. If you hear from him, let us know. And if you happen to stumble upon something that might tell us what happened, I'd like a call." Again, Moretti handed me one of his business cards. "Did he ever pay you?"

"What?"

"We checked his bank statements but didn't see any payments issued to you."

"No, I guess not. I'll have to work on streamlining our billing process."

"Well, if you're worried about getting paid, perhaps

you'll be able to track him down. Good luck." Moretti got up, followed by Renner. "You know, there's one thing that's been bugging me."

"What's that?" I asked.

"Knox reported everything that had been stolen from his house in great detail, including a championship ring. When we searched his house for clues as to where he might be, we found the ring in his desk drawer."

"Odd," I said.

"Isn't it?" Moretti asked. "We'll leave you alone now."

THIRTY-EIGHT

The police thought I was involved in Knox's disappearance. That's why they went to the bar and came by my office. They wanted to rattle me. Moretti brought up the ring, but I didn't react. It meant nothing. But for the next few days, I couldn't shake the feeling that I was under surveillance.

The cops didn't tail me in blue and whites. They used surveillance vans, as if I wouldn't notice. So I kept my head down and my nose to the grindstone. I had doctors' appointments and meetings to fill the hours.

When I wasn't meeting with clients or having MRIs of my back or my nose reset, I had plenty to do for the impending move. Construction would finish on the new offices by next month. The basic bones and structure had been finished. Now they just had to set up the layout the way I wanted.

I had to order equipment and hire movers and take care of a million little things. Keeping busy helped keep my mind off the blade swinging above my head. As each day passed, the chances of getting caught lessened. No one came for me. Maybe Knox had freaked and fled.

With the constant police tail, my investigation into his disappearance had stalled. I didn't know what was what.

My gut said the police thought I'd eventually lead them to Knox. So far, I hadn't, which is why they continued to linger like a bad cold. Eventually, they'd get tired and give up. I just had to be patient and stay focused on work.

During a break between meetings, I found myself bored and studying a database on scuff marks. The ones I'd seen in Knox's bedroom might not have been from the heels of his shoes. They could have been from wheels on a piece of luggage.

I'd barely looked inside Knox's closet, but most of his things had remained. Still, he could have packed light and vanished. Knowing Knox, he would have taken whatever remained of his precious collection with him before he fled. I tried to think, but I didn't notice anything missing from the shelves. However, after the break-in, most were bare.

Maybe he ran. Vasili's men tried to kill him the day before his disappearance. I wouldn't have blamed him. Running might have been his safest move, especially if he owed other loan sharks or other gangsters money. Deciding to believe that, I slid the Knox files out of pending and into the closed file. Since I couldn't investigate with the police sniffing around me, I'd have to let it go.

I'd just closed the drawer and retaken my seat when I received a message from one of my contacts who I'd reached out to about the sports memorabilia. Apparently, someone else had been asking around about acquiring a championship ring. My contact didn't have a name, but he gave me the person's handle.

It took a couple of days, but I traced the handle to an IP address. The user was located on a small tropical island nation without extradition. After that, I did more research and made some calls.

"I don't think Trey Knox is dead," I said to Justin. "I think he's hiding in a non-extradition country."

"Okay."

The implication hung heavily in the air. Knox fled for a reason, and if he went to a non-extradition country, it wasn't for his own safety. It was because he was afraid of getting arrested. Curiosity killed the cat. It almost killed me, but I couldn't let this go. I'd spent the last week in physical therapy because my muscles and nerves were wound so tightly from the stress and cold brought about by this lying bastard's case. The thought of him sipping pina coladas in a tropical paradise made me sick. I had to confront him. I had to find out the truth.

After making travel arrangements, I went home and packed. Justin agreed to call all our clients and tell them Cross Security and Investigations would be closed for the next couple of weeks due to the move. He'd get some time off, and I'd get answers.

Luckily, the police didn't stop me at the airport, and I boarded the plane. For the first time since the detectives stepped foot in my office, I would finally be able to investigate the Knox disappearance and figure out precisely what happened.

*   *   *

The white sand reflected the early afternoon sun. I'd spent the better part of two days searching for Knox, but I finally found him. He had a room at the resort under an alias. From what I'd gathered, his passport and credit cards were under the same fake name.

"I'll have what he's having," I said to the woman working at the tiki bar.

Knox spun on his stool at the sound of my voice. "Lucien."

"You're a hard man to find. Didn't I tell you to pay your bill?"

"Jeez, I'm sorry."

"You should be."

Knox stared at me as I took off my sunglasses. My eyes were no longer black, and my nose had started to heal. Aside from some swelling, it looked the way it always did. "What are you doing here?"

"I was going to ask you the same thing, except I had a lot of time to think about it and conduct research while on the plane. It's insane the kinds of things you can find on the dark web, especially once you have a person's handle."

"I have a cabana reserved. Let's speak in private."

"Fine by me."

I picked up my own tropical concoction and followed Knox across the white sand, past the resort's pool, and off to the side, near the individual bungalows. He stepped into the cabana and took a seat on one of the cushioned, wicker chairs. I sat beside him and stared out at the picturesque green-blue water.

"How did you find me?" he asked.

"Your obsession with that ring led me straight to you."

"It means a lot to me. You didn't happen to bring it with you, did you?"

"No, I'm done breaking into the police evidence locker or stealing from crooks. I'm also done working for crooks."

"Crook?"

"Don't lie to me. I'm tired of it."

"When did you find out the truth?"

"Too late for my own good."

"It happens to the best of us."

"So what happened? You realized as acquisitions manager you could move plenty of things in and out of the country without anyone noticing?"

"Pretty much. My profession taught me a lot about international travel and trade. I could get things in and out without anyone noticing. Forget import/export. I was magic."

"Except Vasili Petrov noticed."

"Actually, it was his idea. I'd never even considered it before he suggested it." Knox slurped on his drink. "My gambling debts were real, even if that had been years ago. Instead of paying him back with cash, he waived my debts in return for a favor. He wanted me to bring in a shipment of guns. All I had to do was stick an additional package in a cargo container that the company had already approved. It was easy. But it didn't stop there. Vasili wanted more, and since I'd already broken the law once, he said he had proof and would turn me in as a smuggler. So I did him one better."

"You decided you should become an actual smuggler?"

"Brilliant, isn't it? It took time. Lots of time, but eventually, I got the names of his contacts. His contacts knew who the overseas buyers were, so it wasn't hard to cut him out."

"But he found out that you were moving stuff on the side using his people and his buyers."

"Not right away. It was just little stuff at first, but I started to expand. That's when I got in trouble." He studied me. "I wonder how much you know about."

I sensed the danger in his statement. "I'm not here to bust you. I'm not even here to bring you home."

"Why are you here?"

"The police think I had something to do with your disappearance. They figured you were dead. I had no reason to disagree and wondered if whoever came for you would eventually try to find me."

"Guess you don't have to worry about that," Knox said.

"I guess not. But you used my services, and you didn't pay me. I feel like a whore you ripped off, and I don't like that feeling."

"Should I have left the money on the nightstand?"

Turning to him, I lowered my volume to something lethal. "I saved your life. If I hadn't intervened, Vasili's men would have killed you and left your body in the street. None of that had anything to do with my actions. That was all because of you."

"Do you want an apology or just money?"

"I want to make it clear that no one uses me or my company as a distraction to escape from a dangerous situation, especially not without my consent. I won't forget what you did, the damage you caused, the danger you put me and my friends in. If I ever see your face again, I will end you."

"Now you're threatening me?"

"It's not a threat. It's a promise."

"What are you going to do, Lucien? Take care of me the same way you took care of the Russians?"

I didn't know how much he knew, but it worried me. He'd blackmail me or threaten to, the same way Vasili had. I couldn't let that stand. "You can't extort me. I'll expose you for what you are. You don't know what I've found on you or the info I have on your various aliases, so I suggest you do us both a favor and stay away."

"Lucien, you're no angel. You can't do anything to me and still come out smelling like a rose. It'd be a shame if your actions were to come back and bite you in the ass."

"If they do, you're getting bit too."

"This is a non-extradition country."

"You should keep in mind, Mr. Knox, I have dozens of Special Ops trained mercenaries on my payroll who know a thing or two about international travel. They won't have a problem grabbing you in the middle of the night and taking care of the problem. Understand?"

"You're bluffing."

"Quite possibly, but do you want to risk it?"

Knox reached for his wallet. "You realize you said you don't work for criminals, but you still want me to pay you. Do you see the hypocrisy?"

"To be honest, I didn't come here for the money. I just came here to see what you'd say, what lie you'd try to sell me this time. I'm surprised you came clean. I guess you just don't care anymore."

"You can't hurt me. I've got a new life and a new business. Here, I'm practically untouchable. Maybe we can help each other. You shouldn't be so quick to dismiss the benefits of knowing a man in my position."

"Fuck you. You used me to free yourself from Vasili and expand your arms dealing. The cops will figure it out eventually, and I might even help them, unless you agree to stay gone. If our interactions have taught you nothing else, you should know you don't want to get on my bad side."

He held up his palms in surrender. "Fine, have it your way. I just have one final question. Will you send me my ring?"

Turning, I walked away. This job had almost cost me my life. It could cost me everything, even my sanity if Knox knew as much as he pretended to. I'd spent most of the plane ride debating if I'd turn him in, but I couldn't do it, not when he claimed to have dirt on me. I didn't know how much or if anyone would even listen to him, but I didn't want to risk it or deal with the headache.

Knox wasn't going anywhere. He'd stay here, in

paradise, with his money and the protection it could buy him. Eventually, he'd piss off another Vasili, and he'd pay for that. Karma would come around and take care of things. I had to believe that.

I'd already wasted enough time and energy on Knox. I wouldn't make the same mistakes in the future. I wouldn't take clients I didn't trust, especially ones who lied to my face, and I'd learn to function at one hundred percent even with distractions. I wouldn't live in fear of being arrested or killed. I'd wasted enough time on both of those worries this past month. No more.

I had a natural talent for reading people. I just had to trust my instincts and listen to them instead of dismissing them. This job would take everything from me if I let it, and I wouldn't.

On the plane back to Los Angeles, I decided I'd start my training right away with a few days of high-stakes poker in Vegas. That was the best and most surefire way of practicing reading people and flushing out liars. It was time I brush up on those skills.

Once I landed, I changed flights and booked a room at one of the casinos. Then I called Jade. It went to voicemail. "Hey, I don't know if you've had time to consider my proposal, but I'm going to Vegas for the next couple of days. No strings, just gambling and hanging out. I'll have a ticket waiting at the airport in your name. If you don't use it, don't worry about it. It's refundable, and the suite is already booked. I'd like to see you, but I understand if I don't. And I won't bother you again."

I hung up, boarded another plane, and set off for a fun and safe way of honing my skills. No one would kill me if I got it wrong, but it'd cost me thousands. With those kinds of stakes, I'd figure things out quickly. This was sink or swim, and I didn't want to do it in frigid water at the dead of night ever again.

* * *

"Sir, are you going to call?"

I shuffled a few chips in one hand while I tapped the

edges of my cards against the felt. "I'll raise." Tossing another grand into the pot, I leaned back in the chair. I wanted the move to look like a bluff, even though it wasn't.

"Call." The player to my left tossed in his chips.

The next one folded, and the one I'd been analyzing for the last two hours raised again. I matched his bet. The fourth player folded, which I knew he would, and my opponent flipped over his cards. Depending on the river, he might have a flush, but I already had a full house. The dealer placed the final card, and I took the pot.

"Cash me out," I said, smiling at the gorgeous redhead who'd been ogling me for the last hour and a half. Talk about distractions, yet I was walking away a winner. After tipping the dealer, I took my tray of chips and headed over to the lounge area. "What do you want to do today?" I asked.

Jade smiled. "Don't you want to sleep? You've been at that table all night."

"No, I haven't."

"You snuck out of our room at three a.m."

"See, not all night. Just most of the night." I kissed her. "Thanks for meeting me. I hope you haven't been too terribly bored."

"That's not even possible with the spa and pool." She grinned. "We should go to the pool." She looked down at the container of chips in my hand. "And then shopping."

"Agreed." My back and legs needed to move after the long hours. I'd have to work out a better schedule with my trainer and physical therapist once I got back home. I took her hand in mine as we went to the cage with my winnings. "I'm glad you came."

She wrapped her arms around me and clung to my side, nuzzling her face against my neck. "I think these casual, no strings meet-ups will be good for us."

"Me too." I smiled down at her. "They're lucky as hell."

Don't miss the next book by G.K. Parks, *Past Crimes*:

Eight years ago, Lucien Cross covered up a murder. Now Alexis Parker has to prove he didn't do it. Except, she's not convinced he isn't guilty.

Ever since Alex went to work for Lucien Cross, nothing's been the same. She's always been wary of him. Now, she finally knows why.

The police discovered a body and enough evidence to put Cross in a cell for the rest of his life. He won't offer an explanation. He hasn't even said he's innocent. The only thing he wants is Alex to work the case and clear his name. But how can she do that when every bit of evidence points to the contrary?

Available in print and ebook.

ABOUT THE AUTHOR

G.K. Parks is the author of the Alexis Parker series. The first novel, *Likely Suspects,* tells the story of Alexis' first foray into the private sector.

G.K. Parks received a Bachelor of Arts in Political Science and History. After spending some time in law school, G.K. changed paths and earned a Master of Arts in Criminology/Criminal Justice. Now all that education is being put to use creating a fictional world based upon years of study and research.

You can find additional information on G.K. Parks and the Alexis Parker series by visiting our website at
www.alexisparkerseries.com